GAVIN CORBETT

GREEN GLOWING SKULL

FOURTH ESTATE • *London*

Fourth Estate
An imprint of HarperCollins*Publishers*
1 London Bridge Street
London SE1 9GF
www.4thestate.co.uk

This Fourth Estate paperback edition published in 2016

First published in Great Britain by Fourth Estate in 2015

1

A catalogue record for this book
is available from the British Library

ISBN 978-0-00-759432-0

Printed and bound in Great Britain by
Clays Ltd, St Ives plc

For Lilian

A round unvarnished tale is that delivered to our representative by Mr. J.F. McCormack, the Irish tenor, who has just returned from St. Louis. Mr. McCormack's narrative is a model of moderation, and contains ample internal evidence that he has exaggerated neither in one direction nor the other. From what came under his own observation it is plain that there were at least a couple of disgusting exhibitions of stage-Irishman antics … If the matter ended at what Mr. McCormack saw himself it would appear that there has been a good deal of high colouring in the charges levelled against the management of the theatre. The narratives of Mr. Digges, Mr. Ewing, and Miss Quinn, of the Irish Literary Theatre, have, however, yet to be obtained, and it may well be that they will supplement the facts related by Mr. McCormack.

From a report in *The Dublin Evening Mail*, July 21, 1904

A thought ... will fly from us and only return again in the darkness crying in a thin, childish voice which we may not comprehend until, with aching minds, listening and divining, we at last fashion for it those symbols which are its protection and its banner.

JAMES STEPHENS, *The Crock of Gold*

the golden and only age of airship travel and she had an ambition to bring back this method of travel. Somebody put it to her that the gases that had been used in airships were dangerous. She said she would not use combustible gases in her airships but normal air filtered of the heavier pollen released by genetically modified crops and urban tree cultivars. Before she had a chance to rope Rickard in in some way on this folly or on some other aspect of her life he was gone.

Now he was idle and, thinking of things he could do to occupy himself, he settled on trying to realise a recent and half-baked ambition to become a singer. Lately he had discovered he had not only a certain unrefined talent for singing but a repertoire of songs within him that he had not known was there. All of this emerged on his last night in Dublin when his parents put on the traditional emigrant's wake. This had been an unexpected move on their part because his father did not have much of an attachment to Irish traditions and his mother had a learning disability. To the last minute they misunderstood why he was leaving for America. They thought it might have been because he was angry over his sweetheart. He was angry over his sweetheart, it was true, but people do not move away from the sources of their anger unless they have been told to do so by a counsellor or a court. No, he left for America mainly because of his parents: he had been an only child and he did not want to have to care for them and he could not suffer to see them decline. About his absence from their lives, he hoped that they would remain healthy enough to care for one another to the end of their days, and that they would die more or less simultaneously. He comforted himself with the thought that they had good neighbours and many relatives, and that he was not, in any event, very entertaining company for them.

He did not like to think about his parents now because thinking about them, and how they had driven their son to the brink of suicide and ultimately America, made him feel like a tragic cabbage-scented character in an Irish rural drama. But happily there was another reason for leaving Ireland that he could dwell on, and this reason was wholly of the modern world.

In the end, leaving his parents in Dublin had proven not as difficult as leaving his job in Dublin. The company that Rickard had worked for in Dublin was called Verbiage. It specialised in 'the mining and re-purposing of online text'. Only two people had worked for Verbiage – he had been the familiar of a man who looked after all the computer and techno-logical aspects of the job. Quite suddenly Rickard had come to loathe the tasks being asked of him, and the feeling would not let go. There had been no possible way to move sideways within the company with just the two of them working there, and so to leave his position he had to leave the company, and the only good reason he could give for leaving the company was that he wanted to leave the country, 'to explore new horizons', etcetera. His boss was upset to hear this, and tried to convince Rickard to stay. He asked him wasn't he a little old to be starting a new life abroad, alone, which only hardened Rickard's resolve all the more, and not because he wanted to prove that he was young (which he proudly was not; he was forty-one), but because he felt that his boss (who was twenty-six) was being ageist, and he wanted to show that a forty-one-year-old was just as capable of starting again, abroad, alone, as a young person was. His boss, again and again, and finally (with his face in his hands), said that Rickard was irreplaceable, and that he would be admired and appreciated in time. 'But this is just the problem,' Rickard did not say. At the end of the exchange Rickard realised that he had committed himself to leaving the country, and that the unpleasant sensation he now had (with eyes closed) was one of floating in or falling through space, his insides pressing against him in all sorts of new ways, and that he was about to be reborn. He put his hands to his face just as his boss had done, cried with him, felt his face become hot and wet, opened his hands, and enjoyed the fanning of circulated air.

Alone, again, abroad, in his accommodation in New York, he understood that one of the reasons he had left his newspaper job in New York was that he was worried it might have taken a similar turn to his job in Dublin. The pattern would have gone something like this: he would recognise a sarcastic and assertive tone in his voice, and he would only have to find this tone once, as surely he would, because it was easy to be

6

on a guitar and an accordion were produced, and a cousin cleared the lid of the piano of boxes, and by the small hours the blue-painted wall in the living room, which was the inside of a cold gable wall that faced the sea, was damp with condensation. They were all in their turn called on by one of the more socially confident neighbours to sing a song. When it came around to Rickard he sang the music-hall standard 'Come Off It, Eileen'. It was not an imaginative choice but it was said to him that night that no one in their life had heard a better version sung. He went on to sing, to everyone's astonishment including his own, selections, some obscure, from the songbooks of Challoner, French, Ffrench, Balfe and Moore. He was told that he had great volume and vibrato, which he understood to mean that his voice wobbled to pleasing effect. These were certainly things he was aware of as he was singing, although he may have been helped on the night by the acoustic qualities of the corner into which he sang.

The next morning, feeling sorer of head than he would have wanted before a long flight to America, he was presented with a 1908 edition of Chauncey Challoner's *Airs of Erin* of 1808. His father said he had been inspired to root it out after Rickard's performance the night before. He described it as a sacred 'codex', which Rickard thought was a strange word, suggestive of future or futuristic technology, for this repository of songs gathered in long-gone romantic days of muzzle-loading firearms and symbolic bitterns. The cover was green and sticky and embossed with shamrocks, harps and gold lettering, and a reassuring beeswax-like smell rose up with the purr of the pages. Every few pages a colour plate or a title would cause him to pause and realise that he should not have been surprised to know such essentially Irish songs as 'O Truncated Tower', 'The Clover and the Cockade', 'Wigs on the Green', 'Dempsey of Dunamase' and 'The Order of the Emerald' (in school they used to deliberately mishear it as 'The *Ordure* of the Emerald'). Other titles – 'The Snow-flake on Art's Greying Lip', 'My Grand-father's Fighting Stick' – were not known to him but were enough to evoke a world.

Afterwards his father attempted to impart some wisdom to him before his leaving. He began by mumbling unintelligibly in Irish as if scanning his stock of the language for a pithy phrase. This was another surprise, as although his father was a speaker of Irish he hated it because he had had it beaten into him by religious brothers who had also beaten ambi-dexterity into him.

Switching back to English his father said, 'You must know at least one phrase of the Irish language. If you are on public transport and you see a black person and feel the need to talk about them to someone else for whatever reason, do not refer to them as a black person but as a *dinna gurrum*.'

Then his father got on to what he really wanted to say:

'New York is a tough city and it would be easy for a man to fall on hard times. Don't let this happen to you, son. Fortunately for you, there is an institution in that place where you will always be welcome.'

His father of course was referring to the Cha Bum Kun Club, of which he was a long-standing member. It had clubhouses in all the major cities of the world, plus Thule, Greenland; Puerto Williams, Chile; Leverkusen, Germany; and Ceduna, South Australia; and several clubhouses in remote locations through the Korean peninsula and islands.

His father gave him a shining leather tie box.

'I went to Rostrevor Terrace yesterday and finally got this off the President. These are not handed out at random. Only one scion per cell every six years is allowed to possess a tie. They had been considering my application for weeks. I am so relieved to present this to you. You will never go hungry or homeless with one of these. If you wear it to the New York clubhouse you will be given a room and a stipend until you are capable of supporting yourself. But you must wear it in the special way.'

The tie's design was of left-to-right-slanting blue, orange and cream stripes. Overlying the field of stripes, at the thickest part of the tie, was the black, white, blue and red Cha Bum Kun roundel, and below the roundel a white box inside which were stitched, in blue, the characters '< V.V.': V.V. being Rickard's father's initials and < signifying 'less than'.

His father showed him how to tie the knot in the special extremely tight manner, so that the knot looked less like a knot than a hard seamless node.

he hoped that Toni would come to New York herself, looking for their dream, and that they might bump into each other on these streets.

Those first weeks he experienced all of the newly arrived immigrant's pangs and few of the excitements. His cheap guesthouse in the northern Bronx was in a mainly Irish neighbourhood that prided itself on being a tightly knit community. The shops sold Irish teabags and Irish chocolate and Irish black pudding and damp-tasting Scots-English biscuits. Everywhere there were murals that depicted sporting and para-military activities and featured Celtic script and men with basic eyes and very pink faces. Many of the build-ings were in the faux Irish-village style just like many of the buildings in Ireland. The land of his birth had never seemed so far away. People moved as if they had all the time in the world, following cracked cambers with their hands behind their backs; or idled as if they had all the time in the world, slumped against cham-fered corners below dowdy eaves laughing pile-driving laughs. They seemed so at home, and he felt so locked out. He spent every spare hour he could in Manhattan where even the men in suits spun about as dazzled by the place as he was, though it was not ideal boulevard-ing territory owing to the regular stops put in the flâneur's way by the town planner. One day in one of the less frenetic streets of Midtown a photographer told him he had 'crossed' his 'line' and ruined his photograph. After this Rickard told himself to be understanding of US ideas of social involvement and he became careful not to disturb people's 'personal space'. He took 'personal space' to mean the space between people and the objects of their concentration, or that aura-like area around people through which the energy by-product of their concentration was diffused. For example, in subway cars he would try not to look people in the eye or would be wary, as he was taking a seat, of sitting on a stray bag strap or body part. And in book shops he would not walk between people and the books they were looking at on the shelves and thus he took tortuous courses and was left face to face with books he had not in the first place been looking for.

He did not like the idea that anyone wished him ill but he felt that the billionaire's widow at the newspaper wanted only evil to be visited on him because she could not have him. She had tried to kiss him with her doughy, immobile and always-damp lips as he was leaving the offices for the last time. He recoiled from her, backing into a filing cabinet, which fell backwards into another filing cabinet, which broke a window. The glass, original to the building and warped with age, crumbled to grains. The rest of the office staff rose as one.

'See what you bring to the party,' the billionaire's widow bellowed. 'Only blue funking dudgeon, to use a local expression.'

With no job, no daily routine, he found himself careering, and for long listless weeks; he ate only sweet things and slept odd hours and never felt bothered about seeking work. His behaviour became erratic, sometimes risky. He engaged madmen – people happy to violate his own 'personal space': street preachers, or rap singers on the make who handed out leaflets with website addresses on them. He went to the famous Waldorf Astoria one night and tried 'the green fairy' – absinthe; and he told the barman from County Mayo to fill her up again. Rush hour one evening he climbed down to the subway track to salvage what in any case only turned out to be a potato.

Once, worn out, and feeling sentimental for home, and knowing that the pubs of his neighbourhood were anything other than public houses, he went to Mass. The priest had a whispery voice like chalk on a blackboard, but coughed often, spoiling the effect. Rickard woke on a cough to hear the priest deliver a homily on the dangers of leaving Mass early. He said that leaving Mass early was like finishing a course of antibiotics early, and that if one didn't finish one's course the germs of sin would grow stronger and become resistant to the medicine of the liturgy. Rickard, aware that he was in danger of falling asleep again, and that he was a snorer, decided all the same that it was best to leave before the end.

Near Christmas he went, in indifferent mood, to a late-night rhumba party on a pier in the Hudson River to see if he could meet a US girl. He never told his landlady where he was going or at what time to expect him back. Nothing happened at this rhumba party, which was exactly as he had wanted, and he walked all sand. His new apartment building shook with tremors generated by shallow-lying tunnelling machinery and it also had a cockroach problem. A significant factor in his decision to leave Ireland had been his fear of the European house spider, but he soon grew to hate and fear the American cockroach with equal passion and dread. Daily they seemed to increase their dominion; taking the words of Charles Stewart Parnell out of context he would lift his hand and say to them, 'Thus far shalt thou go and no further.' One evening he was putting on a moccasin when he noticed one of the maroon scurrying pests inside it. He opened the window of the apartment to shake the creature out. 'Shoo, shoo!' he said, and ended up letting the moccasin slip from his hand. It dropped eight floors and beyond retrieval. His other moccasin, water-stained and curled from drying out, sat at his feet looking like an artefact from a museum of agriculture. This, after a day in which he had suffered the hauteur of people in shops and the service industry. He wept for forty-five minutes and thought of moving back to Dublin. He thought about this – moving back to Dublin – paralysed slightly in movement, and partly in thought itself, for the rest of the day. Late in the night he tried to sing. He willed his diaphragm to flatten like a weakling pushing a plunger, and he intoned. His plans to be a singer now seemed altogether pathetic. He knew no way of going about being a singer – and how juvenile and risible of him to have even dreamt of it. He took Lyons tea and felt that perhaps it would be nice to return to Dublin and embrace the kind of love that was sympathy. But it was painfully easy too to imagine the great stigma of being delivered, pitied, in a squeaking cage like some kind of King Puck, brass crown askew, with divergent eyes. No; no. It was true; he could not return to Dublin so soon.

There was of course another option, another way that an observer of his situation might have told him would improve that situation; but it was one that Rickard had never been, nor was now, prepared to entertain. He had felt, from the moment his father had introduced the idea, that to go to the Cha Bum Kun clubhouse would be to walk into a trap. His father knew that Rickard would only have approached the lodge in the most miserable condition. Down at heel, pining for home, and sitting across a room from old men, he would be squarely in front of the cause of his flight from his parents.

No, no, he decided. He would attack his problems with great conviction. Encouragement came from an unsought source. One of the books in a book shop that he was left face to face with that he was not in the first place looking for was *Atlas Shrugged* by Ayn Rand. Lessons emanated. He would strain at his balls and sockets from the down-suck and make money. This was America, this was New York, the beating and – importantly – not geographical and not rutted heart of America. Men here had made art deco facades to provide footholds and handholds to the clouds. Later in the 1980s men had made the same things in polished granite that was the colour of both the inside and outside of salmon. Now new walkways were emerging on elevated platforms, and gleaming silver tubes on skyscraper roofs pumped beautiful pure clouds into clear blue skies. Young people, no longer afraid to revel in youth and money, were running with the spirit. Many wore ironic pilot goggles in a nod to the spirit of early aviation. A new dawn, or a new young spirit, was rising, or abroad.

In the meantime, in a time, some time, in the middle of that, on a day when no ATM in the city would accept his PIN, a woman in the bank persuaded him that – yes – he should get a job because his funds were rapidly depleting, and assured him that the problem with his card would be resolved by the next morning.

'But if you don't mind me saying,' this banking woman with beautiful Greek almond eyes decorated with platinum eye shadow said, 'it's all fine declaring that you're a professional singer, but when you've got no income from it, it isn't worth the name that you give it. New York is an expensive place at the best of times.'

This was true, Rickard knew, but he had said 'professional singer' without any belief that that's what he actually was and only to make it seem that he was not a layabout.

'But then I realise the kind of person you are,' continued the woman with the Greek eyes, 'and it's the kind who will be satisfied only with following some "art and craft" pursuit.'

18

'Yes, I'm afraid so,' said Rickard, taking in the woman's stern high-waisted navy skirt and then looking at his hands on his knees.

'There are plenty of creative opportunities in this city if you look around you. New York is full of reminders that you may not be wasting your time if that's the life you feel you must live. There are signs in the smallest gesture on the street and in the grandest building on the block.'

Perhaps this woman was not Greek after all: Rickard had only thought so because his thinking had become contaminated when he noticed the Greek-style columns in the hall. And then there was the question of him taking advice from a person who was obviously under the spell of these trashy fashionable novels that dealt in symbology and conspiracies: a copy of *The Gordion Quorum* by Cole Tyler lay on her desk.

'New York,' said the woman, 'is a city built by cults who begat cults who know very expertly the art of making cults. And this is my suggestion to you: that you find a cult of your own. There is a very large one in the city right now that you would do well to be a part of. Lots of people young and old are part of it and it worries those of us who are not! I'm talking of course about Puffball Computers. You won't have failed to notice its adherents. They carry Puffball products with them wherever they go, and they look in ways unconventional, yet every element of their appearance is discrete from the other elements around it. They are so clean and ready for this world that they've shaped for themselves. We in the bank are always happy to help a person who looks like this.'

* * *

Breaking point came one evening when he fought a hopeless battle against a translucent close relative of the cockroach, the water bug. Long after the creature had scuttled to safety he was still rattling his tongue scraper back and forth through the crack behind his water cabinet.

'Die! Die! Die!' multiplied ten thousand times he screamed.

Afterwards he went to his bedroom, sat at the end of the bed, and began to do the one thing he'd been doing a lot of recently to comfort himself. Most often he would select a song to lift his mood, but occasionally he let the mood dictate the selection of song. That evening the most morbid ballad in the Challoner canon, a song about expulsion to the penal colonies, poured from him:

> *'Diemen, smother my face*
> *And have what you will,*
> *For the bread I have taken*
> *Is making me ill.'*

As he sang, he looked from his window to the night sky and the full moon above. He saw it as a spot at the end of a beam of light moving across clouds that were not, on this coldly clear night, there. A call for help, or to arms, in other words. Then he looked at his Challoner book on his bedside stand and considered again his home, his father, his mother's porous brain, his genetics, Toni, and his funds. He saw from the corner of his eye a movement on the wall – a plain cockroach. He leapt to his wardrobe where his Cha Bum Kun tie hung on a hook on the inside of the door, made a loop with it, and went to crack it against the bug. But he pulled back at the last moment; and then began the complex and arduous process of putting on the tie.

New York City's Cha Bum Kun clubhouse was a townhouse-height Venetian box of white and smoky-blue stone, in Murray Hill, Manhattan. Tall windows tapered to sharp points and the impression of verticality continued through many twisting chimneys and flues. Inside, the air smelt of brass polish and coconut hair. A flying-buttress-style walkway vaulted the width of the grand stair hall. The walls to second-floor level were crusted with dozens of skulls of mystery beasts.

'Rabbits, hares and cows,' said a receptionist, a Pole, or Russian. 'All killed by Kunians, or their Pak Doo Ik forerunners, in the New York area when it was mainly forest and silica.'

He beckoned Rickard to bend his head towards him. Pulling Rickard's tie across the desk between finger and thumb, he worked slowly towards the knot, appearing to examine the threading. When he got to the knot, he pinched into it with his nails, then produced a thumb tack and tried and failed to puncture it – testing it presumably for hardness and layering.

'What is your name?'

'Rickard Velily.'

Now he looked into a diary, scanning down through a series of paragraphs in tiny squarish handwriting. He turned over two pages until he found the entry he was looking for.

'Rickard Velily. Yes, yes. Velily. Yes. Okay, just give me a moment. Yes. Velily. Your father rang ahead some weeks ago and told us, uh … to expect you?'

'He did?'

'Yes, he did. Can you wait here for a little while until the President arrives?'

Clicking feet descended the stone grand stairway, and a 'Hello' sounded from two flights up. The President embraced Rickard with overbearing warmth. He looked every centimetre the reluctantly retired company executive with his figure-hugging silver suit, his Latin tan, and his side-parted grey hair held in place by a perfumed product.

He introduced himself as Paulus.

'Rickard, the first thing to say to you is that we'll ask no questions. You're among friends here. We'll ask nothing other than that you don't play loud music in your room, that you smoke only tobacco, and that you eat only in your room and not in the dining hall, and only off your plate and not off your lap or bed sheets.

Rickard settled for now on the drawing room. The room was hot as he entered, and he felt his face flush. A fire blazed in the grate. Set as it was into a gigantic tableau carved from green-grey soapstone, the fireplace resembled the centrepiece of a tall satanic grotto. At first glance the tableau seemed to be an oppressive mass of ribs, roots and boils, as if made of continually melting and solidifying wax. As Rickard's eyes adjusted he picked out the details: foliage, weaponry, fauns, sheep-people, Korean farmhands, men from Europe. It was an attempt to represent the legend of Cha Bum Kun. Here were the gryphons and dragons of his childhood; there was the Moon Baby that brought him dairy produce from the West. It was a random and confused scene, and therefore a good representation of the story. Nobody was sure of the details of the story of Cha Bum Kun or in which order the details came. Nobody knew, either, what Cha Bum Kun's message was, or even if he had had a message, or what lessons could be drawn from his life, or even if he had ever lived. In truth, Cha Bum Kun was not a figure that was taken very seriously. It meant that the Cha Bum Kun Club had no rituals – the tie business aside, and despite the vocabulary around its workings – and no ethos. It was, and always had been, just a club where men from all over the world could meet each other in its lodges, make useful connections, relax and play games. Usually these men were of such a disposition – meek, or odd – that they found it hard to get on in the world despite significant financial means. (And, usually, they were of significant financial means.)

There was just a single free chair in the room. It was so positioned that Rickard could not help but face two men. One of these men was bald on top, perfectly round-headed, and had an underbite. A pad of spittle had collected at a corner of his mouth. The other man had a full head of greasy white hair, long and pinned back behind the ears, and a face that tapered to the nose and lips like the blade of a Stone Age hatchet. They were snoozing, and easy to imagine dead.

Recently Rickard had been given to imagining that any elderly person he saw looked dead. Perhaps this was because the elderly were the easiest of all people to imagine dead: their corpses, in the main, would not look so different to the living versions of themselves. Something of the fear of death would disappear with this visualisation, although when he thought of his parents at home he saw them face down on the floor beside each other and hollowed out and grey like hot-counter chickens. But this bald old man would not be quickly corruptible. He would remain apple-cheeked and full in the mouth – no collapse in support behind the lips. Rickard imagined him too in a giant glass tube, in a bubbling rose-coloured liquid.

The other man – the flint-hatchet one, rigid in his chair, one hand loosely holding the other – would find the transition to corpsehood traumatic. His face was whittled, Rickard decided; had an eaten quality, been blasted, from having seen too much. He had uncanny foresight. Or, rather, uncanny experience: he knew, somehow, the advancing horrors. In the first moments of death the microbes would swiftly – and not for the first time – get to work; the tissue in the face would subside ply on ply and the hard edges above would harden further.

But even haunted by death there was something elevating about this man. He would be long and limber and heroic and become one with the relief carving in his likeness on the lid of his tomb. The tomb would be made of alabaster and in the dark it would glow. And in death the other man too – there would be something grand and glorious. This man as a crusader at rest, and that man at peace in his bubbling tube: and now the tableau behind glistened and quivered. Rickard saw in its details other creation stories; he thought of Romulus and Remus, Europa, and of the Milesians. He saw in it too evolution: the squirming tissue oozing more of itself, regulated by an electronic pulsar; but in the embers something seasoning – a glimpse of another world, arcane and outlasting, beyond bosses or bailiffs.

The heat of the fire had lulled him to sleep – a thump of the heart brought him back to life. He saw the bald man taking him in with querulous rousing eyes. The other man fully awake. The fire roaring again with fresh fuel.

'New blood?' said the bald man, with a discernibly Irish accent.

Rickard was afraid to open his mouth. It would give

him away and then they would be off on that predictable old track talking about the same old bull.

The other man looked him gently up and down, and said, also with an Irish accent, but Americanised, and slightly lispy and high, 'Sure leave him be, Denny. He's only settling in. You're very welcome anyhow. I'm Clive Sullis. Your friend here is Denny Kennedy-Logan.'

'He's not normally so forward and confident,' said the first man, Denny, leaning now with ladsy familiarity towards Rickard. 'The club makes him feel very secure. In the street he's a lamb.'

Well, he would have to be out with it. He told the men his name – established that Denny was from Dublin, Clive from south Donegal ('though I went off to Dublin as soon as I could escape'). Both had been in New York a long time.

'And so they've given you that attic room, aye?' said Denny. 'They gave me that room when I first came here. But they boot you out once you find your way again. I wonder if they'll ever give it back to me. What do you think you'll do with yourself here in this city?'

'I'm not sure,' said Rickard. 'Perhaps I'll stay with the newspapers.'

'You look like a print-room boy, all right. Do you know about the hierarchy of aprons? You won't get anywhere in that game unless you have the right length of apron.'

'But,' Rickard cut back in, 'I've a bit of an old hankering to become a singer, that's what I've set my sights on.'

'Nothing in that game either. I knew a "rock and roller" in Dublin called Pádraigín O'Clock. You've never heard of him because he never amounted to anything.'

'I don't want to be a rock-and-roll singer, sir. I want to be a tenor.'

'A tenor!' Denny guffawed, clapping his hands together as a log exploded in the grate and hissed in its half-life. 'Clive, would you listen to this! And how is your voice?'

'Untested. Untrained,' said Rickard. 'But it's all there, I think.'

'You must try and coax it out so. Have you thought about getting lessons?'

'Yes, this eventually would have been the plan.'

Denny sat back into his seat and turned to his companion. 'Well, Clive, what do you think?'

Clive, to Rickard, said, 'Denny here is a tenor of note.'

'And better known than Pádraigín O'Clock I was in my day, too!'

'He was,' nodded Clive, 'I can vouch. Sure Pádraigín never made it to acetate, and you made it to America.'

'True enough! True enough! Did you know that Pádraigín's real name was Pádraigín Cruise? They always give themselves these jazzy names, these "rock and rollers".' When Denny had finished laughing, he said to Rickard, 'If it's lessons you want, come to me, and we'll see what you're about.'

28

He took a notepad – personalised with his initials – from the pocket of his cardigan, and scribbled his home address.

'We'll say this time tomorrow, at my apartment. What do you think?'

Before Rickard had time to answer, Denny, to Clive, said, 'New blood, what did I tell you?'

became a little angry, thinking of how he'd been manipulated. The old man would have him, before he knew it, wiping his bottom.

But he had a surprising bounce, Denny, to his walk; a combative bustle and energy, as he led the way into his apartment. He was forward-angled rather than forward-leaning or forward-stooped. Rickard could picture him in leathers, in a garage, at three in the morning, failing to kick-start a Triumph motorcycle; on his way to a confrontation or to playing a mean prank on someone; unwittingly and unknowingly kneeing a child in the skull in the course of a purposeful stroll.

A darkened passageway brought them to an inner room, softly lit and warm in colour. A brass or bronze arm projected from a wall and held a barely luminous globe. Rickard perched on the edge of the seat he was offered, under the arm. An upright piano created an obstruction in the middle of the room. Floor-to-ceiling bookshelves flanked a chimney breast and the space on the shelves in front of the books was cluttered with trinkets and ornaments, as was a mantelpiece, a wake table, a whatnot and a small chest of drawers. Larger ornaments – slim glazed pots and a couple of wooden figures such as might have been prised off the front of a medieval guildhall or from the alcoves of a reredos – sat on the floor against the wall behind him. The place smelt either of dog or popcorn, Rickard could not decide which. As if in answer, a ginger-and-white dog with a squidgy pink-and-black face came skittering into the room and rolled on its back by its owner's feet. The old man pulled up a chair so that he could sit down and tickle the dog's belly. After a minute he turned the animal over and toggled the flesh on its head until its eyes watered. 'My little poopy frootkin, my little poopy frootkin,' he said, and continued to jerk the dog's head.

'You found me all right,' he said, still looking at the dog.

It took Rickard a moment to realise that the old man was talking to him. 'Your directions were very good,' he said.

He sat back into the seat, warily, expecting broken springs and plumes of dust, but discovered a plump and yielding easy chair that smelt most definitely of dog; for split seconds he remembered the two dogs of his childhood, Jumpy and Kenneth. This was a comfortable, lived-in sort of place, he admitted to himself. Something about the randomness of the clutter and the softness of the light reminded him of the living room of a wealthy Irish country home or townhouse. It would be nice to live in this way in this city, he soon found himself imagining; in a dim few rooms near the service core of an old apartment building surrounded by the stuff of a lifetime. He spotted high on the bookshelves a cherrywood radio set like the one in his father's clubhouse in Dublin. He remembered seeing it on Spring Open Day. A man called Wally had said, 'That is just like the one in my grandfather's country kitchen. My grandfather was a great man for the ideas and one day he had the idea that there was a little man inside that radio and he smashed it up with a hammer.' He chuckled gently at the memory, forgetting himself.

'I'm sorry,' said Denny, 'would you like some shaved ice?'

'No, thank you,' said Rickard. 'I haven't long finished my dinner.'

'I have a machine inside for it.'

'I'm fine, really.'

'I don't drink alcohol any more, so I've nothing to offer you in the way of that. We said nine o'clock?'

'Nine o'clock was the time I thought we agreed in the club last night.'

'I must have meant four o'clock. I'm usually thinking about bed by nine. But all right so – nine o'clock.'

The old man made playful faces and noises at his dog, then spun it around and sent it racing away with a loud smack on the backside.

'Here for the night we are, then. Oh well, I'll enjoy the challenge.'

He stood up and, with his shins, shuffled an ottoman towards Rickard.

'At least have the footrest,' he insisted, manoeuvring the item under Rickard's feet. 'You should come and see the outside of my building in the daytime. It's been said that it looks like the Treasury in Petra, so grand and serious does it look in this street, and so suddenly does it come upon you.'

'It's not an area lacking in grandeur.'

'No it is not.'

The old man sat down again, on top of his yelping dog, which had already skittered back into the room and settled itself up on the chair.

'But the pity then it has all gone to rot. The cross-streets are not so bad but they funnel you, with no by and by about it, to the main drags. If I take a stroll anywhere these days it's on West End Avenue.'

'I have been on West End Avenue,' said Rickard, indulging him. 'It's a very beautiful thoroughfare.'

'What do you like about it?'

He thought about it seriously and could not come up with anything better than, 'I like that it doesn't have any shops.'

The old man sat perfectly still for a moment, then added, 'It brings to mind, for me, the old world, or at least old New York, with its old associations. And something of the world of the tango, and of depressed beef barons. But mostly, yes, it recalls a great European boulevard. In its scale, in its idiom and, when I think about it now, its shape. Not so much because it curves, which it doesn't, but because it undulates. Like keys rippling. Under a virtuoso's hand. Spelgelman used to live there, as did Rosburanoff.'

These revelations delighted Rickard, although he had no clue who the old man was talking about.

'Tell me now, Rickard Velily' – he said his name mockingly, Rickard sensed, throwing in an extra '-il-' syllable, and became distracted with the taste of it on his tongue – 'Velily, Velily, Velily. Is it an Irish name?'

'It is. It's also a village in White Russia.'

'They are Bialy this and Bialy that in New York. Many people originate from places that were once part of Antique Poland or Lithuania, or Greater Austria or Russia. Velily is one of those names that is Irish but might not be. Like Costello, which could be Italian, or Egan, which could be Turkish, or Maher, which could be Berber.'

'Or Walsh,' offered Rickard, 'which could be German.'

The old man looked at him testily.

'You mustn't make any jokes around these parts about the war, you'll learn that smartly enough.'

Rickard protested, 'I –'

'You're a recent immigrant, we've established that?'

'I've been here just a few months.'

'Ah, you'll fit in well enough. We always do. There are American people today called Penhaligon and Thrispterton and the like who say that they're Irish. And they probably are. Anyhow, she's doing well, I believe, Ireland?'

'She has been doing well, it's true,' Rickard confirmed, hoping that the matter would be left at that as he did not want to be drawn into a discussion on economics, of which he knew nothing.

'I hear that now we're a force on the world stage, that everyone seeks to imitate us. I have read that there are companies that will kit out your pub in Moscow or Peking in the Irish style, with advertisements for Whitehaven coal for the wall and Nottingham-made bicycles to hang from the beams.'

Rickard's eyes wandered about the room, to the left and right of Denny, through the ornaments and vases, and settled on a small mottled wall mirror.

'Perhaps,' said the old man, evidently noting the pattern of Rickard's scope, 'if someone from one of these companies, someone less forgiving than myself, stood on the threshold there and said, "How much for the job lot?" I might agree a price. We have trouble moving these days for the bric-a-brac, isn't that right, Aisling?'

Rickard glanced back at Denny and saw with some alarm that he was not addressing his dog but the ceiling or a point beyond. He guessed that this 'Aisling' was a dead wife, and he had no wish to hear about her, or about the old man's being made a widower, or to be involved in his affairs by this knowledge and have it implied to him that he should care.

'It's not, though, as if I bought it all in one go. Although I have had to move a quarter of it twice, and half of it once, and arrange it in new ways, in different places. Though the last time it was a different place only to the one before it, and not the place it is now.'

Rickard was tiring already of these spiralling formulations. 'Do you mean this present apartment?'

'Yes. A fitting home for my belongings, I think it is. Did you notice the tracery in the hall?'

'I did,' said Rickard, lying.

'It reminds me of Stapleton's work, and the work of those great Italian stuccodores that came to Dublin in the eighteenth century.'

'How long have you lived here?'

'Oh. Twenty-one years. Twenty-one from last September.'

The old man tapped the dog's head, nestled in his groin, evenly and gently now.

'I have done more living in this building, in these rooms, than in any other building since I came to New York; many moons ago now. If living is taken to mean man-hours, and in this building, in these rooms, is taken to mean just that.'

Rickard detected self-pity creeping in. 'It's not such a bad space to spend time. A fitting venue, as you say, for a man of refined tastes.'

'It is that. But, well … refined tastes. I must tell you, all this' – the old man gestured magisterially with his hand – 'this, ornamentation, all these pretty-looking things, you probably wonder if I'm a bit of a funny sort. Well I am not this way inclined, I would like you to know.'

'I would never make judgements of that nature about a person.'

'But these pretty things … What you see about you are monetary investments.'

He leaned forward in a manner that suggested he was about to say something very important, though the lower part of his face wrestled with a smile.

'You're not a – hoo hoo hoo – thief, are you? You're not one of these drag-racing hooligan bucks who would twist an implement inside an elderly man and rob his things?'

'No, Mister Kennedy-Logan. I have come here to be taught how to sing.'

'Shall I tell you what is the most valuable of all the items in this room? It's those curtains.'

He pointed to dark red drapes, drawn across, on the end wall.

'You wouldn't think to look at them, would you? They're from Turkey, from the early nineteenth century. They look better tied back in the wings, I feel about it, where the gilt threading picks up the light, but they add an element of drama to the nightly act of blocking out the evening.'

He remained leaning forward, with a slump, as his dog trilled enquiringly and tried to catch his eye.

'But I do not sleep in this room, so it's an act best described as a ritual, then.'

At this moment Rickard felt that he could have risen from his chair and walked out of the room and apartment undetected, such was the completeness of the trance that the old man appeared to be in. Instead, in a life-changing intervention, he said, 'Mister Kennedy-Logan, I am booked in for a singing lesson tonight, yes?'

'Booked ...'

The old man grasped, peevishly, thin air, as if he might have found an appointment book there.

'Singing lesson ... Yes. Do you have a song that you could sing so that I can gauge the quality of your voice as it is?'

'I do,' said Rickard. 'I usually like to warm up with "Come Off It, Eileen".'

'Good choice. Not too challenging. Away you go.'

'Now?'

'Yes.'

'Unaccompanied?'

'Yes.'

'All right. Here you have it, so. *Ahem.*'

Rickard stood up, cracked back his shoulders, and began:

> *'With a nerve to match her rosy cheeks*
> *And a cheek to pique my nerves,*
> *My brazen Eileen, mo cushla ...'*

'Stop there, stop there.'

The old man lifted a hand, his forefinger extended; and he was chewing, seeming to be assessing Rickard's efforts with more than one sense.

'You have very good vibrato.'

'Thank you,' said Rickard, still frozen mid-pose, his arms stretched around an invisible keg at his chest.

'And more. And more.'

Rickard laughed, in astonished gratitude.

'Yes. You have quite a range of gifts.'

'I've been told that I have excellent control in the middle to upper register, if only you would give me the chance to show you.'

'Oh yes ... control ... middle to upper register ... I can tell that, I can tell. No, you're ready.'

'When you say "ready" ....?'

'I could do with a young man like yourself, and a

42

voice like yours, pure and not so fraught with the years.'

'I'm not as young as you think,' said Rickard, with a suddenness and even a venom that surprised him, his arms dropping by his side. For some reason the use of the word 'young' felt like an attack on his very sense of himself. His reaction seemed to jolt the old man.

'Do you not consider yourself young?'

'I have not considered myself young for many years, even when I was young. Even the pop vocalists I admired when I was young were people who sounded old, like Kaarst Karst of Kaarst Karst and the Iron-filers.'

'When did you technically cease to be young?'

'I could last credibly claim to be young five years ago when I was in the middle of my thirties.'

'You're young in my book. It's unusual for someone of your age to be interested in the old-style tenor singing. Your soul may creak but, I tell you, it's exciting for my ears to hear a virgin voice like yours. You should revel in the light voice that you have, your spry and tinkling tone; do not be after some character that you do not possess. You would be ideal for a project I have in mind. I and the man you met in the club last night, Clive, wish to form an Irish tenor trio and we are on the lookout for a third person. We will play the front parlours and concert venues of this city, whose people's appetite for Irish ballads and art songs and the singing styles of John McCormack and Joseph

"The Silver Tenor" White I believe is dormant but has not disappeared.'

Rickard was still brooding over the 'young' comment.

'Mind you,' the old man went on, looking Rickard up and down, 'young though you are, it's not as if you'll be attracting the attention of the ladies. Your thighs are swollen like upturned bowling skittles and you have hips like a hula hoop and your face looks like it's been split with a hatchet and has gradually fused back together after many setbacks in a humid region of the world.'

It was an easy decision to make in the end. If Denny Kennedy-Logan could continue to offend him, Rickard would not feel so bad about spending time with the old man and not his parents. The next evening, finding him in the drawing room at the clubhouse again, Rickard said he would join his trio.

gabled houses. But the real Dublin was not so bad, he said; it was where he had learnt to sing, and learnt all the songs that meant the most to him, and it was the city of his father and mother, and the city that gave birth to them: the floral Victorian city; and of the generations preceding them: the stout Georgian city; and of a less-easy-to-define lineage. (Twice in three weeks Rickard listened to Denny tell the story of when, as a young man of seventeen, he was invited to 'Glena' by the marsh, the home of John McCormack, to view the body of the tenor-count in repose, and how grand he looked in that cucumber- and lily-scented room in his dark blue papal uniform and his lilac sash, with a medal pinned to his breast and a ceremonial sword by his side, and that surely in such resplendence he had graduated to the ranks of the most exalted heralds.) They spoke of the entertainment that was had in the Theatre Royal on Hawkins Street. Clive bemoaned the day that establishment was razed (which he remembered well, because he'd been there the day that it happened, and he remembered not just the wrecking ball and the clouds of dust but the lament of many voices that came to his mind: Jimmy O'Dea and Maureen Potter and Noel Purcell crying for Dublin in the rare aul' days and the big American variety stars who had graced the Royal stage down the years and under it all Tommy Dando's organ playing a dirge). Denny dismissed that version of the Royal as 'a seedy penny gaff', and Clive as 'an old blow-in', and preferred to talk of the previous

Royal on the site, the building that burnt down in 1880, where his great-grandfather had seen Pauline Viardot in *Don Giovanni*.

They spoke, both of them, about Ireland with such ardour and colour that it was as if Ireland were the only country that mattered to them and all their years in America amounted to nothing. But the Ireland that they spoke about was not one that Rickard recognised wholly from reality. It was an Ireland, perhaps, with 'Dovelin' as its capital; one that he knew only from the romantic Irish songs they practised. It was the Ireland of *Airs of Erin*. It was Hibernia herself. It was the Ireland that glowed brightly in the minds of a certain class of dreamer in about the 1840s – Thomas Davis and Gavan Duffy and the Young Irelanders.

It was a dream Ireland, yes, they both admitted, finally and without any provocation; but it was an Ireland that they once had been prepared to fight and die for to make real, just like those Young Irelanders.

'Well, maybe not you, Clive!' said Denny. 'You were only in the movement because the Davy Langans was the only club in New York that would have you!'

'Who were the Davy Langans?' said Rickard. 'Militant Irish republicans?'

'Militant Irish patriots,' said Denny, and stressed again: 'Militant Irish *patriots*. It wasn't from Marx or Thomas Paine that we drew our credo. It was from "Bright Fields of Angelica". We were after a dream country, oh to be sure, unbound and unburdened by any social realities, or any of the other realities.'

'It was there in the constitution all right, all of that,' said Clive, with a drop of the head. 'But by the end of it were we anything other than a drinking and gaming club like any of the rest of them? I don't know.'

Denny glowered at his companion, causing Clive's head to drop further and turn away. 'There you have it! There you have it! As I said: Clive was only in the Langans for want of a roof over his head! There were some of us still in that movement idealists and activists! Some of us to the last meant to take the dream home and rescue Ireland. If only more of you understood what the Davy Langans was for and it might still have been a force today. But it's all gone now, and a pity. The last branch of it died out in the Cape Colony some ten years ago, I believe. We once had been a very active branch here in New York.'

'Ach,' said Clive, 'long ago, long, long ago, before any of us –'

'We died on his watch!' said Denny, wagging a finger in Clive's direction. 'He was both secretary and treasurer when we went under. All North American funding for the movement came through New York. A sudden disappearance of money killed us off! There are questions still unanswered! We died on his watch and he has to live with that!'

'The writing had been on the wall for a long time,' said Clive, laughing it off. 'We folded anyhow, and we merged with the Cha Bum Kuns up the street, and the few of us left in the branch were taken in here, at a reduced subscription for a while.'

'"Merged" is a good word for it!' Denny adjusted himself in his seat. 'Eaten up! Utterly subsumed! By golly, if they'd known there were some of us would have borne arms for a cause would they have taken us in so fast?!'

* * *

It was difficult to sing through all the many interruptions. There was one pesky club member, a man from an old Dutch family, who took enjoyment from bursting into the room. Usually this man had been enjoying wine somewhere else on site.

'Here they are again!' he boomed in one evening. 'Oh, they'll love you, the hussies! You'll have them lining up outside the stage door at the Carnegie Hall.'

'Go away now!' said Denny. 'I won't have this, or any excuses that my friends make for you.'

This particular interruption on this night moved Denny to make a vow:

'From tomorrow we take our rehearsals to my apartment. What do you say, men? The environment here is not conducive. I think it is time to strike out on our own.'

He pointed to the ceiling. It was a chequerboard, of orange and blue panels.

'East Prussian orange amber and Dominican blue amber. The soapstone beside us was shipped from Persia. They've plundered the mineral and cultural wealth of the world. From us they'll take our spirit, put it up there in mahogany in mawkish motifs of fiddles and harps. I've always felt a certain condescension within these clubhouse walls towards the Irish, haven't you, Clive?'

Clive looked uncertain, rearranging the flaps of his jacket at his groin, and dithered over a response.

Denny jumped back in: 'There's a latent racialist sentiment in this city. The reason these pug-dogs are so popular in New York today is that blackface entertainment has been outlawed. There's a latent irrepressible fondness in the people for little white clowns with painted black faces. They will seek to characterise you. I think it would benefit us to take ourselves away from this clubhouse. We must work to extract the essential in what we do and concentrate on it, never lose sight of it. Keep it and concentrate *ourselves* in it. We will not get that here.'

'Hey, you guys! Are you still fighting off the hoes or what?'

'We will not get it with that nincombocker around.'

Denny turned his gaze on the Dutchman until the Dutchman had shrunk behind the door again. His eyes lingered on the closed door for some moments; furious, then pensive.

'I will say though that he has brought to my mind an important issue. If we are to be committed in what we do we must commit fully and no compromises. Both of you would do well to take on board, before the start of your singing careers, a bit of advice. I heard it first from Maestro Tosi, my singing teacher in Milan. I did not pay much attention to it at the time; I remembered his words only too late, and how forcibly they struck. I remembered them on the very day of my wedding. They seemed like the most fearful admonition at that moment. He had said, "Do not go rushing into marriage before your career has begun!" Now let me be fearful with you both – let me be fearful with both of you! But then the time for marriage has long passed for you, Clive! And you, young man – Rickard – no woman would have a man that looked like you!'

* * *

In the privacy of Denny's apartment, away from the taunts of other club members, physical exercises could be performed. The purpose of these exercises was to improve the musculature of the chest walls, diaphragm, lungs, throat, tongue and mouth, and to bring legs, spine, shoulder-girdle, neck and head into the correct relationship.

The first exercise of any evening involved adjustment of the pelvis in a standing position by means of rolling movements so that it was relaxed and the intestines lay relaxed also, as in a basket. The idea was to inculcate good posture. Legs were held in such a way as to cause the balance of the body to shift backwards. To this end, splints and yokes carrying buckets of water were imagined. The singer, said Denny, was no different in a certain respect from the butler or the docker: his was work performed on the feet.

Broad vowels unknown in speech were held to keep the pharynx open. Denny said that eventually he would introduce eggs into the men's throats and that when each man could keep an egg in his throat without breaking it he would know that his pharynx was elastic enough to achieve all the necessary shades of dynamics and timbre. Scales and a system of forced coughs would sharpen the ventricular mechanism. Correct unhinging of the mandible was practised, with particular regard to coordination with lip shapes. Awareness, on singing of the brighter 'ee' and the duller 'ah', of the muscles that closed the entrance to the smelling bulb in the upper nose would burn a nerve pathway to allow the voluntary control of these muscles. These muscles could then be brought into play for tonal manufacture, along with the muscles of the throat.

'The face is a mask for the purposes of singing,' said Denny. 'It is one of our key resonators. The mask has to grow so that it reaches behind the ears. Then it will have the maximum opening.'

To improve suppleness of the ribs, the men vigorously beat imaginary timpani with their fists while singing in the middle voice for thirty seconds at walking tempo.

'Let's be wary at all times, men, of the Bs, Ds and hard Gs, and I am not here talking about musical notes. I am talking about consonants. Firm closure of the glottis could kill stone dead the vibrations of the vocal cords.'

Strength was built in the omohyoideus muscle by saying the word 'omohyoideus' one hundred times at an increasing pace. A strong omohyoideus was needed to keep the larynx lashed to the backbone during singing of the A-range of vowels.

All exercises were ultimately assumed to give native vowel sounds the best possible chance.

'The special character of our songs is held in the vowels. You see, men, in music there is a unique set of Irish vowels. They are rounded like the English vowels but their articulation must never result in the sacrifice of the R sound. The R must, at the very least, be trilled. Our Irish vowels will be found by knowing and practising the Italian, English, French, American and German vowels. They lie somewhere among all of those.'

During exercises a set of charts was tacked to the wall depicting the anatomy of the structures under improvement. These charts were huge powdery things, variegated with minute creases, which had to be unfurled with great care. Denny had taken them from Italy with him. They had originated at the medical school in Bologna. The larynx looked an immensely complex piece of machinery in the charts. The ribcage was simple, stark and frightening. Awareness of these structures would lead, the thinking went, to more nerve pathways.

A formula for sublimation was written on a sheet of paper and also stuck to the wall. It was never mentioned. It read:

100 JOULES OF ONANISTIC FERVOUR = 100 JOULES OF RELIGIOUS ZEAL = JUST AS EASILY 100 JOULES OF ARTISTIC PASSION

* * *

'Tell me more about Denny's time in Milan with Maestro Tosi,' Rickard said to Clive one Thursday evening ahead of rehearsals. They had met outside the clubhouse and were now – having been delivered by the uptown subway – waiting for a crosstown bus to Morningside Heights and Denny's apartment. A smell of caramelisation on the air – a uniquely New York feature of the colder months – tortured them both.

Clive said, 'It was a period so brief and embarrassing in Denny's life and career that it rarely comes up, and I'm surprised that it ever does.'

Rickard said, 'I'm ashamed to say that I hadn't heard of Denny before.'

'I'm not surprised that you hadn't. This was a star that burnt brightly and went out quickly. But a source of historic light.'

'I see it,' said Rickard. 'I see it. It beams through the universe.'

Clive stood stolid, beaky in profile, looking up the avenue at the crest of the hill against the fading pearl of the sky and at the approaching cells of headlights. Rickard was suddenly embarrassed at his own open enthusiasm. An icy cold wind blew through the cross-street. He pinched at his dripping nose.

'Nineteen … when was it?' said Clive. 'Early fifties. I was a young lady in Heet. (Heet is the name of a townland.) My parents left me one night with my brother on our own to go to a concert in Bundoran. I believe it was for the opening of a ballroom. Denny Logan was giving the concert. I did not know this at the time. Only later, after I'd met Denny, and I wrote to my mother, did I know this, did I know anything about Denny. I'm afraid that Denny's time in the limelight had passed me by entirely. He was one of a crop of young Irish tenors in his day, one of the best, so it was said of him. There was no shortage of tenor singers or concerts in those days. For a very brief time. Before the girls' attention moved elsewhere, on to the rock and roll and what have you. Then the tenor voices were forgotten, and with them Denny Logan. You young people would find it hard to believe that tenors were ever a popular success. I found it hard to believe. But the girls went crazy for the tenor voices, they came with flowers to the concerts. The singers used to hand out photographs of themselves in the carte style, and they looked all blushered up in them, bruised below the eyebrows, and flushed in the cheeks. My mother brought home Denny's that night, and posted it, later, to me here in New York. I could not understand the magnetism, but I understand it now I do. You bring me out you do.'

Clive took a long pause.

'You do, you do. You bring me out in Donegal you do. I have not spoken like that in a long time. Must be that you're Irish. I do not like it.'

'I see it too,' said Rickard. 'That magnetism, despite certain masking features. But I don't hear ...'

He checked himself.

'The voice?' said Clive.

'I don't mean to be so plain but it's quite ...'

'Monotonous,' they said together.

'Yes,' said Clive, looking at his feet. 'It is sadly limited.'

'So what happened to that voice in the meantime?'

Clive leaned back against the glass of the bus shelter, then stood forward again.

'I don't know. But I wouldn't be surprised to learn that he had accidentally or purposely disturbed in some way a fairy mound. Bad consequences are known to result from such an action.'

* * *

Within a few weeks of rehearsals Denny, Clive and Rickard had a core of fifteen songs for their set and a repertoire that extended to three dozen more. They were satisfied at last that their voices achieved harmony: Denny steadfastly held the middle; Rickard cleaved to and weaved around him; Clive skirted the top. They had a name for their trio too: the Free 'n' Easy Tones. It was of course Denny's name. It was not a traditional-sounding name, he conceded, but it had a spunk and a jizz about it that might catch the eye of modern audiences.

Rickard was excited about the idea of performing and making money out of it, but he couldn't help wondering if Denny's expectations of how their music would be received in the modern city were unrealistic. Did this residual affection that Denny insisted New Yorkers had for Irish tenor singing carry to the young people? It was hard to imagine, and New York was a young city. The young people seemed always busy and sometimes angry and interested only in young music and fashions. The boys were feminised yet somehow thrusting, like wicked regime-favoured women of mercy-free places of the East. The girls were not people Rickard could imagine in the nursing profession (apart from the girls he saw on the streets in medical scrubs, and there were many of these girls). All the young people were in thrall to the great technology cult, Puffball Computers. In every coffee shop they were bent behind the orbs of the hoods of their Puffball machines; if they were to lift their heads at all it was only for an incoming young acquaintance who they would acknowledge by dislodging then quickly reinstating a single white earplug. He recalled Denny's enquiry weeks earlier about whether he was the sort who would 'twist an implement inside an elderly man and rob his things'. He wondered about how easily these words had come from the old man and whether this was so because he had been violated in a natural or surgeon-made opening of his body by angry young people. Many muscles contracted in him at the thought of several gruesome scenarios and he felt these contractions as empathy. He pondered the cruelness of this city with its dry-eyed young people who would backdrops for them. There was talk too of elaborate three-dimensional stage props, round towers and passage tombs and such, from which one or all of them might emerge as part of their act. The agent said that he knew opera-house managers in Campania and Sicily, including that of the San Carlo in Naples, and that if all went well the Free 'n' Easy Tones would soon be touring the south of Italy and that they would be millionaires. It all sounded too wonderful to be true, and of course it was. Some days later, after another phone call to the agent, Denny was told that the trio would have to audition for a place on his roster.

The old man fumed.

'I have offered him a private concert in these rooms yet still he demands we line up outside his decrepit offices with the sword swallowers and the cowgirl troupes. Well schist and frack to that! He can stick his auditions in his cameo locket and stuff it in his cannoli! And curse his dead mama! We're better than this, boys!'

Then one Sunday evening Denny told Clive and Rickard that he had had a dream during a nap that afternoon. He described it with the solemnness and detachment of a religious mystic, looking away and into himself in recollection of the vision.

'I saw loudspeakers attached to telegraph poles in a bocage-like landscape playing the music of liberation.'

'Were they playing our music?' said Clive.

'They were playing Al Jolson. They were playing Al Jolson. Listen now – we must find a mosque. I believe hundreds have sprung up around the city in recent times. We'll get a willing muezzin – bribe him if necessary – to play our music over his loudspeakers and have it echo down the avenues.'

'We'll need to make a record first, to play it on his stereo,' said Rickard.

'We'll look in the Yellow Pages!' said Clive.

'Yes!'

Denny bounded humpbacked from his chair like an excited monkey. They were all excited – at the way they seemed to harmonise and relay on this gathering idea. They ripped leaves and sheaves from the directory – the hand of one beating away the hand of another – until they reached the R listings. They found a number – one of several under 'RECORD COMPANIES'. Aabacus Records. Denny straightened his back and went to his phone. Rickard took a deep breath, went to the window, tore back the Turkish curtains. To the south, a huge glowing nebula that changed through phases of intensity and colour hung between the great entertainments of Midtown and the proscenium of cloud above. All seemed poised and possible.

'Fellows!' called Denny in a loud rasp with his hand over the mouthpiece of the phone. He beckoned the others near. '"The Caul That Jack Was Born With", all right? When I slide my hand away. On three ...'

Some twenty-five minutes and ten songs ('The Caul That Jack ...' / 'Cogitations of My Fancy' / ''Tis Very

Cold For June' / 'The Malefactors' Register' / 'Empress of the Americas' / 'Evidence of the Glimmie Glide' / 'The "Celebrated" Windy Song' / 'Letters from France' / 'A Pike in the Eye' / 'What I Shall Have Been For What I Am in the Process of Becoming') later they took a pause, took a step back, and Denny signalled that that was enough. They had given the best possible account of themselves. They would change the world.

With the return of the wail of far-off sirens, and as the light in the room seemed to pulse and pitch as on a boat adrift, Rickard realised that it was ten past eight on a weekend evening and that no record company would be open for business. Also, he noticed that the year on the front of the directory was '1961'.

There came then the sound of laughter – cackling laughter, as troubled as it was troublesome – from up the hallway and out in the landing. Denny swung open his front door. A big man, broad as a sandwich board, was creased over on himself.

'Jeremiah! What are you doing?!'

The man stretched to full height, rising to six and a quarter feet. He had flaccid dangling arms like downed electric cables, and his shoulders were held confidently apart. He had short black coarse hair, pale pimply skin on a babyish face, and unclear milk-blue aboriginal Irish eyes.

'Jeremiah! Were you laughing?'

'No, sir. I was crying. I was weeping at the sound.'

The thought came suddenly to Clive Sullis that the creatures who had returned him to his body had at last caught up. He began to run – crab-ways, turning, instep patting into instep. In so far as he was in any state to be observing anything he observed all of the colours at once and only grey. A weather condition rose above the trees of the park. Any and all of the trees, they all looked the same. So did the grassy areas. There was no telling where he was, or in which direction he was going. The sky was the sky; towers towered beyond like the fairy follies. Pathways of chewed chewing gum. Choo choo along, he said. Just keep on, keep choo choo-ing. He spun around and the man in the chewing-gum trench coat was gone. The world continued to spin. He was in a cartoon. More like it he'd had a stroke and all this had been assembled using a computer. He wondered when he'd had his stroke. Because it seemed likely that recently he *had* had a stroke. He was bothered lately. He took more time with decisions. He sometimes did things and was not sure when or why he had done them. The delicate man he was outwardly had started to seep inwards. Fears he had not had since the nineteen pissstained seventies were coming back more wretched, more *fawsach*, than ever. Irish words had been creeping into his speech. Rude words had been creeping into his speech.

He plunged his hands deep in the pockets of his long black overcoat, narrowing his already thin frame, and hurried along a path towards a bright open area. Ah, but he knew this place. The Conservatory Water, according to all the maps and guides; the toy-boat pond, as he thought of it. He would stop by here sometimes, on the way back from the Boathouse, on his way out of the park. He had just come from the Boathouse, in a roundabout fashion.

He kicked up some late-winter mulch and tore at a salt sachet in one pocket. He rested his foot on the kerb that ran around the edge of the pond and tried to rally his nerves. In the water his reflection was in pieces. The man by the wheelbarrow in the chewing-gum trench coat – had he been the same man inside the Boathouse, he wondered; the man in the mould-blue sweater sitting on his own by the bar, tipping at something in a little pot? It was hard to tell. The man by the wheelbarrow had not only been wearing a chewing-gum trench coat but a trilby, or a homburg. He had also been wearing sunglasses.

Clive Sullis thought to himself: Why? But why now? Why were they coming, after all this time?

Why, because he'd been given, lately, to saying too much. He'd given himself away. He'd let the mask slip.

He'd told perhaps rather too many people that he had once been a woman. He realised that now.

This was possibly a condition of his stroke. Or it was a function of his mind. His mind knew what his body did not know by this stroke. His body, at the last, when it came to it, taken by surprise and feeling betrayed, would put up a struggle, pulling in gulps of air and throwing out gobbets of phlegm. It was all it knew to do. And his mind, in its pathos, knowing what was coming, was trying, in its way, to put his affairs in order.

And so he had gone around telling anyone who would listen. And they'd laughed in his face. 'But sure we knew!' they'd all said, in words of that order, or in the way they'd looked back at him. And he'd looked at his reflection and seen that it was true: funny; though he'd been a manly girl, he was never quite the manly man. Perhaps it was in the outline of the eyes. And perhaps it was in the nose – and the surgeon had even offered to take a bone from his backside and bolt it to his nose, give him the pugilist's nose. But he'd worried, stupid girl, that he'd have toppled over while seated.

And it was a pity he'd told so many people because it had been a good disguise until then, he said now to nobody (pulling out the elasticated waistband of his trousers and pouring salt on the sore around where his outlet pipe met his skin – the salt being medicinal). I mean, although I'd never made much of a man, it was still a pretty good disguise – I looked nothing like I did before. I looked nothing like her, that person, me: Jean Dotsy.

And by God Almighty, he'd made a good fist of it. Out of necessity, the very need to survive, he'd given it all he'd got. So that before a year was even out he'd wanted to be the best man there was. She grew into himself, in whole.

But it was a disguise. Still it was. He'd forgotten that. In wanting to grow into it, and in giving it away finally, he'd forgotten that. Why did he give it away? Because he needed everyone to know. Not to know that he'd once been a woman, no. But that it was a disguise.

And he'd go back now, if he could, if he could give his pursuers the slip, he'd go back to the Colombian who sold him his cantaloupe melons, the man, one of them, he'd told he was a woman, and he'd say, 'No – no. There's something else.' And he'd go back to his neighbour, Mia, who he'd told too, and he'd say, 'No – no. I knew you knew that. But have you since wondered why? If I tell you now that it was all just a disguise, a way to go into hiding, would you like to know why it was so?'

And he'd go to Denny, he would. He would go to Denny, who had thought he knew all that there was to know. And he'd say, 'You think you know me. You think you knew who I was, and what I became. But. Listen.'

If only he could be given the chance now. If only he hadn't opened his big bog mouth.

He looked out over the pond for a few minutes. Children and their minders raced yachts and clippers and tourists were spread about. If he stayed here, no harm would come. This was the idea of safety in numbers, this was the feeling of safety that came from being in somebody else's scene, a windless Dutch scene. This was the play of the light. He could wait here for the man. Where was the man? There he was. His form stretched above and below the line of the kerb. He was as still as the bare branches.

Clive watched him and waited for him to move but he did not.

The enemy: safe to think of him as that now. The envoy. He thought back to the wheelbarrow; the way, after he'd spun around, the man had disappeared, gone, into thin air, in a whip and a swirl of leaves. He knew exactly the enemy he was dealing with here. He looked about him, at women his own age and at little children in paper-boat hats. Common birds of the north-eastern United States that did not have a care. The world was spinning. Litter, little weightless scraps, ash, followed a spiral descent. No amount of witnesses, no number of nobodies, would protect him. He knew exactly what he was dealing with. The spy costume no doubt was deliberate. A taunt. This is what we are doing, yes.

* * *

A night weeks before. Clive Sullis woke from a nightmare that was gone in an instant and he was worried about blood clots to the brain. He woke up screaming, screaming. The screams out of him. That was it. Just: 'Pissstains!' 'Jisolm!' Like that, bursting through darkness. Like the original language. The first words after the bang. As if something had broken down and something else was made in its place. False and crude. This was the story of his life. Why couldn't they see him for who he was?

He sat up and patted the bedclothes around him, letting them cool, and his breathing settle.

He had an obscure memory of getting up in the night with a headache and pulling apart the presses for paracetamol. He remembered having a dry throat and that he was nauseated too and that he was convinced a plastic fork was stuck in the root of his tongue and that his head was a head of lettuce and that he was halfway through a prayer when he realised he was praying to Peter Stuyvesant, the last governor of New Amsterdam. This was an obsession now: Holland. This was the trouble after the bang. Memories from now on might only be vague, or split, or not memories at all. Of the moments before he woke, before the outburst, he could recall, he thought – what? Material, chippings. Lines and circles. Ones and zeroes. These things had been falling through his mind against a black background. But of the day before – of the waking day before, he could recall almost everything, he thought. He remembered he had read that because the beaver ate only tree bark its diet was considered vegetarian. Now hold on a minute, he said.

He made himself a cup of coffee and brushed his teeth and swept his jacks across the table with his arm and tried to keep active in his apartment at 1202, The Birches, Stuyvesant Town. He knew who he was, in name: Clive Sullis, self branded. He knew his age: seventy-four. These were the present identifying stamps. But what of his long-term memory? Could he write his whole life story, if given the time, in broad strokes at least? Yes, he felt that he could.

He poured himself another cup of coffee, tipped out the rest of the container of sweetener on the saucer, and dropped in three of the pills. And he had also read of pills that could help with the despair of getting older. And that they worked by giving you a good view of yourself in the world and making you realise that you are unremarkable and that any of the oddities that you worry the rest of the world might notice are not noticeable at all. He thought that he would have to nullify this knowledge if these pills were to work on him, but he did not need to think so deeply now. He did not need to be fretting and thinking or fretting about not thinking. He needed to relax was what he needed to do. He should not be fearing the worst and he should stop being so hard on himself. He should allow for the fuzzy memories, for the confusion, for the bad language, for the worries, given his age and given every change he'd been through.

Later that day he was not so coherent. Parting a way through a scrub of cane chairs under the umbrellas of the terrace he greeted his good friend Denny by saying that some day he would say something, that there were some things that needed to be said, that in all their years of friendship there was one thing, that really there was one thing, that –

'All right, Clive, all right. Sit yourself down and stop making a holy show, will you? The cold is getting to all of us.'

* * *

He made it as far as the subway station. He was under no illusions about any of this. He waited by the steps, in front of the MTA booth, where it was said that you should wait for safety's sake, where behind a pane of glass smeared with scratches a beautiful young woman was absorbed in a magazine. The station was not busy with people. A teenaged boy was spinning a girl around by her haversack and the girl was screaming because she was coming close to the edge of the plat-form. Three youths watched with awe and amusement something on the track. Beside him a woman and her ward pulled at cords of liquorice from a paper bag. The announcer said a downtown local train was two stations away. The commuters gathered themselves. He moved off the steps and to the white line and stared into the ribbed gullet of the tunnel. Choo choo, he said.

One station along, at 59th Street, a large crowd squeezed its way on to the train. His carriage filled up with huge shopping bags stuffed with duvets. There was a collective release of breath, and here and there laughter broke out. He looked along all the people on the side opposite him, then he leaned forward to look at the people on his own side. There was no reason to believe that the man in the trench coat had got on at

59th Street. Why not just have done with it further up, out in the open, on the street? He could have caught up with him if he'd wanted to, on 72nd Street, or on Lexington. That said, somewhere between Madison and Lexington he had seemed to lose the man. He most definitely had followed him out of the park, he was sure, but then somewhere on the street he had gone, perhaps ducking into an apartment-block lobby, or crouching in the flower beds in the middle of Park Avenue.

Or hopping into a taxi. Most likely. Most evidently. This was exactly what he had done: at the other end of the carriage a door opened to a gush of hissing and grinding and slammed shut again. The man stood still for a moment, as if decompressing, or as if preparing to make an announcement. Ladies and gentlemen, a few words about safety. It was comical, almost. The enemy/the envoy. Chewing-gum trench coat and trilby, or homburg. Now he was moving again, all deference, tipping his hat to the woman whose bags were blocking his way.

He sat diagonally opposite Clive, twenty feet away, in clear sight. Nothing was in the section of aisle between them except duvets, folded in quarters. He opened the top buttons of his coat to show a sliver of mould-blue sweater, took off his hat and placed it on his lap. So this was the creature who had staked him out in the Boathouse, had pursued him using all means at his disposal. This physical – yes, physical, Clive was surprised to note – specimen. Thin on top;

wispy strands of red backcombed hair clinging damply to the sides of his head. A colour to his skin. It was not quite a high colour and not quite a tan. He had the complexion of a hearing aid, and almost the glaze: something other than blood coursed through his veins. His head turned slowly in Clive's direction as if on an oiled track, his face set in palsied neutrality. His eyes were watered-down green; they stared into Clive's, looked through him, to say, 'There – we are going to there.' Behind him a poster read: SNUGGLE UP TO APPLEDORN'S HALF-PRICE DUVET SALE. Any second Clive expected the train to derail in a shower of white sparks and feathers.

They pulled into 23rd Street, one station from home. He would make his exit here. He waited until all who were standing had disembarked and then he sprang from his seat with as much suddenness as he could muster. The doors snapped behind him, nearly catching his coat. But he was safely on the platform, out and away. But – there was the man ahead, stepping out from the other end of the carriage without a glance behind, going now with the main flow of people, but proceeding slowly, with deliberation. The back of his neck glared. The skin looked painted on, like the skin on his face – resin on an invisible surface. Once, when Clive was a tall young girl, his brother had attacked the neck of a football hero with a rod because he had disgusted him, he said. The thought came to him now. He could attack the man's neck, cut off whatever was feeding the brain. He could ram it with his elbow, then

76

hand himself over to the law. They might be lenient, if he came clean, told them everything, every detail, right from the start.

Some people were moving against the main current, walking in the direction opposite to the way Clive was facing. They were heading for another exit, behind him. He went with this movement, flipped around, and hurried up the stairs. On the concourse above he was presented with a choice – a choice and a man playing 'Rest, My Woolly Wolfhound' on a saxophone. As he hurried up the steps for 22nd and Park he found himself transported. He thought of the pale cone of Errigal and the honeyed scent of gorse. And he thought that if souls and bodies with them could be transported they would have him where they wanted him, and they would surface with bronze hurls from the prickles, but they would not get their milk because he did not have diddies and they would be even angrier.

* * *

When he first emerged into New York he was still a young woman. Her name was awkward bony Jean Dotsy and her introduction to city life had been a Dublin of livestock sales and Swastika Laundry vans. In New York she had woken into a dream and for a while she experienced a golden time because the city was a place where she could lose herself and at the same time she knew it would tell her everything about herself that she wanted to know. She had for a long time known that she was a woman who loved other women but now she said it to herself and it felt like both the making of her and a declaration. Back in Dublin she was known as an independent girl but in New York she had another word – variant. She was a variant. She got the word from a kind of manifesto in a magazine that another woman who was also a variant had given her. Perhaps she had been magnetically attracted to this woman sitting on a bench in Washington Square Park or perhaps she was simply tired on that day, her first in New York, and had wanted just to observe the assembly of variants who were all gathered to march in support of basic rights for black people. The woman on the bench scribbled down the address of a restaurant where later the variants on the march were meeting. But Jean did not want to promise anything and she was naturally suspicious of being part of groups she did not know much about. And the wet creamy gravel of Washington Square Park patted under her feet in a paste like peanut butter and she had so many things she wanted to experience so soon: peanut butter and Times Square and jelly and jazz and Chew-butter Cracknells and the fish market and the Jews and the diamond sellers.

Of course she was so tired by that evening that she needed somewhere to sit down or where she could put up her feet. She was not prepared to go back to the hostel just yet, for the previous hours had given her a feeling for and a faith in the community of people. Everywhere was the sense of people exagger-

through gloomy arcades in already gloomy streets: scaffolding had sprouted everywhere. On 19th Street he felt the leer of stone carvings, hideous caricatures of mercantile men. He spun around a stanchion, checking through all degrees. At Gramercy Park he knocked a cup of froth from gloved hands. He brushed it, she crushed it. An upshoot of gloop. She screamed, 'You'll pay for that, asshole.' There was no time for recompense. He would die running. They would kill him. He would die under these stone eyries.

He would need a weapon. He knew of a butcher's shop nearby that would have hooks and cleavers and long knives. Perhaps he could persuade the butcher to sell him a hook. Or he might be able to buy a bone, a cow's shin bone, or a buffalo's. In the butcher's shop he found himself behind a line of people. He considered leaving, but then the butcher's assistant asked him what he wanted. He was aware that the other people in the line were annoyed that he had been asked before they had, but he had a base frenzy about him and they would not make a fuss. He scanned across the platter under glass and saw a mound of purple-brown tongues, outsized tongues that were still furred and glistened with pinpricks of light. A tongue was a weapon his pursuer would understand. He could slap him across the face with it and it would have mystical, symbolic significance. He got his tongue for one dollar on account of how late in the day it was.

He slumped into Duffy's Tavern on 23rd Street and sat on a stool at the bar in front of the taps knowing he would be challenged soon. The barman would not care for raw meat on his premises. He gripped the tongue between his knees with his nails. He kneaded his head, his hair, and the knots and mounts beneath. He pleased the barman by allowing him to show that he could fix an old-fashioned but now the tongue had slipped from his fingers and hit the floor with a splat. He kneaded his hair with his other hand, the one he had been holding the tongue with, and his fingers were through his hair before he realised. Oh my God, he thought, his hand shaking. He was a delicate man. He feared people – he feared his good friend Denny, this delicate man. That's what Denny thought, that's how they all thought of him. A delicate man. He didn't want that side, the side that was on the outside, to infect him. He was not this delicate man. She had not made this man to be a delicate man. For the love of Christ, if she was to be a man could she not just be a man? She had howled and wailed at this delicate man. She had tried to command him and watched as he failed her, put on airs, apologised for everything. Her words would go unheard, lost somewhere. The voice was tiny. Tinny. Always she was aware of the great breezy gaps in this largely empty vessel – always she was aware she was the occupant of a vessel. One had never, never nearly, fitted into the other. Now the occupant was shrinking from disaster. Jean, he called to herself, from outside to in. Wake up you feisty thing, you big lumbering bitch.

'Mind if I sit here?'

His pursuer.

Chewing-gum trench coat. Enemy/envoy. Trilby or homburg. The voice was, like his own, an Ulster one. It made some kind of sense to him that this should be so.

He did not look in the creature's eyes and he was uncertain as to whether he should take the hand that was offered. He fastened his eyes on the floor where his tongue was laid out in black blood like a slug.

'Oh, Saint Sybil. What's that? Your dinner?'

He found the Ulster accent placating, like the sudden rush of some mild narcotic.

'Hey. Allow me to introduce myself. Please.'

He looked at the creature's knees.

'My name is Aidan Brown. My friends call me Quicklime.'

The barman dawdled at the taps, waiting for an order. Aidan Brown climbed on to his stool, his trench coat and hat still on him. Clive opened his mouth.

'Yes?' said Aidan Brown.

'Are you a fairy, Aidan Brown?'

'Quicklime, please … No, I'm not a fairy. My friends call me Quicklime because I'm a sailor and I know the best way to treat scurvy.'

'Is that true?'

Aidan Brown shook with laughter.

'No. My friends call me Quicklime because I have pitted thick skin and I'm fast on my feet.'

'*Are* you a fairy?'

'No, most definitely not.'

'Have you been sent on behalf of the fairies?'

'No. I represent only myself and the organisation I represent.'

'Reveal yourself please and do whatever it is you have pursued me to do.'

'May I ask, first of all, *your* name?'

'Do you not already know?'

'It's evaded me, that one, I admit.'

Aidan Brown ordered a pot of coffee. Eventually he took off his hat and got the barman to hang it up for him. He rolled his trench coat in a bundle and sat on it. In the piercing spotlights Clive was able to observe that he indeed had pitted skin. His face was not frozen and palsied now but puffed out and twitchy with tics like that of any regular middle-aged man after taking vigorous exercise. The humanitarian in Clive was glad he had not attacked Aidan Brown in the neck. At the same time he was aware that a game of wiles might have been in play.

'*Am* I to call you Quicklime?'

'If you like.'

Quicklime looked across the arrangement behind the bar. A grid of pigeonholes was decorated with bunting and each flag on the bunting was a county flag of Ireland. Amid the reserves of whiskey, perry and absinthe was a lead bomb labelled 'Replica of Saint Patrick's Bell'.

'You could feel at home in a place like this,' said Quicklime. 'You're from Donegal?'

'Yes. Close by Ballyshannon. I left it when I was eighteen to go up to Dublin.'

'You haven't lost the burr. It's softened a bit, mind. But that's burrs for you. Burrs burr, brogues rattle. I'm from your neck of the woods. The village of Garrison. Caught the wrong side of the border.'

Clive tried quickly to ascertain the layout of Duffy's Tavern. It was a narrow and deep and typically light-starved single room. He looked for escape routes. But he was somehow assuaged by this mention of a real place, Garrison, and the implication that the listener would understand the nuance in the words 'caught the wrong side of the border'.

He traced the rim of his glass with his finger.

'You're a Catholic rather than a Protestant?'

Quicklime laughed again.

'You've been out of Ireland a long time, my friend. Nobody asks questions like that. I'm a Protestant, as it happens. But a nationalist. My parents named me after the great British way station of Aden. Later I gaeli-cised the spelling.'

Some moments of silence passed as Quicklime mopped up coffee from the bar with a handkerchief.

'Look at the two of us here in this pub,' he said.

'And you're not a sailor?'

'I'm not a sailor, no. Nor do I know the best way to treat scurvy. But I do spend most of the year travelling great distances. This is what I do.'

'What do you do?'

He reached into his trouser pocket, winked at Clive, and took out a slim silver case from which he produced a card. It said:

'We're a charity, but as I say to the people we help: don't look on us as a charity. Look on us as a service, a free service. We're in the business of repatriation. We help the most valued members of Ireland's diaspora. The elderly and the wise. Which description are you most comfortable with? Elderly, or old, or aged?'

'I would say I'm comfortable with any of them.'

'We help men who left Ireland as hopeful younger men for places like New York and London and are still in New York and London but with the old form of hope long extinguished. If they have any hope left it's the hope that one day they might return to Ireland.'

He was not looking at Clive as he spoke, becoming absorbed in his spiel, rapping the counter with his knuckle.

'But that hope is laid to waste by worry about where the next bag of fuel pellets is coming from, or whether the cheque will last them the week. They've nothing to be doing only breaking into racecourses and walking the track in the middle of the night. Or mooching in Irish clubs in Cricklewood, say, nursing a pint of sickly English bitter, eyeing that battered box of Cluedo up on the shelf. And they'll be eyeing it all evening, that box of Cluedo, because they'll have nothing else to be doing. And they'll be thinking of all the people they're not playing Cluedo with and of all the people they once played Cluedo with. Does this sound familiar to you?'

'I don't know what Cluedo is. I'm … This is …'

'Or take the man I helped the week before last. Poor lad, went out years ago, in his thirties, to the Niger Delta in Africa to follow the fossil-fuel craze. He had degrees coming out his ears, in oil engineering this and oil engineering that. Thought he might meet a wife out there. But he didn't. The Nigerian women wouldn't have him. And he didn't thrive in the job either. Turns out the oil business down there is run by a cabal of Brits. Treated him like muck. I found him in a bar in Port Harcourt supping bad Nigerian Guinness. Have you ever had Nigerian Guinness?'

Clive remained silent.

'It's not the same. Nothing like the same. It's brewed up there in Lagos.'

'Mister Quicklime …'

'Just Quicklime, please.'

'Have you come to rescue me?'

He took a moment.

'Well. That's up to you. I know little about you, if I'm being honest. All I'm here to do is tell you about Bring Our Boys Back Home. And to tell you that Ireland values her sons even if no one else does. I want you to know that there's help here if needed.'

'But … you must have identified me as someone in need of help.'

'I identified you as a fellow tribesman of a certain vintage, alone in a vast and impersonal city.'

'But really – you know nothing.'

'Which is true. I haven't even got your name yet.'

'I don't have a name.'

'Now come on.'

'I call myself Clive. I've learnt to live with this name, Clive Sullis. It means "sword of light" in Irish. Men with theatrically priapic names such as this you have to wonder about, don't you think? More recently I'm inclined to respond to the name I was born with, Jean Dotsy, though no one ever calls me that.'

'Look. Clive. As I say – a vast, impersonal city. And full of fairies, you're right about that.'

Quicklime began brushing the bar, the patch where he had spilt his coffee, with the sleeve of his mould-blue sweater.

'Ah yes, that'll bring up the grain all right,' he said.

Clive stared quietly at the wood for some moments. Then he said, 'No, I'm staying here. I've been here too long, and this is my home.'

'"Too long" I think is the revealing phrase.'

'Things are moving along now. I have a purpose here. I have a friend, Denny, and … we've started a tenor trio. We've formed a little singing group. We'll sing Irish ballads, play engagements.'

Quicklime examined his sleeve for damp.

'What sort of ballads?'

'Oh … the old ones. Like McCormack used to sing.'

'This is one of the signs, you see. I've seen this many times before, in men like you. The pain of yearning is too much and so they lose themselves in sentimental old songs. It's a dangerous game. These are sad old songs and in their singing the yearning and sadness is perpetuated. And the Ireland depicted in these songs is a fantasy. All harps and rainbows and Glocca Morra.'

'There's nothing wrong with that, no? What's wrong with a little make-believe?'

'Fantasy is the path to madness. And wouldn't you rather come home and see how things are for real? How long is it since you've been in the old country?'

Clive thought about it.

'Fifty years.'

'Ah now, Clive.'

Quicklime flicked the gleaming gold pipe of a tap, making it ping.

'I can show you an Ireland more glittering and more wonderful than any Ireland you'll ever sing about. Ireland today truly is the land of fantasy. You would be amazed. A new age of statuary ... Huge triumphal arches in green Connemara marble ... Gold mines.'

'Gold?'

'In south County Wicklow. They've reopened the mines after two hundred years ... We have ways of thinking about politics that are a cause of wonder to the world. Restitutionalism. Bifurcal assemblies ... They're draining the bogs and clearing the fields on the Roscommon–Mayo border to create a new capital city. New Tara.'

'New Tara?'

'Tara Nua.'

'It sounds all very wonderful. It does. But. I could never go back to Ireland.'

'Of course you could.'

'No, I could never go back to Ireland. It would be dangerous for me.'

'How so?'

'Because ... Mister Quicklime, how much time have we got?'

'Clive, we have as much time as it takes.'

There comes a time, Clive thought, had been thinking all the while. There comes a time. This was the way of healing. This was encouraged, and it was a good thing.

'Just let it all out, Clive, open up.'

'You're a decent-seeming man, it's turned out. You've proved your bona fides.'

'I will listen to whatever you have to say, whatever it is you want to get off your chest.'

'A decent-seeming or any other kind of man, but at least you're a man. At least I'm assured now that you're a man.'

'One to another.'

'Oh no, I'm not a man. At least ... I don't know. As I've told you, I was born a woman. I never intended to become a man.'

'Is this your big disclosure, Clive?'

'No. No. That's not what I need to tell you. That's not my disclosure. I need to tell you – tell someone – about ... what led me, or pushed me, to become a man. And what I became before I became a man. Yes – what I became *before* I became a man. Yes, this exactly. This fact of who or what I am that I need the *world* to accept.'

'Take your time, my friend.'

'But how can I be *sure* you're a man and not a fairy?'

'Clive …'

Quicklime became distracted, his attention switching to some activity beyond Clive's left shoulder.

'Clive, I can't talk to you right now. I've got to go, I'm sorry.'

'But, sir –'

'But please – come back to me. Tell me everything. I'm in town for a while. My number's on the card I gave you.'

Two men had entered the pub somewhere through the back. They were taking stools at the far end of the bar, were broad-faced, platform-browed, and neither was doing a good job of hiding an interest in Quicklime. Clive turned back to his companion, but he had already gone, leaving his trilby, or his homburg, on the hook behind the bar.

Denny's telephone was black and heavy, made of an obsolete compound, and its electrics were partly exposed. The mouthpiece smelt of birdseed and bird markets. He had acquired the phone some thirty years earlier and it was fifty years older again. Its dial wheel resisted his finger like a ship's wheel resisted the maelstrom.

'Clive – a letter arrived this morning.'

'Oh?'

'From a radio station in the Bronx. Called Bettina's Bathtime. Care of. But with my name on it. Denny Kennedy-Logan.'

'Go on.'

'Ultimately from a lady. Named Delma Rosenberg. Do you know this lady?'

'Delma. Fidelma. A good Catholic name … No, I don't know this lady. What does she have to say?'

'Are you sure you don't know this lady? Do you have any explanation for this?'

'For what?'

'For what's in the letter.'

'What's in the letter?'

'Are you sitting comfortably?'

'I am now.'

'She begins':

Dear wonderful Free 'n' Easy Tones. I won't waste too much time introducing myself. My name is at the end of this letter. Let it suffice for now to tell you that I am a music lover. That means that I am cold on modern music because in modern music the percussion is advanced to the detriment of the melody. I think the art of melody has been lost in recent times, don't you think so too? Perhaps that's because so much of the old music has not been heard by younger ears.

You know what I mean by old music of course you do. I mean the old art songs and the ballads of old. I was raised on these songs and I'm afraid that they have spoilt me because nothing else in music can compare with them. I had long given up that this kind of music was around today as a living form but that's 'O.K.'. I simply don't expect to hear the old music of my youth performed today and its essence intact.

It was a stroke of good luck that I had my radio tuned to Bettina's Bathtime on the evening that you were on. I was having some 'bath time' of my own. I rarely leave the radio on when I'm in the bath because if something offends my ears it's hard to change it in a hurry and then there's always the risk of electrocution. There was nothing offensive about this show on that night however. I stopped turning the dial when I heard 'Clair de Lune' by Claude Debussy and there I left it. Then came some Hoagy Carmichael I think and then the Moonlight Sonata. And then the presenter introduced this great new singing group. Well you know who!

I can honestly say that I have not had an experience like it since I was perhaps fifteen years of age. I felt more than that – no! – I was transported further! I felt like one of those rose-cheeked girls in a Pears Soap advertisement from the nineteen hundreds, reclined there in my bath tub under imaginary velvet and green jungle plants! 'Who were these men with these magical voices?' I wondered. Magic! It's the only word to describe it. A cracked and haunted quality that I have not heard from living men. I mean to say 'live' but 'from living men' is as good a phrase for it.

I mean, I've gone to concerts by the Galway Tenors and the Shamrock Singers but these acts are terrible – don't you think? perhaps you wisely don't attend their concerts? or do you know them personally? oh God! if you do – because they seem to me like parodies of great artists like McCormack and they don't treat the music they sing seriously at all, they are like circus acts, although technically they can be quite good, not that I know fully because I am technically illiterate, but there is no life in their music somehow and they are not for me I'm afraid.

Those Irish ballads when sung must hold a certain spirit, a mysterious spirit which the phonograph companies of the early years of the last century captured on those cylinders and later those great heavy discs. This is the spirit that rubbed up against and warmed my own when I first sensed it through the records my mother owned. I was raised surrounded by Irish families close to the water in Steinway. This must have been where my mother developed her interest in authentic Irish music. She acquired her collection over many years. Possibly some of her discs were 'hand me downs' from her own mother who was also a lover of Irish song. I grew up with a great attachment to all things Irish. I sometimes feel that I'm 'more Irish than the Irish themselves'! I had an obsession with the Kennedys at the height of the days of Camelot and do you know I felt a spiritual attachment to Black Jack who was the riderless and well-behaved horse that took part in Jack Kennedy's funeral procession?

Anyway what I mean to say to you is that the music on my mother's records was the sound of my youth and that it nourished my spirit in those and my later years. Since hearing your singing my soul has not for a long time felt so well fed! The Free 'n' Easy Tones – what an apt and evocative name! But I must say I almost caught pneumonia waiting until the last note was sung – the bathwater went cold and cloudy around me!

Now let me get to the nub of why I am writing to you. I am the patron of a charity for nervous illnesses. On March sixth we are holding a benefit concert at the Amsterdam Avenue Armory. We already have a girl who does show tunes and a soprano who will sing some arias but if you were to accept my invitation I would love to add you to the bill. Indeed on the basis of what I heard on the radio you will receive star billing! Please do accept! We have a little under a fortnight until then but could you take not more than two days to confirm your availability? Perhaps that is enough time for you to fret and say no! Please don't!

Yours admiringly, Delma Rosenberg.

PS I noted on the radio that you sang *a cappella*. If you like you could use an accompanist of my recommendation or you may choose to use your own.

Denny took a moment.

'And there you have it,' he said. 'Clive?'

'I'm still here.'

'What do you make of it?'

'I'm as mystified as you are. Except, perhaps ... When we rang the record company that time, and sang down the phone –'

'What?! We were singing into *space*, man! There was no one on the end of the line. The line was dead. You heard it yourself.'

Both went quiet.

Then Clive said, 'Still, we're being offered a concert. You know? Denny?'

'So it seems.'

'And –'

'But …'

'Hello?'

'This is not the answer.'

'The lady is offering us a concert, Denny. Top of the bill, she says!'

'I don't know.'

'What is there to know?'

'This, exactly.'

'Maybe we should just –'

'I have a hazy … pre-Christian sentiment about it.'

'I know she says it's not a paid concert, but –'

'Give me some time to think this through.'

'But she says we only have –'

'Just give me some time, man!'

'Yes, Denny. Of course.'

Denny put the phone down and went immediately to his kitchen, took some mince from the refrigerator and tipped it into Bit's bowl. The dog had been fed less than an hour before but did not complain; it ate the mince with gusto. Then Denny went to the living room, and his piano stool. He sat in the heat, dripping, elbows on knees, and later also in the dark. He did not turn on a light. Always in the colder months the apartment was hot like a botanical glasshouse. Below the building Jeremiah and his goblin brothers made sure the boiler was full and firing through the day.

At some point in the evening the smell of Bit's faeces drifted into the room. He heard the dog warble.

'Good boy,' he said, seeing the sparkle of Bit's eyes in the doorway.

He held its gaze for some moments.

'Come here now.'

Bit did not respond. Its eyes disappeared in the dark. Denny resumed his slumped posture. Later he turned to face his piano square. His right hand idled over the higher notes. He felt the faint and satisfying *shup* of keys, then held down a chord. The words of one of Arthur Sullivan's songs came to mind:

> *'I know not what I was playing,*
> *Or what I was dreaming then,*
> *But I struck one chord of music,*
> *Like the sound of a great Amen.'*

He allowed the notes to decay as a melody swirled in his head, building and collecting. *Clamor. Clamor.*

Before the notes had faded to silence he had it. In the dark night all noise is quieted: Otello and Desdemona's renewal of their vows of love. *'Già nella notte densa s'estingue ogni clamor'*: the peerless tenor Francesco Merli, his favourite performer as Otello.

He tried singing the Moor's lines himself but nothing would come; his throat – tightening, stoppered – ached with the effort. Now his fingers did the leading, searching for the melodic accompaniment to Otello and Desdemona's great love duet. It was a kind of automatic playing: harp and horns and bassoons filled the auditorium of his skull while in the dark outside he pushed for a way through. But his playing was heavy, his joints stiff. Clamour, clamour, it went. With the quiver of violins that brought the first act to a close his fingers weakened on the keys until the soft beat of wires on felt came to him again.

He wept, leaned forward to the shiny black box. His cheek pressed the panel in front, his hand the panel at the side. Wood and metal rumbled inside with the disturbed air. He was no longer hearing Merli soaring now. He was hearing Paolo Silveri. In Dublin, 1959, dying.

Dying.

(He told anyone who asked that she had died. And dead she probably was now. They had been the same age and he was all of eighty-three and half of Western humanity did not make it as far as eighty-three.)

Aisling.

She had come off her bicycle. It was a terrible tragedy.

The next day he decided to get rid of his piano. He put an ad in the newspaper:

UPRIGHT PIANO. BLACK, GOLD LEAF AND
BRASS. GERMAN. MID-CENTURY.
HAS STAYED TRULY IN TUNE FOR 45 YEARS.
$750 o.n.o.

Two days later three men came to carry it away. A woman in mustard angora, the mother of the new owner, stood back, directing their movements, little Bit jigging like a jumping bean among these strangers' ankles.

'You must show these beasts who's boss,' he said to the woman, stooping to smack the dog's bottom.

'Yes, they are making it awkward for themselves,' the woman said, 'though I can see why you thought it was too big for the room.'

The men carried the piano out the door, down the corridor, down in the service elevator. In the lobby, doorman Emmet helped them the rest of the way.

'Mind it,' Denny couldn't help calling out, though it was no longer his to care about. 'Good riddance,' he said, 'and bye to that.'

Emmet came back into the lobby shaking his arms from the shoulders down.

'Ee-yaye, yaye, yaye,' he said.

'Heavy?' said Denny.

'Painful,' said Emmet.

'Emmet,' said Denny, 'I want to talk to Jeremiah about his electric piano. I'll need a replacement for my own now.'

'Excellent for tight spaces, Mister Kennedy-Logan.'

'Is he down below?'

'Just follow the noise.'

The basement was in fact quiet when Denny entered, except for the hum of a tumble dryer or two coming from a side passage. Past the passage, on the left, was a door to a vestibule, then two of the three goblin brothers' living quarters. Past Jeremiah and Breffny's living quarters was, somewhere, a set of workshops.

'Come in,' said Jeremiah.

On one side of the vestibule plastic trays filled with oiled nuts, dirty rags and various cranking and turning tools were stacked to the ceiling. On the opposite side, sitting on a stool, was the middle though largest and yet youngest looking of the goblin brothers. He was eating a sandwich, and wearing shorts and an upside-down US Mail bag with holes for head and arms. To the left of him was his electric piano on a serifed-X-shaped stand. To the right was a wooden lectern desk.

Jeremiah was a quiet and private lad, but the residents often remarked on his talent. He played in the day or in the evening when he was not on door duty, which was most of the time. Whenever Denny came down to wash or collect laundry it seemed that a vamp or fugue or riverine tinkle was coming from Jeremiah's cubbyhole.

(The lectern desk, Jeremiah had explained to Denny before, was for the business of producing manuscripts. All the goblin people and varieties of that kind in the world worked flat out to make history and artefacts to give a delusion of past beyond human beings' living memory.)

'What can I do for you, Denny?'

'I have always liked the sound of your electric piano. Are they expensive?'

'Are you in the market?'

'Can you demonstrate for me please what your machine can do? I believe the keys on these things are not satisfactorily weighted.'

Jeremiah slowly savoured the last bites of his sandwich, then dragged his stool to the piano. He quickly ran through a scale.

'They're fine. Your fingers get used to it.' Lifting his head and crossing his arms now he said, 'The brother tells me you were wanting to get rid of your old lovely upright.'

'Just been rid of it,' said Denny, loudly exhaling through his nose.

'And why would you have done something like that? The tone off of that instrument was easily the finest in the building.'

'A woman, of course.'

'Sit down there now,' said Jeremiah, offering his stool. He went into his room and fetched a fold-up chair for himself. 'Same woman?' he said, settling down again.

'The same one.'

They listened to a fit of croup from the boiler for some moments. (The goblin brothers had illegally redirected steam from public services into the building's heating system.)

Finally Jeremiah said, 'I wouldn't be in any position to give advice on that.'

Denny considered this point. 'It's true that I have never seen a goblin woman, or even assumed that such a variant existed. How *do* the goblin people generate themselves?'

Jeremiah angrily slapped his hands on his knees. 'Why do you persist in calling us "goblins"? We are fairies or shee. Is that such a hard idea to grasp? Do you not believe I'm a shee?'

Denny was sorry he had said anything to hurt Jeremiah, having thought the words 'goblin' and 'fairy' and 'shee' were interchangeable (though the words 'fairy' and 'shee' clearly now were, and this was noted).

'I have no difficulty at all believing that you are a shee,' he said.

The Mac An Fincashel brothers belonged to a clan of lowland fairies, isolated by bogs and cuts, who were famed for their jam-making but equally for spoiling jam. After a blackcurrant blight they came to the new world as stowaways in the hull of a steamship, or at least a ship that was powered a great length of the way by steam and partly by electrics. It was in the clanging compact chambers of this vessel that they had learnt all that they knew about plumbing and electrics. In America where there are no blackcurrants they turned to blueberries, and because of the tremendous nutritional value of blueberries the brothers grew to an abnormally large size. Denny had no difficulty believing that the Mac An Fincashels were shee because two of them (Emmet and Breffny) had tenacious beard shadow despite shaving every day, and one of them (Breffny, the youngest) had dark wrinkled skin like a defecated husk. Also, he had no difficulty believing that they were shee because he, Denny, belonged to the city of Dublin, the most magical city in Ireland, which sat in a saddle between the Hill of Howth, where the queen Aideen was buried, and the Hill of

Kilmashogue, which was a known haunt of the god Aonghus Óg.

'Although,' said Jeremiah, caressing his forehead, 'I've observed this about women: they don't have the power to overpower men and yet they walk about care-free as you like, so delicate' – his caressing became a forceful strumming – 'around the hollows of their ankles and in the glides of their necks and at the houghs of their knees, as if they are never in danger. I'm not sure if that's of any use to you.'

Denny, studying him with an ambivalence of pity and awe, said, 'No, Jeremiah, it is not. Is there anything more useful you can tell me about women from your vantage of bemusement and dispassion?'

Jeremiah looked back at him with rubbed-red bright smiling eyes.

'Is there anything you can tell me from your vantage of great experience and knowledge?' the shee said.

Denny, stroking his chin, said, 'You are blessed by your nature, Jeremiah the Shee, and you're as well away from them.'

'I think I would like to know more about women.'

Denny, thinking for a moment, said, 'Some informa-tion you might like to know about women can be found in this song.'

He noticed something slosh across the muscles of Jeremiah's face, like a wave in a tray of water. A smirk broke from the shee's lips. Denny closed his eyes tightly and gave it as well as he had it within him, sing-ing 'Two Sisters of Outstanding Charms':

> *'Then one day I knew what it was –*
> *My poor benighted mind!*
> *This charm was but an illusion of sight*
> *And was I ever but blind?*
> *One sister was the half of her head*
> *Where feel and instinct wrought.*
> *The other close sister was the half*
> *Of soundness, nerve and thought.*
> *Wasn't I the fool to ever believe*
> *The marriage was her and me?*
> *The union true was prestidigitator*
> *And the woman that I could see.'*

A distressing fact of Denny's singing, and one that he wondered about others detecting, was that he could not meet anybody in the eye when he was in the act.

He placed his knees neatly together and his hands on his lap.

Instead of articulating a response Jeremiah said, after a moment, 'The sounds you hear now are of tunnelling and underground exploding. All sorts of groupings are in on it. New York City is being undermined.'

Denny believed he could feel the vibrations of this activity through the legs of his stool.

'Tell me this now,' he said. 'If I called a tune, any tune, like the one I have just sung, would you be able to play it?'

'I'd be able enough to have a crack at it. If that doesn't sound too proud.'

'I don't doubt that you would be able. I have heard you play, and you have a rare ability.'

'Have you a specific task in mind, Mister Kennedy-Logan?'

'I do. I have a concert upcoming on March the sixth and need someone to play the piano for me.'

'That doesn't leave a lot of time.'

'No it does not, I suppose.'

'I mean this with the greatest of respect.'

'I hadn't considered it a slight until now.'

Denny inclined on the arc of his arm, racked with a surge of internal insubstantial misfirings.

'And tell me this now,' he continued. 'Was it you or your brothers behind this radio-station business?'

Jeremiah gave a big open smile and tilted his head.

'You've got me in a corner and I cannot tell a lie. It was me the cause of it all right.'

'A shee's machinations. I thought so.'

'Only machinery. And benign espionage. Mister Kennedy-Logan, I must admit that the last time wasn't the first time I stood outside your door listening to your singing. And not the final time either.'

'How did you know to come? Did the neighbours complain?'

'No, no. You've been perfectly discreet. But to be in charge of plumbing in a building such as this is to have an ear in every room, you'll understand. The pipes led me to you. And most Thursdays and Sundays now I've liked to stand outside your door enjoying the nice sound. All these songs of home make me feel sick for Ireland, but in a good sort of way that brings me right the way up before they sluice out of me again as a purgative and leave me feeling tired and wanting more. And you sing them very well, all of you. But do you know, the first time I heard you through the plumbing it was all warmth and not so much clarity. Outside your door I get less warmth but better clarity. I think the latter is the better of the two compromises. But a compromise is a compromise and I can't encounter a problem within my jurisdiction without wanting to try to fix it.'

'And how was that accomplished?'

'Well, the door, I felt, was a boon, acting like a resonator, or a tympanic membrane, as it were, and I knew that I would keep the door, and so I didn't bother to knock on your door to ask your permission to stand the other side of it with my recording equipment. A bit of that then, but also the software I have on my computer there behind. It took a bit of fiddling, but after a time I felt I had a file showing the Free 'n' Easy Tones' singing to its best advantage. It was a very beautiful piece of sound production, if I may compliment you. And compliment you I will, as the beauty did not originate with me – I was merely the usher of the beauty.'

'Thank you, Jeremiah.'

'You're welcome. Yes. No. For a time I found myself wondering if it was vanity had come over me, listening over and over again to the music in the file; was it that I felt proud admiring my own part in its effect? And then, after I would turn off the computer to rush upstairs to listen outside your door of a Thursday or Sunday evening, I realised that a more honest admission was that it was a weakness for beauty caused this obsession.'

'Thank you again.'

'You're welcome. And when you finished singing and I rushed back down below I became very sorry that by having to switch on my computer again the beauty was locked away de-constituted at all. And when I did reopen the file it made me terrified with a thought: the perilousness of it. How easy the zero negates the one; how greedy is the interstice for that which bounds it, for it is tropic to the void, which is all beyond the bounds, which is the rigid simplicity of nothing, which is the opposite of beauty. It is no wonder we are all so afraid of the dark, for the dark itself equals nothing, it is the encroachment of nothing, it is the overlap of space. Turning on the lights or making the most of the hours that the sun graces our yardages of earth is just about all we can do in the midst of it. But there is another thing we can do: we can try and give back to that infinitely large and sublime space the immaterial beauty fully constituted it begs for. Which is why to my mind came the idea that I would send the file of music, on a disc, to a radio station, where it might be decoded and the beauty transmitted in the straightest of lines that would cut away from the curvature of the earth and continue for ever and ever into the darkness.'

Denny had been squirming about on his seat as if he had worms in his bottom.

'That's all well and good, Jeremiah. But the upshot is that I now have a concert date and I don't have a piano. Nor have I had time to organise an accompanist.'

At that moment young Spanish-coloured Breffny emerged from the door to his room. He had a little hammer and some rattly bits of blue metal in one hand and was wiping orange axle grease on his trousers with the other.

'Good evening, Denny,' he said, and again: 'I said: Good evening, Denny.'

'Good evening, Breffny. And what are you making for the benefit of the world?'

'Some braces for the brother above.'

'To hold up his trousers?'

'To straighten his teeth.' He showed Denny the pieces of metal flat in his hand and shook them. He went on: 'Denny, I hope you don't mind but I couldn't help hear you say that you needed an accompanist for a music concert. And what, with the greatest respect, were you all this time thinking by not having an accompanist? Why don't you ask the brother here?'

'Jeremiah?'

'You know of his talents. Call any tune and he'll play it. Sing something now, Denny.'

'We've done that bit,' said Jeremiah.

'And I have no doubt he would have accompanied me perfectly,' said Denny.

'What about it, Jeremiah?' said Breffny to his brother.

Denny said: 'As a result of your machinations, Jeremiah, the Free 'n' Easy Tones have been offered a concert on the sixth of March. I came down here to ask your advice in buying a portable electric piano. Now I feel that you owe us your assistance in playing the piano.'

'I think you are very kind,' said Breffny. 'Jeremiah spends too little time outside of his basement making himself better and fresh for the work he has to do. Some day we fear he will place his head under the clock weight of the elevator in despair and then he will be no use to us at all.'

'You are not the master of me,' said Jeremiah with a snap.

There followed a heated conversation between the brothers in Old Irish, only a tiny fragment of which Denny could understand. Eventually, though, an amicable and indeed amusing consensus seemed to have been reached.

'What are you so giddy about?' said Denny, leaning in and wanting to join the fun.

'I was just saying,' said Jeremiah, 'that you have a most unique voice.'

'Oh dear,' said Breffny, pressing a knuckle into a swollen wet eye. 'Yes. You'll be all right for this concert. Jeremiah will do a fine job for you.'

* * *

Denny went back to his apartment with the goblin men's laughter ringing in his ears. It continued to bother him through the day. He did not like that these indeterminately young persons had cheeked him, their de facto employer, and he especially did not like that he had not had a plan in place.

Oh to hell with the idea, he thought. They would use this woman's accompanist or they would sing unaccompanied: that was always the plan.

There was never a plan.

Drat it, Aisling.

He was alone again, in his living room, with no piano taking up space, no piano to walk around. An imprint, buffed at the edges, soaked wet in one corner, marked the site on the carpet.

'Bit!' he cried.

The brothers saw things more clearly than he did. Poor Jeremiah, Jeremiah who was so awesome and pitiful, he was not so pitiful that he could not speak the truth as he heard it. And he had heard it with his own ears: Denny could not sing above or below one note. Jeremiah might tell him which note. The D flat of the cuckoo. Worse – the gargle of the magpie.

Denny could not sing. He had a stone in his throat. He could not sing: say it loud, he said to himself. He was saying it, he thought. There is no one here to hear it.

'Bit!' he cried again.

That is saying it.

And so. The plan was.

Bitching heat.

'Blasted heat!'

The plan had been.

Simply this. To sing again before his time ran out. To clear his throat of that stone. Not much more thought-through than that. He would enlist his friend, Clive. (Clive? Really?) And somebody else, the some-body else who happened to be the boy with the ill-fitting hemispheres for a head.

The plan: to see that stone on the floor, reddened and wrinkled. That would be swell.

Stuck there since the day she left him.

The irony being there had been such grand opera in their parting.

'You will not survive on your own! You will die! I hope you die! If you think you can sing for your supper – well! You'll never earn a penny! You've never had an ounce of talent! It was me who had all the talent! I was your "meal ticket", Aisling! I curse that I ever met you! I curse that day!'

'And I curse you!' she had said. 'I curse you!'

He drank ten bottles of porter that night, tried to sing for the boys in Mulligan's. Nothing but pain for all. They patted him on the back, punched him in the stomach, told him to put it down to grief. It's humours, toothless Billy assured him. Your bile is black from trauma, your throat is heavy with the weight. Humours or possibly tumours. Oh machree, machree, he said. Make it go away. It never went away. She haunted him, always and still, did Aisling.

113

Did Aisling.

It meant vision, it meant spectre.

Too painful, too painful.

His little cornflour rabbit. He would feel the smoothness of her cheek with his finger. If only she had come to America with him and she would have been his little malted milk ball, his little malted milk ball.

Aisling that meant 'vision', as every Irish schoolboy knew. The spectre of Mother Ireland whose appearance heralded a revival in fortunes.

O!

And what a vision she had been when he first saw her!

Eyes, two eyes in a room. Sleepy kind eyes behind mother-of-pearl lids. In a neat, somewhat 'Continental', face. A prim, laterally, but full, longitudinally, set of lips. Straight feet. Small figure, but sharply outlined. She would be up to no further than his chin, which was important. By far the best he had seen in a long while.

He saw her first one Saturday afternoon while standing in a cold and bright and echoey hall. Vehicles passed in the near distance. The shouts of some corner boys came from over the wall outside. Easy to know the ones who will die young and those who drink their milk, he thought. Many thoughts came to him. Thirty expectant faces stared at his. She was wearing a green woollen suit; he was wearing a waistcoat that was intended to look serious. This was an intermediate and

114

uncertain time in his life. He had a foretelling of the seizure to come when he found he could not summon a note. It is possible, he thought, that many of these young men and women, many the same age as myself and many attendees or recent graduates of the university, have heard of the ignominy of the months before in the pages of their *College Tribune*.

But all he had to do was look at those kind encouraging eyes and he felt a flap of feathers in his heart. He realised that the terror that had seemed to go on for an hour must only have filled him for a second. Suddenly everything was well. And he sang, eventually, like a nightingale. He sang 'Claim Me in Spring'.

This was a time in Ireland when you married the first girl that you met and loved.

* * *

As agreed, following his performance Missus Dwyer, the choral-society president, asked him questions in front of the group. They were very searching questions. Evidently she had got her mitts on that copy of the *College Tribune* that carried the story of his defeat and embarrassment in Italy.

'Well we knew you would be good and aren't you "the business". But tell us now about your time in Milano with Silvio Tosi. Did he find that there were limits to what he could teach the Irish tenor? We are not at cellular level so "hot" on the high B flats, are we? I'm told it's to do with the positioning of our clavicles in relation to the ribs around the other side. The audiences in those opera houses in the small towns really "know their stuff" I have heard.'

'They are demanding people, but they are not wealthy people, so they are naturally demanding,' said Denny.

'They let their feelings be known, to the debutante as well as to the singer of many years' experience, if they don't like what they hear, isn't that true?'

'I don't know about that, Missus Dwyer.'

He looked back at the girl in the green suit and found that her sleepy eyes continued to show encouragement and also a curious tolerance. It gave him the strength not only to carry on under this line of questioning but to not be afraid of speaking about his failings.

'No, no, I mean to say, indeed they do, Missus Dwyer. And the same audience does not give you a second chance. Well – there are some regional opera houses that might give the beginner a fresh start, it's true, but by that stage Maestro Tosi had already decided that an opera career was not for me.'

He said all of this with his eyes fixed on the girl.

'Are you determined now to prove that his judgement was wrong?' said Missus Dwyer.

'No I am not,' said Denny. 'Don't you know what pride comes before, Missus Dwyer? I will never enter that world again. I will make my name instead as a singer of the type of ballad I have just sung for you. I see myself very much of that world instead. It is a world more humble and in almost every way more honest than that of Italian opera. Give me the moon rising over Gougane Barra over the sun setting on Sorrento Bay any day, Missus Dwyer!'

'Such an interesting and novel and sentimental outlook, Mister Logan.'

'Let me tell you a piece of bunk that Maestro Tosi once told me.'

Warming now to his oratory, he made sure the eye-to-eye connection with the girl was firm and unmistakable.

'It came in the form of a piece of supposed advice on the art of acting. "Play-acting" in all senses of the term. He said that in order to win over the women in the audience you must project your understanding of the character of the role you are playing to the farthest one of them, in the same way that you might project your voice, the hope being that they will develop feelings for a figment of your imagination. Well let me tell you about another piece of advice, much better advice, not from the Maestro but from a weary baritone in his circle. This man had said: The things that give the most uncomplicated pleasure are most connected to our survival on earth. And these themselves are uncomplicated things. Eating, love, assembling fires – but most of all love! Love is all that matters in the end. (Forgive the imagery, Missus Dwyer.) And when you find love (and please forgive my Italian accent here too), thissa granda lifestyle of the opera house willa disappeara, no notta really, but I mean that it willa seema that way and it willa not be a disaster.'

'And what is your reading of that?'

'It is open to interpretation, Missus Dwyer. Something to do with falsity, and honesty, and the first overcoming the second through learned behaviour, and how this might be reversed. This baritone was a grown man of great experience, and he could diagnose something in me that I could not see myself. I speak now as one youth to the very best of youth before me. I say, away with the pomposity and the grandiosity! Go with what is in your heart! Let the gold leaf lift and the stucco crumble and show you are as brittle as the balconies that keep men in the gods! Better to tell a girl that she is beautiful and that you are a fool.'

He let his words hang in the air and watched the motes float above him to a ceiling rose plugged and clotted with eras of paint.

Afterwards he waited for the girl outside. He caught her by the gate, by the arm – somewhat brutishly, he worried for an instant – and blurted: 'Won't you come for coffee with me?'

She gave no immediate and clear response. Her mouth hung open, the 'Continental' face was pale, and the eyes that had seemed so sleepy and reassuring were now alert and panicked. He wondered if he had misread the look she had given him in the hall. But he had such an unshakeable feeling within him, damn her, and she had put it there, and he could not accept that it did not exist within her also.

She went to her friends, two girls who had stalled between the gateposts, and the three of them gathered in a huddle. They were giddy and all the while cast glances back at him. The whole scene was very 'American', it struck him, and how must he have come across, he wondered – so brave and forward and American-seeming in standing his ground and waiting for an answer? Or did they see him, in fact, and in spite of his and Missus Dwyer's best efforts, in the mould of the romantic Italian tenor?

He would be resolute now and show her he was a man of will and then, by and by, after she had got to know him, she would see the man he thought she had seen in the hall, the man he knew himself to be and had spoken about, the young man so uncertain of himself.

She turned and came to him – and those eyes now! He would possess them like she possessed them. He would not care if anyone else might think of them as ordinary, he would carry them in a box in his pocket if he were allowed and eat them with herbs and butter.

'Don't you know,' he said, 'that you have eyes that would bring peace to warring nations? You have the eyes of a lobster. Do you know what an anagram of lobster is? It is "bolster". You have eyes that would bolster a man before a day's work.'

'Excuse me?' she said. 'I'd like to think I have a wider set of functions than that.'

'Oh you do, no it's true, I wouldn't doubt that at all. Please, let me buy you coffee and tell you what you have done for me this afternoon.'

6

Rickard Velily stood on his bed in his attic room and looked out of the open porthole. For half an hour he watched the night sky, lulled by bleeping lines, readable left to right or right to left: aeroplanes and helicopters; the helicopters equipped with heat cameras, Rickard had learnt, to find illegal factories in attic spaces like his own. He was not on drugs – he was not in favour of drugs – though the porthole plate, flipped flat in front of him through a diametric fulcrum, would have been ideal for spreading out this or some other drug. Time could be spent like this, standing on the bed, or lying on the bed.

He was feeling dreamy, nostalgic, romantic. A minty moon, a *paper moon*, unmoved by aircraft distress signals, shone brightly for, and only for, this bailiwick of Tin Pan Alley. It was at one time the home of song – and would be again! (he thought with sudden determination). Into this silver pool of spinning life the minstrel cast lines from his heavenly perch. Lovers birthed from electrical charges danced to his jigs and swayed to airs carrying the sadness of older worlds and times. Well it was that Americans were passing through a time of change again and the fixative of nostalgia and meme of melancholy would be dominant once more in music. Rickard would send the message from the concert stage and he would sell songs from an office and build new words yet again on old airs. In winter and autumn he would do this, in society season, when people came back to the city. In summer he would harvest his airs in Ireland. He would receive blind harpists. Scenes from *The Severe Dalliance* played out in his mind. He thought of Toni again. He was unhappy again, quickly.

On most nights that were not practice nights Denny and Clive could be found downstairs in the drawing room. Mostly Rickard would leave them be, and usually he spent the time – if not in his room, or outside meandering – in the clubhouse library. But there was not even a good range of books in the library. Every book, as in his room, was on the subject of business. The only material he could find on music was in a volume called *The Brill Building: An American Production Line* and another called *Why I Dropped Out, What I Reassessed, And How I Came Back More Eager Than Ever*, which had a chapter on Gregorian chanting. How hungry he was to learn and improve. He felt ignorant beside Denny's knowledge and past, and so, he suspected, did Clive; he and Clive were merely enthusiasts, when it boiled down to it. He had come to his art by whim, really; but then he might as well have, for it was all whimsy, what they were doing, these this room, in the form of a diary, a logbook, a tablet of ogham. A section of the floorboards came away at Rickard's command, lifting, in a block. He stared down into the hole beneath, puzzling how he would move to the light switch without falling into other sections of hole around him. There was some light in the chasm: faint granules that illuminated enough in their vicinity to reveal a network of pipes, wires, resistors – circuitry. He knelt down and leaned into the gap. He felt heat on his face, and heard ticking and whirring. A chaffinch's metallic note of 'tchirrit'. It would be work for another day to find this diary, in better light.

After his breakfast, off-premises, he went again to the library. He liked to sit here before it got too late in the morning because it was east facing and it gave him the banal sense that the light that streamed in was the distilled first light of an American day. One of the oldest club members was also taking in the warming light. This man was about Denny's age although unlike Denny he looked every day of his years. He was like a crumpled sheath that had lost its skeleton – so folded and formless that even his eyes were buried. Rickard began to amuse himself by putting the thought that the man was merely the sloughing of a man together with a nightmare about the internet he'd had during the night. In his nightmare, he'd had to come up with an 'avatar' for a false version of himself. The idea that this thing would be a homunculus, a hobgoblin, a sprite or a celebrated piper seemed terrifying in his sleep. But seeing him sitting here now in the library, his legs crossed, thigh over thigh, the effeminate way, made him laugh. He laughed thinking of those legs running amok in that great unmanageable wilderness, dancing across all of history and rumour and oceanography.

'We are in the company of a genius, you know,' he said to the homunculus in a slightly bullying tone that was unintentional.

'Oh?'

'Oh yes, don't you know?'

'Know what or whom?'

'Denny Kennedy-Logan, the great Irish tenor and club member.'

'Now why do you tell me this?' said the homunculus, sitting forward as his eyes extruded from their hoods.

'Led by whim again.'

'Whim has little to do with it,' said the homunculus. 'We are never led only by whim.'

Soon after, Rickard joined the New York Public Library system. His ostensible reason for doing so was that the clubhouse library was too small, but he recognised also a need to move closer to home. (In the simple visual display by which this thought was represented to him, the move to home was a bubble encompassing his New York experiences, interests and contacts that expanded [even if the contents at its centre did not] so that it combined with and expanded that past bubble of his life.) This was confirmed to him on his first visit to the main library branch on Fifth Avenue when he ordered up from stacks the Dublin telephone directory. The effect of what happened next took him by surprise. He was amazed at the slimness of the volume he was given; it had been a long time since he beheld any edition of his home city and county's phone book. Its smallness, and the smallness it seemed to contain, only emphasised the immensity and grandeur of the reading room he was in, and the great windows, gangways of sunbeam, high ceiling and burning silence of the place increased his pity for and embarrassment at the place he was from. He went out to the street, and the roar and soar of Manhattan had never felt so new.

A short walk from the library Rickard found exactly what he was looking for – a telephone booth, open air, just like in the movies. He dialled Toni's work number. It was 1.18 in New York City, 6.18 in Dublin. For too long he had waited for chance to happen and now he was going to do something about it. 6.18 was pushing things, although his father had told him that he believed Toni had reached such a status in work that she never, in fact, clocked out. Asked if it was possible that not clocking out meant simply that Toni carried her work home with her, his father hesitated, saying then that once or twice at around eight in the evening he had seen from the slip road all the lights on in Toni's office. Picturing those lights now as violent slashes in the permanent grey that enshrouded the addressless place where Toni's office was, Rickard considered how necessary it was that he got through to Toni at work rather than at home, and that what he would say to her was less important than what she would hear.

He closed his eyes and allowed the soundscape to disturb his emotions. There was nowhere in the world that sounded so like itself as New York City – all hollering horns and saxophonous sirens. He plugged his right ear with his finger and listened through the earpiece as mediated by the mouthpiece. Eyes open too: there was nowhere so like itself as New York City. Fifth Avenue stretched away to the north, to a little cluster of red and yellow, and sped the imagination along its lines to beyond this vanishing point and on to other places, times, and the products of other people's imaginations. It put in Rickard's mind one of the most famous scenes in *The Severe Dalliance*: Tyrone's homage to the avenues, as delivered in monologue over black-and-white montage, while an epic Harold Campbelltown score suggested both the wonders of human achievement and (via the use of saxophone) giant vats of viscous human sleaze. Columbus and Amsterdam, according to Tyrone, were psychic transporters to early European America; the ancient holloway of Broadway, which cut across all the avenues, gave passage to, as it admitted, pre-Columbian time; the Avenue of the Americas continued as a highway through the southern cotton fields and Mexican cordillera, across the no man's land of the Darien Gap, and as a golden road connecting the cities of the Incas; Fifth Avenue was America's revolving carousel, its permanent World's Fair pavilion: a showcase for the best of this modern nation of bright ideas and fierce competition.

He closed his eyes again and tried to imagine what Toni would imagine. His finger was still in his right ear. In that ear all he could hear was his blood, cruising like a jet engine. In his left ear was a horrible piercing tone, like bats. He clattered the receiver on its hanger and waited for his coins to drop into the refund trap, but there was nothing. He went back to the library, where he checked the phone book again. The number he had taken down was a fax number. He patted his trouser pockets, hoping for the hi-hats of loose change, but all he got was the phut of his pudgy thighs. In exasperation, his head flopped back on his neck and his feet pushed out in front of him.

When eventually he looked back up, the yellow rods of sunbeam had disappeared and the windows were panels of peacefully glowing ivory. Stirring himself further, he opened one of the other books he had ordered, *The 'Eir-Lite' Book of Whimsy*. A medical tendency to hyperfocus, which usually attended physical exhaustion, did not kick in, and instead he went to sleep. He entered a state of lucid dreaming: so lucid that he was not able to concentrate on his dream and only on the fact that he was loudly snoring, but he was too tired to do anything about it.

After-hours, Rickard stumbled around the back of the library to Bryant Square. Feeling thoroughly stale, he paused to take in the enormous Puffball building that dominated one side of the square. In a newspaper a month or so before, he had read the building described as a 'fastness' or 'alcazar'. This was intended as negative criticism of its visual effect on its surroundings. In the same piece someone else had described it as 'the omphalos of all that is hip and innovative, which in New York today are often correlative qualities'. The article was divided into 'against' and 'for' arguments. The word 'alcazar', in particular, now resounded in Rickard's head. It seemed to him an accurate description, not because it was intended as negative, but because it had an exotic or fantastical flavour, and the other person in the debate, a young person, Rickard seemed to remember, had thought of the Puffball Store as a sort of centre of dreams. Rickard was not quite sure what an alcazar was, but it made him think of dreams, fairy tales, and of the Challoner song 'The Earls at Corunna':

> *'The dust not settled on their tracks*
> *From Cordova to there.*
> *Beware the power at their backs,*
> *From Finisterre they glare.'*

* * *

The Puffball Store was one of many innovations personally envisioned by Puffball's messianic founder and chief executive officer Townsend Thoresen. It was a destination in itself, so it was said; Rickard had passed it before on his daytime walks in Midtown, barely noting its presence, which was obvi-

131

ous mainly for the backpack-wearing crowds that milled around on its piazza and the shrill collective noise that they made. In the evening, with the crowds thinner and with the benefit of artificial lighting, he could better appreciate the structure, or what was visible of the structure, for most of it was underground. Above the street, set well back on the piazza, was a great glass dome, composed, wondrously, of eight interlocking sections. It was lit from inside, and the light was so concentrated at the seams of the glass that the dome appeared to be held together with green laser beams.

The dome protected the entrance to a spiral stairwell, also made of glass. At the bottom of the stairwell Rickard found a quiet shop floor. Instantly he was placated by the atmosphere of calm. Lighting was low and easeful; cream marble floor tiles, smooth and concave like old worn flagstones, softened the clunk of his boot soles; wall tiles bore the imprint of prehistoric ocean life. Lines of machines on long white counters cast users' faces in a lunar pallor. Shop staff seemed aloof; strangely so: they stood apart from one another at even widths with their backs against the wall, lit from underneath like deco idols.

Rickard took a machine in the centre of a bank of unused machines. With great self-awareness he held a casual pose. Before long, the calm he had felt disappeared, and trepidation overcame him.

He had had a bad relationship with computing technology to this point. In his job in Dublin, in

Verbiage, the text-mining company, it had never been his business to use computers in a comprehensive way. Before then, long before then, at an early age, he had decided that he would not use computers in any way at all. Resolve had quickened to principle. He was seized now in inaction, bent forward at the waist, arms splayed, elbows locked, heels of hands numb, as if guarding against something that might fly out of the monitor. This, he knew, was a 'hardware' problem: exposure to a mere screen and keyboard brought him out in a lather of sweat.

(Did technology, in the course of his passive absorption of its ethereal communications, detect his hostility? It did not seem so outlandish a thought. The world of information, he was told, was not just a paperless one but a wireless one now too. The medium was the air – even matter – itself; its bore limitless. Moving in three dimensions these days was to move through a fourth dimension, and for it to move through him. This was an increasingly self-governing and self-perpetuating ecosystem. Washing machines implanted with microchips sitting in utility rooms in the Cook Islands conversed with the factories that created them in the Netherlands while their unwitting owners dozed on verandas outside; cars were guided by bodiless eyes from behind the stratosphere. Encrypted military communiqués, scrambled recordings of Mozart symphonies, disassembled pornographic images – on every ordinary day all passed through his body on their way somewhere else, unprompted by human fingers. What messages were these pulses picking up from the electrical exchanges taking place in his nerves and cells, and what were they making of them?)

Four hours easily slipped by. His eyes became dry. He spent time on a website devoted to *The Severe Dalliance*. So strange for him to see this, *The Severe Dalliance*, made in 1976, cooed over on a computer by people who claimed to appreciate the warmth of the celluloid print. There were categories: FAN FICTION was one. The idea was appalling, the thought of these 'fans', hypocrites, rabid and proprietary in their enthusiasm, internet communicators, entering data by rows, by columns, intersecting with each other, forming cells, swapping TRIVIA – another category.

His movement – he had straightened suddenly – must have caught the attention of one of those members of staff in praetorian pose: slinking out of the beam of her floor light, into shadow, and into soft, diffuse light again, came a girl. She was in her twenties, no older than twenty-five, dark haired. Her eyes were the most supernaturally wolfish grey, and her fringe hung in a silk curtain ending in a straight border just below her eyebrows. A name tag on her T-shirt read FONDLER.

'What can I do for you?'

He had no answer, but said, finally, 'I'm looking for information.'

'Information? On ...?'

'Um.'

Her eyes, Rickard saw now, were not in fact grey but the deepest black: the grey had been a reflection in her pupils of the light from the screens.

'On a product?' she said.

'No, not on a product. Information on the internet.'

'On …?'

'The internet.'

'Does your query have a specific application to any of our hardware or software?'

'I want to look something up on the internet.'

He gestured to his screen and an animated caricature of Townsend Thoresen that had appeared.

'As you can see, the internet has vanished.'

'That's a screensaver, sir. Press any key and you'll be on the internet again.'

The rest of his time he spent looking up Toni on social media and other websites. She was surprisingly easy to find – surprising, because she was not a sociable or voluble person. But here, she was everywhere, with an opinion on every matter. Most of her sentences ended in exclamation marks, but she rarely exclaimed anything in reality (meaning the real, speaking, face-to-face world, which, Rickard had to remind himself, was a world that he and Toni occupied together, at the same time, a very long time ago now, it seemed).

* * *

'Well, it looks like we've landed ourselves in the image-sourcing business,' said Rickard's boss at Verbiage,

Robert, overwhelmed, on his return to the office from the western midlands of Ireland where he had been trying to solicit work.

'Images?' said Rickard. 'Landed?'

'Oh boy, yeah,' said Robert, resting his head back into the sling of his hands, and looking even a little expectant now. 'I had a bottle of whiskey with the head of the syndicate two nights ago. They're building a tower in the bog, eighty floors high, with a quarter of a million LCD screens on the outside and inside. He needs a different image for every single one of those screens. He's calling it the Europa Tower. Each of the pictures has to be a painting by a famous European artist. I told him that I could deliver the images before anyone else could. He said this time six months would be fine. The money's not great, but I think I could get more business out of these people.'

Robert set to work finding free pictures on the internet. By the end of the day he had collected some fifty pictures of paintings and put them in a folder on his computer. This folder was also accessible via Rickard's computer. (The computers were connected in some way.) While Robert was on his lunch, Rickard opened the folder to see what his boss had found. When he clicked on one of the picture files it opened not a picture but a page of gobbledegook text (the text-encoded binary data that Robert often harvested for concrete poets). It was so stark and ugly and unantici-pated – like a spider on the back of his hand – that he panicked, stabbing his keyboard and adding some text, though he immediately deleted what he thought he had added.

A couple of days later Robert announced:

'Brilliant, Rickard! The syndicate thinks it's great!'

And then:

'Come on, I know you manipulated that file! I have an electronic record of when you go into what. It's okay, Rickard. And anyway, the head of the syndicate knows what we're about. I told him we're chiefly a text-extraction company. This intrigues him. And he loves how Quentin Massys's Notary's eyes now appear to have swapped around.'

For the next six months Rickard's job was to change the text versions of pictures that Robert found on the internet; the pictures, when opened as pictures again, would then have changed too. At the start, Rickard thought that the syndicate would soon tire of the gimmick. For the next hundred pictures that he changed he made no more effort than he had made for his first picture – he simply randomly inserted text into the code by stabbing the keyboard. But this consignment only increased the head of the syndicate's enthusiasm for the project – he came back to Robert saying he thought the alterations 'the work of a genius'. Deemed such, Rickard found himself taking his task more seriously. Now there were greater expectations of him, and he thought: I got lucky with one hundred and one of these pictures; what if my luck runs out, as surely, mathematically, it will over the long course ahead?

For every set of code behind each picture in the next batch he stared at his computer screen until his eyes and head throbbed with pain. He knew – or rationality told him – that there could be no making sense of the reams of Roman and Hebrew and Cyrillic characters that comprised the text-encoded binary data without knowledge of how the computer translated the binary into this gobbledegook. But then he did not want to leave his success to chance again. And so he told himself that a careful reading – again, he knew this was ridiculous – of the gobbledegook, a more thorough exposure to it, would enable him to understand how it translated back to binary, and how the binary translated to a picture.

And then a funny thing happened, four and a half thousand pictures into the project.

Plain words within the text would sometimes give a clue to the title of a picture, or who had painted the original; one day he went home knowing that the last picture he had worked on was called 'IKB 191'. When he got home he took his *Great Art Book* from the shelf and looked 'IKB 191' up, discovering that the original had been painted by somebody called Yves Klein. The picture in the book was basically a solid block of dark blue. He knew straight away that the picture he had been looking at in text form earlier had been of a different blue to the blue of the picture in the book. He knew all this from the pattern of the code he had been combing through that day. When he went into work again the next morning he returned to the picture. He could, he knew, if he'd wanted to, have changed the picture to something near the shade of blue in the *Great Art Book*. He changed sections in the centre of it to a bright red instead. He understood not how he was able to know how to do this.

With every set of code now he could tell exactly what the picture looked like; fields of textual scree collected at the bottom of his mind and gathered upwards as great artworks. Not only this, he knew how the electronic renditions of the pictures – even, perhaps, something of the original versions – came together, and how they might artfully come apart; to achieve 'X' or 'sigma' effect he knew precisely what to do. He was no longer happy with randomly scrambled images; he conceived of and executed thoughtful deconstructions, though none required any great expenditure of effort. If what the head of the syndicate was seeing over in the western midlands was 'the work of a genius', then this, he supposed, as he raced through a day's images, was how geniuses worked. They just understood, and they just set about. Genius! Genius! If someone had suggested to him only a few months before that he was a genius he would never have believed them. But then genius was not something that a person was born with; it was arrived at through hours and hours of practice: Mozart's twenty thousand hours, or Mondrian's ten thousand hours, and though Rickard had not spent ten thousand hours exposed to these encrypted pictures, perhaps he had received the equivalent in compressed form, or perhaps even had been assimilating genius itself.

'Rickard! Rickard!' came Robert's voice from the muffled auditory world and the receded and blurred visual one.

'Rickard?' he said.

Well, he had another task for him. It was this:

Though they were some thirty thousand pictures away from completing their project for the syndicate, a Brazilian publisher and art connoisseur had seen many of the deconstructed pictures and wanted to bring out a book featuring a selection of them to coincide with the opening of the Europa Tower. The head of the syndicate had put the publisher directly in touch with Robert, who, the publisher had been led to understand, dealt vaguely with the written word. He wanted now 'this genius' – the head of the syndicate's reference – responsible for the deconstructed pictures to write the introduction for the book. Because Verbiage was a company that re-purposed online text rather than generating original text, Robert insisted to Rickard, as a matter of professional justification, that they work from pre-existing sentences. These sentences he got from a website on which people had pasted examples of bad technical writing. Rickard's own suggestion was that they used not the sentences as they read in English, but as they translated in code form.

'Is that possible?' he wondered aloud. 'Can the sentences be translated to gobbledegook just like the pictures were translated to gobbledegook?'

'A-ha' – as in 'Leave it with me' – said Robert.

By the end of the next day, Robert presented Rickard with hundreds of encoded excerpts of bad technical writing. Or rather, the excerpts plus a sort of frosting of gobbledegook, as Robert explained; what was seemingly the bad technical writing translated to code was actually nonsense excess text that had accreted around the excerpts after Robert had emailed them to himself. (And indeed, there, embedded in the accretions, were the original excerpts in plain English, so to speak.)

'So where does all this extra stuff come from?' said Rickard.

'I don't know,' said Robert.

Then: 'From the fairies who live inside the internet.'

Rickard went to work on the accretions (he ignored the excerpts themselves) with the confidence he had gained and with the same rigour he had never ceased to apply while working on the pictures. This new project, however, seemed to take a lot more out of him than even the earliest pictures had. It was harder to say something in rearranged gobbledegook than it had been to rearrange something in rearranged gobbledegook. The point, of course, was that he would say something from what was already there, but from the beginning it was apparent that, to create something rather than deconstruct something – that was to say, to say something – he would need to draw on something extra that he had not needed to draw on for the pictures. Then he remembered how he had known how to put the patches of red into Yves Klein's 'IKB 191', and how he had known how to change the tint of blue in it too, and soon after he chanced to catch – to actually read, or listen to, or in any case perceive – one of his own thoughts in the moment it took to relay across his brain, and he realised it was not even in English or any other spoken or written language. These things revealed, and with the confidence he already had, he knew he had everything he needed.

The idea of an introduction for this Brazilian publisher's book explaining blah blah blah was soon abandoned. (Indeed so was the idea for a book, although the picture project was completed to the syndicate's enormous satisfaction.) Quickly Rickard moved on to the possibility of notating thoughts untainted by having to be carried in a human language. Knowing he was on to something great emboldened him; his thoughts – characterised in mysterious symbols culled from online gobbledegook – became definite, brave, truthful, and finally incomprehensible to his bodily, delimited self.

Robert merely indulged him to begin with (the syndicate had paid them handsomely), but soon he was enthusiastically encouraging his employee. He, Robert, was an 'imaginist', he told Rickard. He scrunched up his eyes, walked in figure-of-eight circuits, and told Rickard that he thought the company was 'finally going where I'd always wanted it to go; we're getting to a level now, Rickard. I think we stand on the threshold of a new conceptual framework for non-augmented non-experiential eventfulness.'

Hearing such gobbledegook from his boss had a sudden and profound effect on Rickard; it was then that he realised that the thoughts he had been notating were not even his own. They had merely been transmissions, intercepted unknowingly, and sent on their way again. Arrogance had buried the deep but incandescent conviction that the thoughts were false ones, and just because the thoughts had been smoothly transcribed into a language that he couldn't, as a human being, understand, didn't make them any less false.

Other truths crept up on him. He was not what he had become. He touched his hand to his computer that always remained cool; he had never cared for these machines and the intangibles that floated between them. He preferred those other intangibles, the ones that no one was ever sure about: romance, imagination, the soul. And of tangibles, he liked, so he told himself, their limitations: the limitations of the analogue world, as he had known people describe the world just gone; and words on his clodding tongue, his voice sounding stupid, vibrating through bone and fat.

And so he was lowered in a great bell into the place of his imagination, where was to be found his soul anyway. The bell sealed off a circle of earth and the air inside was laden and spicy. The air only grew heavier and heavier with the traces of the dead, and, constantly circulating, gave life to the dead. Daylight came down through an oculus punched in the top and sealed off again with glass. Landed and sucked to the earth now the bell was a redoubt. Passages made of wood and hair and regurgitated paper clung to its outsides, their floors sloped in an outward-falling pitch. The passages layered and pleated the space that they carried and let in something of the outside air. The permanence of the central redoubt, the certainty of its form, the security that came from knowing it would give shelter in a catastrophe, only showed up these passages for the flimsy constructions that they were. Because of the breadth of the bell around which they wound, and because they were never built to expedite at any rate, a walk in the passages could result in lengthy and spiralling journeys. In them were encountered many lost men. They had grey and glassine faces. They came here in their distress and confusion and built the place in the shape of this confusion. They hobbled on crumbling ankles and with the pitch of the floor. Their walk was catching; caused Rickard to palm the walls. Pictures of golfers and golf holes came off in his hands. Books on business – only ever books on business – tumbled from the shelves. Some of these men had business plans, or ideas that would contribute to a larger business plan. Apart from this that they had in common – their confusion, and, for some, their business plans – they shared nothing. The point of this sanctuary was that they would be left alone in it, another silent node in a network. Rickard imagined all the nodes in the network silent and anxious, across the world. More and more he thought of these nodes as fortifications spread widely through hostile territory. Increasingly he was aware of contingencies for a future conflict.

He found himself opening a door, and then another door, and exiting the clubhouse. He was in an alleyway filled with trees whose spring blossom gave off a smell of cats' urine. One end of the alleyway was open to the street. He came out on to the street and walked north-wards and westwards and adumbrated certain thoughts he had about the coming conflict.

Meanwhile he arrived either inexorably or with militant purpose at what he considered the enemy ompha-los. On the way he thought of himself as a basking shark, but not in the usual way that he thought of himself as a basking shark. Denny often encouraged Rickard and Clive to think of themselves as basking sharks. A basking shark was basically an immense cone that was nothing if not for the water that flowed around and through it. Stretching his ribs and muscle and circular cartilage to the maximum extent the singer could be in balance with his medium – external, eternal feeling – until he became the medium. The idea was to give oneself up to the currents of feeling and let them have their way. But taking the temperature of the outside air Rickard had felt nothing. And so he simply became a basking shark that was either numbed by intent or dead and given up to other currents. But that was not to say he could not at a future time find feeling on the air: the leaders of one side in this coming conflict would do well to remember that all on their side were owners of special human gifts.

He observed the tourists in the plaza in front of the Puffball Store gathered in clusters like seahorses on the sun-warmed reef. Among the seahorses glided sharks – not basking sharks, but clean and consolidated species like mako sharks or great whites. His eyes alighted on one young man – in a plain blue T-shirt and baggy brown trousers and glasses with thick frames and carrying a shoulder bag – who might have been the very emblem of this type if he did not move as sluggishly as he did smoothly, and whose beard was as untidy as it was neat. Rickard had tended to think of the combatants on one side as Youth, or Whites, or Sharks, and on the other side as Lived, or

Blacks, or Eagles/Owls, but he would come up with better names, because this young man exhibited none of the characteristics of a shark.

It was easy, too, to identify the one person who, in the glut of his totality, was firmly on the other side: the flushed and flabby sixtysomething standing on the spot, dabbing from one foot to the other, owing to fallen arches, or to feeling lost, or probably to a combination of the two. This was a creature to be pitied, and naturally to be allied with. What was he doing here? This man had come to the plaza to see what all the 'fuss' was about. Now he knew what the 'fuss' was about. The 'fuss' was a fuzz that rattled along every nerve and told him on a sub-awareness level exactly what it was about. For now, and likely until such a time as violence shuddered him to full knowledge, all the man understood about the 'fuss' was a sadness. At some time in the past, this square, for this man, had been the most public of New York's public spaces. Perhaps like others he had dreamt of one day announcing his fame here. He didn't know what form this announcement or fame would take, just as he didn't fully understand why neither of these would now happen. All he could clearly picture was a bunch of sad carnations in his own terrified hands. Both he and Rickard had made their way, on this day, each for his own reason, to this seditious detail on an enlightened planner's map.

As Rickard had walked to this part of the city, directed upwards, he came to appreciate what a bloody battleground narrow Manhattan Island would be. The island would be divided more or less into a southern section and a northern section. The stronghold of one side – Youth, or the Whites, or the Sharks – would be the south. The stronghold of Lived, or the Blacks, or the Eagles or Owls would be the north. Enclaves of Lived in the south – such as where he'd just come from – would be relentlessly attacked. Youth's bases were scattered across Downtown, and off the island altogether, but its holy site was right on the front line, here, in Midtown, there –

(He tried to send his thoughts across the noise to the man.)

The conflict would be an intergenerational one, crudely speaking. It would not simply be between a younger age group and an older age group but between those who chose to affiliate with one generation or another. On one side were the harvesters and users of information, the people in control of the systems of society. On the other side were the latecomers, the pussyfooters and the intransigents. The first side seemingly had all the advantages; it had, in the main, the advantage of youth. The combatants of the other side – human beings, as opposed to beings – at least housed all of their insubstantial components, but were none the cleverer or more organised for it. In fact it would have done them good, somewhere along the line, to have offloaded, or uploaded, some of these components. How and ever, they were where they were.

151

Many might have said that Rickard, as a forty-one-year-old – on the threshold of two generations, or belonging to an in-between one – had a decision to make. He had no decision to make. The decision was already made. He saw his stand as a stand against the proponents of a new and awful definition of beauty. Their aim was to sublimate our diffuse and random and damaging inner lives to another dimension, leaving the world of solids as a zone of calm perfection. Their watchwords and gospel were 'streamline' and 'synchronize' (absolutely with a 'z', pronounced 'zee'). Those damaged inside and out and living in the zone of calm perfection would not be tolerated. Rickard and this man who carried so much of the old world still with them were targets. The complicated and carbuncular, the flabby and the jagged, even the sublime, were incompatible with these tyrants' ideals. Incompatible formats were, needless to say, also incompatible. Their logo and livery was a pure and infinite field of white. It symbolised the blanching out of opposition.

(Now he caught the man's eyes on the full with his own. Instinctively the man moved his hand to cover his eyes and, in the same movement, collapsed to the ground.)

Rickard glanced about the plaza. The tourist shoals giggled and bowed among each other as if nothing unusual had just happened. Rickard advanced the twenty yards or so to the man. He was enormously pudgy, and wearing a huge leather coat that creaked as his weight and shape rolled him slowly on to his back. His face looked dead but retained its flushed colour. He was at Rickard's feet, and Rickard guessed that it was his responsibility now to see that he was all right.

He went down on his haunches and put a finger to the man's nose, detecting the faintest movement of breath. The man had passed out, Rickard surmised, on what was the first truly warm day of the year. Oddly, there was not one bead of sweat on his face. Rickard pressed the backs of his fingers to the man's cheek and felt a sort of dead warmth, as if the flesh, like the granite slabs, had been heated only by the sun and not by a source inside. He took in the whole face and decided it was the most hideous face he had ever seen. There wasn't a specific hideous feature on it, but taken as a whole it had the look of a face constructed by a ham-fisted forensic anthropologist on a skull.

Now Rickard, meaning to antagonise the man to life, took a good pinch of cheek and felt it slide and squidge like goo between his finger and thumb. When he released his grip the ridge of cheek retracted slowly, like a snail's head. He was so disgusted by the sensation and sight that he did it again. This time he accidentally pulled the cheek beyond its elastic breaking point and a tuft of flesh – more or less the entire cheek – tore away. At the bottom of the pit was another tract of skin, blotchy with a white marshmallowy glue. The man's eyes beat beneath their lids, then opened.

He gathered Rickard's hand into his own, which felt gloved.

'Not here! No, not here!' he said in a distinct north-of-Ireland voice, slapping the ground – three times, in a fluster – with his free hand. When he tried to roll on his side Rickard made to stand up. The man gripped Rickard's hand tighter, and Rickard, feeling himself pulled towards the ground and not wanting to make a scene, hauled him to his feet. Then the man shuffled away, across the road, with surprising speed, towards Bryant Square proper, where he collapsed on the far side of a bush.

'Why the disguise?' said Rickard, catching up with him, only to find that the man had fallen unconscious once more and was heaped on the gravel. Again Rickard looked around, worried about the commotion. The square was stippled with shadow and light: light made brilliant by the mirrored glass high above but softened and scattered by the gently moving leaves. The effect was woozying.

Rickard guessed that the man was stewing to death inside his padding. He pulled at the already-displaced bowl of blue-grey hair to find that it was rooted in a rubber cushion. The removal of wig and cushion left a crater exposing a bald scalp daubed in tracks of this marshmallowy glue, which was melting with a film of sweat into a suncream consistency. Rickard worked his fingers under the edge of the prosthetic forehead and yanked, ripping away most of the rest of the face in a single flap. The face underneath was a mess, mottled with the adhesive pith and damp with perspiration. Something about it surprised Rickard. It was a similar version of the face that had been, but altogether more human: pinguid, distended with the heat and by age. Rickard had expected a face that was less human: a lizard, or a robot.

Now he found he was joined by a homeless man.

'Hello,' he said almost inquisitively to this hobo by his side, who was ransacking the north-of-Ireland man's shirt, ripping at the underarms and patting – almost punching – the shoulders.

The north-of-Ireland man twitched and grunted again.

'Wait,' said Rickard.

Hands shaking, he began to unbutton the front.

'Fucken hurry up, bitch,' said the homeless man.

Underneath was a cushion, covering the whole of the front of the torso, made of the same rubbery material as the wig-plinth. The homeless man slipped the cushion out and scrambled away, mumbling vaguely about conspiracies.

Rickard tried once more:

'Why the disguise? Were you following me, Irishman?'

'Irishman?'

The man's pupils at last settled on Rickard, contracting to tiny holes. He said, 'Irishman – yes, you're the Irishman.'

'And so are you, by the sound of it.'

'I'm not you.'

'No – who are you?'

'I'm … You're the singer, aren't you?'

'I'm … *Yes.*'

155

The man stiffly jacked up on his elbows and surveyed the square.

'Yes. You see plenty folk these days playing cat or horse for some Eastern earth deity but that which you were doing there on the plaza was a diaphragmatic exercise. You're a singer, I'm guessing. Were you getting ready for a performance?'

'Who are you?'

'On the street too. I can spot a singer a long way off.'

'On the street?'

'You asked was I following you. I saw you on the street and said: "That's a singer."'

'Am I so obvious?'

'To most people, no. But I've known a lot of singers in my time. I know your type. They are conscious of the fluid around them. Air is a fluid too, and that's a fact. It's very heartening seeing your kind.'

'And this was why you followed me?'

'I wasn't following you.'

'You said that you were.'

'Are you a solo tenor or part of a group?'

'Part of a group.'

'Named?'

'Listen –'

'Named?'

'We're called the Free 'n' Easy Tones.'

He grabbed Rickard's hand again, went to say something, but stopped himself.

'Who are you? What is your name?' said Rickard. 'And for how long have you been following me?'

'Can I give you one piece of advice the same as I give any Irishman in the big city?'

He put his weight on one elbow and leaned in to Rickard. Then the seriousness and sincerity that this pose suggested dissipated as he said in a mechanical and idle way, 'Get out before too long and don't become the poor old tragic proverbial.'

And then, as if snapping to:

'But don't leave too early.'

'Why?'

'Hmm?'

'What proverb are you talking about?'

'You have a destiny you must fulfil. The Free 'n' Easy Tones. But tell the boys there's help here if they need it. It's never too late to get out.'

His eyes liquefied out of focus again, and he returned to the fully supine position, making small effortful gasps at each degree.

Rickard remained on his haunches, puzzling over the man's words. Nearby, a game of boules was in progress. Its participants had not at any stage intimated by their behaviour that they were aware of the mummery nearby. He thought about leaving the man in their custody.

'What have you done with it?! I can't be seen!'

The man was back up on an elbow, pulling strings of glue from his face.

'You were overheating,' said Rickard. 'You needed the air on your skin.'

'What have you done with my fecking face?'

Half of the man's face lay in the gravel, the sticky side lumpy with grit.

'What are you trying to do to me?' he said. 'I'll be a goner.'

He rolled to his knees and got to his feet, went this way and that way, then paused at a rubbish bin. Head and arms lowered together. He came back to Rickard his face a collage of bottle tops, strips of foil, banana peel, cheese, refried beans, sunflower-seed shells and Chew-butter Cracknell packaging. As he spoke, items of rubbish dropped off his face.

'Must hurry away now, but please give the boys my best wishes. Thanks for the name. I'll look out now for your Free 'n' Easy Tones. Goodbye, and mind the pipes.'

He shambled off, like a kidnap victim in a sack.

Strange to consider, but Rickard had only just begun to enjoy the familiarity of their scene: their messy, un-American, un-modern, little congress under the plane trees.

He stood up, feeling no small amount of pain in the backs of his creaking knees, and wandered over towards a belvedere, of tubular aluminium and plastic sheeting, behind the library. It was surrounded by circles of chairs that were made of cast iron so that they would make effective tethering posts for dogs. He pulled out a chair, falling into it, then rotated it so that he could look into the square and away from the dogs because their eyes seemed so demonically human. The sun had disappeared behind a building but was visible as a pale purple-tinged kidney on the surface of the Puffball dome. The sky was cold pointillated green, like a test for colour blindness. The words 'fastness' and 'alcazar' came to his mind again.

> *'The Earls, the Earls, are on their way*
> *To take back love and land!*
> *Toledo steel to win the day!*
> *That day will be so grand!'*

He supposed an 'alcazar' was a type of 'bastille', and he thought of how the word 'bastille', once a symbol of tyranny, had come to represent a reversal for the good. But then the word 'fastness' sounded like 'vast-ness' – an immeasurable largeness, slippery like the air. Several empty chairs away the homeless man was thrashing a chair with the rubber-foam chest plate he had ransacked from the north-of-Ireland man. When he was satisfied that it was soft enough to sit on he laid it on the seat.

'Fucken 'roids been givin' me hell lately.'

Two scenarios played out in Rickard's head. The first was that this man, finding communication diffi-cult and frustrating, and seeing fifty things where most people only saw one, would finally beat Rickard to death with his rubber cushion. Nobody would notice in this monetised public space except for the schnau-zers and labradoodles, but they would only notice because they wanted to lap up Rickard's blood. The hobo would then urinate on the work he had made.

The second scenario was that the north-of-Ireland man would shamble back and beat Rickard to death, making a martyr but being the wrong perpetrator, and making the martyrdom meaningless but proving everything right.

* * *

He vowed to call her before his martyrdom and make her sorry.

('Toni. Toni. Do you hear that now? Listen. That's Manhattan. That's New York.'

The silence at the end of the line went on for ever, over which time Rickard could hear his own whimper back at him, and a blanket of hum.

She confirmed:

'It's just noise.'

Her voice had a smell. Of tobacco, and of other men's breaths. And sometimes of those boxes of cheesy breadsticks that she ate. He imagined her with a box of those in front of her now. Perhaps crumbs down the front of a T-shirt with 'LepreCon '96 Gaming Symposium' printed on it. Crumbs on her shorts.

'Listen to you,' she said.

The enamel frames of her glasses clinked against the receiver. She sighed through her nostrils.

'Am I taking up your time?' he said.

'Yes.'

Silence above the hum for a moment.

'I can't believe you can't hear that.'

'What am I supposed to be hearing?'

'Toni …'

'How much is this costing?'

'Toni, do you ever think of coming to New York?'

'No.'

'Why not?'

'I'd be scared of running into you.'

'That would never happen. It's too big.'

'Pfff.'

More silence.

'So how are you getting on over there?' she said. 'What do you do?'

'I'm a singer.'

She laughed, perhaps.

'Like Pius in *The Severe Dalliance*?'

'Yes.'

Silence.

Then Rickard said:

'Do you ever think of *The Severe Dalliance*?'

With tiredness: 'Yes, I do.'

'And not even that would make you want to come?'

'No.'

'What do *you* do with yourself? Do you still eat breadsticks?'

'I've given up wheat.'

'And … you *never* think of leaving that *dreary* place and coming here?'

'No. I'm perfectly happy where I am.'

'I don't believe that. How could you be?'

'I'm like you, I have a rich inner life. Except mine makes me happy.'

'Oh.'

Perhaps Toni understood Rickard's inner life better than he did. This was a possibility.

'All that gaming stuff and science fiction makes you happy?' he said.

'Yes. In an escapist way. But there's more to my inner life than you know about.'

Rickard shoed at a patty of dirty chewing gum.

'Secrets?'

'Pfff. Things I've developed since you left. Writing.'

'You've been writing a book?'

'No. Ideas, just. Fan fiction.'

'Oh! You're not one of those *morons* I've seen on that website, are you?'

'My work is different from other people's. I don't stick to the tropes.'

Tropes: now she was in 'LepreCon '96 Gaming Symposium' mode. Her eyes would be scrunched shut at this point.

'What?' he said.

'A lot of that fan fiction is embarrassing. Mine's more like a personal diary. Or an autobiography. That's how it feels.'

'I don't follow.'

'I'm not afraid to show my hand. Sometimes I pop up in these stories that I write with other people's characters in them and I point out the essential artifice. And it feels like autobiography.'

Silence again.

'And that makes you happy?'

'It feels good to put something out there. It makes me feel not so sad about not having added to the world's biomass.'

Silence. Bafflement.

'Come again?' he said.

'If you have to ask that question –'

'Am *I* in these stories?'

'Pfff.')

* * *

Okay, he said. Okay.

O and – indeed – K, he said.

He would refocus. What had Ayn Rand said? She had said: Grab the world with both hands, take matters into … (Account?) Do not rely on luck. Break out on your own.

Perhaps he did not need the others – this was an idea. He once saw a man selling film scripts from a trestle table in a cobbled street in SoHo. Perhaps he could sell lyric sheets for old Irish songs, in front of the Time Warner complex. There, he might attract the interest of someone from the modern entertainment industry.

He went as far as buying the briefcase in which he would carry his songs – a battered cardboard briefcase, a century old, the type that fell apart in the rain. He gave it a good kick to knock the dirt off, and started to cough, and then to cry, imagining that he was choking on the ashes of pogroms and the dust of indifference. He imagined what it might once have contained – a few tools, of the wrong gauge: metric, useless in the

163

new world. Or something more universally useless, like a magic set.

It fell apart even without the rain. Tapped him on the knees. Abandon me, it said, and abandon ambition. 'You might as well,' it said, like a big animate whoopie pie. Damn it, he said, kicking the case again and sending it scraping across the pavement like a hockey puck. He lifted his hand to passers-by in acknowledgement of his violence. He felt keenly alone in the abscess of space that they left around him, and different from them. He experienced a passing, limb-weakening humility with the destitute, as if he were Saint Francis, and New York was his Assisi, and the destitute were his animals. It was in and out of him like a gunshot, for as long as it took a bag lady to tell him he was a 'dill hole'.

Okay, he said.

He arrived in Morningside Heights dehydrated and exhausted. Outside Denny's building he noticed a small skip – or dumpster, as they were known in these parts. In the skip was a lot of smashed-up plaster. On closer inspection there appeared to be, in the rubble, pieces of broken pottery and crockery. Even closer study revealed complete items of brassware, including a couple of spear-bearing monkeys, and the head of a cherub, flaking and freshly chipped, with a cork for a neck.

The old man's living room was clear of most of the clutter it had held previously. All that remained were the books, the chairs and wake table, and a few unobtrusive items on the mantelpiece. Bit sniffed sorrowfully along the skirting board where the reredos figures once stood.

'I prefer the word dumpster myself,' said Denny. 'Skip seems too light for the item that it describes. And to me that item looks like a giant turtle dumped by a giant bird.'

Seated was Clive, as expected, but also Jeremiah, who lived and worked in the building. He had in front of him an electric piano on a stand, set low so that the keys could be comfortably played while he sat. A plate with a large mound of fruit balanced on the arm of the chair. He was so big – not remarkably tall, but broad – that he seemed to be wedged into the upholstery.

'Rickard, you've met Jeremiah from the basement rooms. His brothers have been very kind to me. They have placed my more valuable items in storage in a pantechnicon. They have promised to earn me some money in these flea shops that are "all the rage". And Jeremiah will be a great help too. A great help to all of us.'

'You'll be playing with us, Jeremiah?' said Rickard.

'In a manner of speaking,' said Denny, before the younger man, who in any case was engrossed in his machine, could respond.

Beside Jeremiah, Clive nodded emphatically along, as if he had already been informed of a plan and was convinced again of the wisdom of it.

'We have some good news anyhow,' said Denny. 'Jeremiah, showing a barefaced disregard for ethics, but an admirable dynamism, has been recording our

165

singing. He has sent the recording to a radio station. The radio station has sent it into space. It has travelled in a perfectly straight line. Is that all correct, Jeremiah?' (Jeremiah, delighting in his fruit, murmured an affirmative.) 'A lady has heard our singing. And now we'll be playing our first concert on March the sixth.'

'Ah,' said Rickard. 'Ah,' he said, 'this is good news,' though the news was like bright light to his dry eyes, and he felt dazed, dazzled, a-muddle, and he was not sure, come to it, it being real now, if he wanted any of it any more.

'Which is why,' said Denny, 'we've enlisted Jeremiah, who has a terrific ear.'

'You'll be able to pick up all the tunes, Jeremiah?'

'Jeremiah won't be picking up any tunes,' said Denny. 'He'll have a more localised job on the night and, here's to be hoped, on many others too.'

Clive nodded with especial fury now. Jeremiah remained a million miles away.

'You'll have noticed,' continued Denny, 'that I've got rid of that awkward upright piano. Jeremiah and I have been shopping for a replacement since. We have acquired a sleek new device. What's it called, Jeremiah?'

'It's called the Reformer,' said Jeremiah.

'Is she "booted up"?'

'It's on, yes, but just having a bit of a snooze at the minute.'

Jeremiah ran his finger from side to side on the shiny white cladding of the keyboard. Within the cladding the ubiquitous Puffball orb burned upwards until it was all the one intense brightness and its edge was sharp. Quickly it settled down to a gently pulsing ember and the edge became hazy. From inside the machine the juice of it, or a spinning part, made a faint and steady hiss.

Rickard stepped forward to examine the machine. It was barely a keyboard at all; the keys were not objects but markings on the cladding. The corners were rounded; there were no bumps or attachments or holes or dials or switches. It encouraged touching, though he resisted touching it.

Denny took a rectangular box from his wake table, about the size of a big man's fist and wrist and the same white colour and gloss as the keyboard. The box opened with a click. It contained what resembled a small flat horseshoe with two curled fronds attached to the ends.

'The machine only works with this device, and this device works by means of laryngeal violation. I place the main part under my tongue. The tendrils unfurl and find their own way to my vocal cords. The device takes all the sound from my voice box and transmits it to the main unit. This is where Jeremiah does his job. He plays not the musical backing to our songs but the vocal parts. That is … my vocal part. He takes the substance of my voice and bends it to the song. His machine then communicates with any amplifier within reasonable distance.'

'Where will the accompaniment come in?' said Rickard.

'There won't be any. Jeremiah's job will be to serve my voice. The machine can produce various effects too. It can make me sound like McCormack, or Merli. Or Dame Nelly Melba, if I so desire it.'

'We will be in effect an *a cappella* group, then?'

Denny's face soured.

'And what about it? We've operated as such so far in practice.'

'In practice, yes, but always on the understanding that when it came to singing a concert we'd be accompanied on piano.'

'On whose understanding, now? It was never my intention to have musical backing.'

Rickard knew this to be untrue. He looked for a doubting expression in Clive, but Clive showed only the most earnest and patient attention to Denny.

Denny continued: 'There are too many tenor groups about now, all the same, all ruined by schmaltzy accompaniment. I don't want schmaltz in my group. It belongs to a different culture. I want to capture a spirit of an earlier, more traditional Irish music culture. One that came from material poverty, is simple, minimal.'

Rickard said, 'We've chosen the wrong songs if that is so.'

Denny did not rise to him.

'We must be honest in our interpretation of these songs,' he said, 'as we should be in how we live our lives. I am a man in the modern world. There – I've said it! Look at Clive – Clive is a former woman and is not afraid to tell people.'

Rickard thought of a flaw in the plan:

'And this concert on the sixth ... This lady who heard our singing ... Surely she has put us on the bill on the basis of the sound she heard. Your voice unchanged is fundamental to that sound, Denny.'

'I am not the fundament of this group! I am the sinew, the ganglions! Damn this ... You and Clive concentrate on *your* voices, and let me and Jeremiah concentrate on *my* voice!'

Denny put the oral device back in its box. Took it out again immediately. Rickard was frightened and filled with remorse.

'This programmer, the Rosenberg woman,' said Denny, 'she is of the old way of doing things. She has fixed ideas. The range of her interests is as narrow as her ambition. I am not interested in death and preservation but in the continuum. I believe in giving life to the past and in bringing forward the bright future. Now – let me demonstrate to you how this technology can be used to our great advantage. Jeremiah!'

Denny eased himself to his knees, and then on to his back. Jeremiah placed a draught excluder under his neck, a positioning that encouraged Denny's mouth to open to as full an extent as the lips and cheeks permitted. Then Jeremiah took the oral device.

'I'm putting it in now, Mister Kennedy-Logan. Are you ready?'

'Ah-ah.'

'They say think of sipping water through a straw. It stops the gag reflex.'

169

'Wait!' said Denny, putting his hand on Jeremiah's wrist. 'Before you do that …'

He sat up, turning to Rickard and Clive, and announced:

'I meant to tell you. The name of the trio has changed. We are no longer the Free 'n' Easy Tones. We are now the White-Headed Boys.'

'The White-Headed Boys?' said Rickard.

'The White-Headed Boys,' said Clive, a half-beat behind.

'The White-Headed Boys,' said Denny, lying down again on the floor. 'It means the propitious, the chosen, the favoured. Re-enter me, Jeremiah.'

The device in place, Jeremiah helped Denny back to his feet. The old man faced Rickard. He was almost unintelligible as he said, jabbing Rickard's chest:

'Now – the Emergency ditty "Eat Your Goodie". A young pup like you wouldn't understand what it's like to live with the thunderclap of war just over the horizon. Listen to how well I sing this one, the feeling we produce.'

Jeremiah switched on the amplifier he had hauled upstairs from his basement bedroom. He sat at the keyboard and rubbed at the cladding again. Denny turned to him for the nod – and was away, moving his jaws as Jeremiah fingered in time. From Denny's mouth came only silence. From the amplifier, a voice that sounded, to Rickard's ears, unlike anything Denny had produced before in singing or speech. It rocketed and plummeted and quarked in mid-air, making queer shifts in pitch and glancing off the diphthongs and sending Bit scampering away to the kitchen:

> *'bREAD aND bUTTER – bUILD iT uP!*
> *bUILD tHAT bREAD uP tO tHE bRIM!*
> *lAYERING sUGAR aLL tHE wAY,*
> *aND pOURING mILK fROM pAIL oR tIN!'*

(Here Denny did a twirl on the spot, flapping his hands like a little clucky hen.)

> *'eAT yOUR gOODIE! mASH iT uP!*
> *lAP iT uP, oH gOODIE-oH!*
> *tHE wHITE tHAT'S tHERE iS wHITE fOR bONES,*
> *iT'S wHITE tO hELP yOU tHRIVE aND gROW!'*

At the end of the song Denny, with all the urgency of a naval surgeon, plunged his fingers into his mouth, tore out the device, and ran to the bathroom. Retching noises and a splashing of vomit were heard.

He emerged again into the living room, dabbing his chin with toilet paper.

'Where would we be without our suffering artists?' he said.

8

Now they had not much time and their rehearsals took on an added intensity. Now, with Jeremiah's help, they practised daily, and into the nights, counting down and losing count of the days. In the heat of concentrated activity they did not feel time pass. They forgot at times the closeness of the air but it seemed that it was a good medium for the thick bars of music that powered from Jeremiah's speaker. In the quiet periods they imagined the buzzing and groaning electrical and heating services were listening, and made jokes about the critics blowing hot air. Poor little Bit was having to listen; it had no choice. The creature could not bear the strangeness and danced amusingly like a naughty girl to catch their attention. The globe at the end of the projecting brass arm cut out with a ping but on they went. They forgot feeding times but some nights a good old Texan eatery delivered 'South in [their] Mouth[s]': cornbread and meatloaf and root beer; and cakes – cherries instead of carrots for Denny. Now and then they sprawled on chairs, feeling like real artists. Denny said he wished for a cigar. His curtains remained closed all these days and nights. When they felt they could do no more practice they wished the concert was tomorrow.

When this happened they sat about the room and looked to the clock, but the clock had been sold and the calendar had not been changed. For a time no one was certain what day it was or whether the concert had indeed passed them by.

Rickard came and went but his copy of *Airs of Erin* remained all the time. They plundered it for songs. Jeremiah came and went too and indeed went missing for most of the later time.

For a time in the earlier time Denny felt he had been singing like his older self, his younger self. When this time passed he became aware of himself again as simply a collection of spaces and resonators. This feeling that he had associated with the singing from the speaker, a warming fuzz around the heart, had been tricking his brain.

He opined that 'the fronds on my oral device touch certain membranes, softer palates, the same that these Irish nose and throat singers use to send vibrations out into the body, like a sonar to find the soul, or the omphalos. Do you know about these nose and throat singers, Clive? You are probably out of the country too long, but then so am I.'

Clive said, 'I am thinking of going back one day. Been thinking heavily of this.'

Denny said, 'You will not be thinking of that while you have a job to do over here. You are thinking too much about death. Or is it that it is following you around? You never need to go back, you know. It follows me around, old son of the sod. One thing that consoles me is that the loam and the silica over here preserve you better.'

Clive said, 'Being here as we are preserves us well enough.'

Then Denny said, apropos of an earlier thought, 'Bloody English, Velily.'

Clive was walking around the living room, divining, clacking his shoes one in front of the other, led by the position of the chairs and by a pattern on the carpet, biscuit coloured, apparent to him now, and embossed, like the back of a biscuit. He had been thinking of the powers unleashed by furniture arrangements, and of other older -ologies, dynamat-this-and-that, with their whirlings and their circles of progression.

Denny said, 'If we are to be honest singers then we should *be* honest, as I have been trying so hard to tell you. Let us play a game among ourselves. It's a game like dare, or omphalos gazing. Tell us again about your being a woman at one time, Clive. "What gives?" as they say. No, I want to know what Rickard has been up to. Anything you'd like to tell us, Mister Piltdown Man?'

Rickard, who was in the room again, said, 'I once threw a roof tile at a cousin who kept putting "-tastic" at the ends of words, for example, "sandwich-tastic", "gas-meter-tastic", etcetera.'

Denny laughed loudly and harshly.

He said, 'Do you know how my dear wife Aisling died? I'll tell you – she walked out on me. There was a real game of dare. I said I was a modern man, a man of the modern world. There were others around me were doing far worse and I asked her to give me the freedoms that these men enjoyed at that time in history as artists. And when she would not stand for it, I took them anyway. And she said she would prove this was a time in the world for women too. And she went after her freedoms too.'

Clive said, 'I am curious to know exactly how this machine brings out the noise in you, Denny. I want to be assured that there is firm science behind it.'

A grinding sounded in the corner: a light came up, the light from the brass arm – Jeremiah was back in the room.

'Twenty-four-hour hardware,' he said.

'Of course there is firm science behind it,' said Denny. 'Biology and sound waves. It resonates with my mitochondria.'

'I cannot help feel that a deal has been done.'

'No cash changed hands.'

'I can sense in its outgoings something above and beyond you and it and Jeremiah.'

'There'll be a certain amount of leakage that will have all of our mitochondria moving, that is only natural.'

'There is a well-established link between music and the otherworld.'

'But anyhow I held out for Aisling, and holding out requires a certain amount of holding in. I wonder if that did all the damage.'

* * *

One Saturday afternoon when Jean Dotsy was a young child an American aeroplane came from over the border and scudded into the bog where her older brother Patrick did casual work on weekends. The pilot, a brown-haired man with a face that suggested he would go on to achieve great things, climbed out of the plane uninjured. On landing, it had ploughed up a huge curl of turf which now, collapsed into divots, largely buried the nose. Patrick observed the pilot, wild still with panic, scoop further bundles of turf in his arms and try to pile a rick on the wreckage. Sensing that he was being watched, the pilot turned around to see Patrick observing him.

'Help me with this, kid – quickly. Take your spade.'

Patrick was a big strong lad but the plane was a job to cover because, as well as being massive, it had a fin that stuck up in the air.

'What about the wing?' said Patrick – one of the wings had broken away and was lying on the ground fifty yards behind.

'Goddamn,' said the pilot, and the two ran to bury the wing as well.

The light was dim by the time the job was as good as could be done and the pilot asked Patrick if there was somewhere he could shelter the night. Patrick brought him the couple of miles to the family home. The pilot explained to Patrick and Jean's mother and father that as an American and an ally he was no threat to them.

'Technically, you are not an ally,' said Mister Dotsy. 'Make up scones and some of that serviceman coffee,' he said to Missus Dotsy, and then to the pilot again he said, 'Young man, have yourself a wash,' before disappearing for half an hour.

Later, over stout with Mister Dotsy, the pilot, whose name was Joe, played between his knees with little Jean, who remembered his tanned face and sharp nose and not-disfiguring wrinkles, and his white teeth, and the way those teeth and his mouth were set in his face in a way that she would later have described as 'goofy'.

'I am fighting the war for people like your little girl,' he said to Mister Dotsy.

He sat unembarrassed in long johns and in a yellow gansey of Patrick's that was only a little too small for him. The two men faced the fire, drowsy from the stout. Behind them sat Patrick, in Joe's pilot's jacket and not much else.

After a while, Joe remarked: 'I feel quite at home here. My ancestors are from the opposite corner of Ireland, I believe, but now I feel they are close by me.'

Over the radio came the voice of the great John McCormack, though he was great now only in reputation for he was well past his prime. The concert being broadcast was one of a series he was giving in Britain to raise funds for the war effort. Mister Dotsy said that he did not 'have the ease of movement through the notes in the higher register that he once had, and why would he, for McCormack is not a young man and he's exercised by this burdensome schedule'. Nonetheless the voice was sweet; lacking its vital and piercing sonority of old, but it had a richness it couldn't have had before, and induced the memory of comfort such as one might have got in better years from Ovaltine or burnt brown marmalade, and it seemed to lull the airman further as it sang of harps ringing out through once-royal halls and pale maidens across the seas.

'I think my radio set does him justice though,' said Mister Dotsy.

He was fascinated by the workings of machines, and could not resist boasting of how he had built the radio himself from a kit. He was a member of a group of enthusiasts that met regularly in Omagh.

There came a mighty thump on the front door. Mister Dotsy turned out of his seat, stayed Patrick with his hand, and left the room with no great concern apparent on his face. He returned with two helmeted officers of the Local Security Force.

'I am sorry, Joe,' said Mister Dotsy, 'but I was obliged to inform the authorities of your hereabouts.'

One of the officers, a man of less than five feet in stature, elaborated: 'Neutral Éire will detain until the end of hostilities all combatant personnel found on its soil or within its waters.'

Joe, who looked as unruffled as his host, calmly rose from his seat, requested his jacket back from Patrick and the rest of his clothes from the laundry sack, and went off with the two men and a 'So long, Mister Dotsy.'

About a fortnight later, Missus Dotsy opened the door to Joe again. This time he did not look contented or collected but in a state of distress.

'I've cycled all the way from the Curragh Camp of Kildare, Missus Dotsy.'

A bicycle was dumped flat on the drive, and Missus Dotsy dared not imagine how it had been acquired.

Joe, still wearing his pilot's outfit, was covered in the slime of the bog, just as he had been the first time he'd arrived at the Dotsys' house. In spite of the filth, and in spite of his distress, he retained a great shining ineffable allure.

'I'm not sure if I should be admitting a fugitive to my household, Joe,' said Missus Dotsy, admitting him anyway.

A few minutes later she had him down to his skivvies and into Patrick's gansey again. She noted that he shook with nerves, and how in the couple of weeks he'd somehow both gained and lost definition, like a bit of grey dried wood on a beach. Afterwards she got him a bottle from the outhouse. In it was a clear liquid.

'This is my secret medicine, Joe. It's made from potatoes, with some clove oil to numb the throat and honey to make it go down. It may help to steady you. But go easy on it.'

When Patrick came home from school she said to Joe, 'I have to head out for a little while but Patrick and little Jean will look after you.'

Missus Dotsy took the bicycle on the drive and went off down the road.

Forty-five minutes later she was back. Joe was gone wild with distress again, pacing two steps back and two steps forth in the small space of the parlour. Missus Dotsy snatched the bottle of dew off him and hid it for the time being inside the dresser. The two children were frightened. Jean was under the table in the kitchen, crying. Patrick, normally so fearless, sat at the table shaking his head and saying, 'Mammy, I'm sorry I ever met that mad cowboy on the bog.'

Not long after, Mister Dotsy's car rolled into the drive. With him were the two officers of the Local Security Force. Their arrival seemed to pacify Joe.

'Okay, Joe, okay,' said Mister Dotsy, easing coyly towards the young airman, all the time holding his gaze as the officers formed a pincer guard on either side. 'Why have you returned?'

'I'm just stopping by, sir. I was at the moor again.'

'But you've come all the way from the Curragh?'

Joe took a step back and said, 'Mister Dotsy – can we have a drink, all of us?'

Missus Dotsy jumped in: 'There's some stout left under the stairs.'

In this moment Mister Dotsy put his hand on Joe's shoulder.

'What's the bother, boy?'

Joe sank back into a chair and said, 'Goddamn.'

He put his arms on the table and flexed his fingers from purple through to white in front of him. He looked downwards and far away.

The three men pulled out the remaining kitchen chairs. Missus Dotsy opened five bottles of stout.

'How did you escape?' said Mister Dotsy.

'There was no escape. I could come and go as I pleased. They gave me a cottage on the camp. All of the prisoners had cottages. I shared mine with three homosexual English sailors who'd jumped from the deck of the HMS *Pluck*. We had a little picket fence around our cottage, and behind the fence, a little privet hedge. There was a little squeaky gate right in the middle of the hedge and fence. There was a rose bush in the garden – there were two rose bushes. We used to go into the town whenever we wanted. Goddamn.'

'That's the second time you've said that,' said the diminutive officer. 'Mister Dotsy won't have it.'

'It's all right, Marky,' said Mister Dotsy. To Missus Dotsy he said: 'Will you build up the fire inside, Mammy?'

'Nobody sees it,' said Joe with a snap. 'There's no urgency. It's all rose gardens, all privet hedges.'

'Now, now,' said Mister Dotsy. 'The Curragh Camp is based on the English Quaker model, don't let it fool you. The ordinary Irishman is hardened by toiling with stones and is ready, believe you me, for Herr Hitler when he lands his jackboot.'

Engineers and pilots, and technicians from the Lockheed company, all side by side. But there's another bunch of something in there too. I don't know what to call it – or them. A couple of spark plugs went missing, that's the first thing we noticed. This we could handle, to begin with. But then a lot of spark plugs started to go missing, and we stopped cursing about it, and the less we cursed about it and the more spark plugs that went missing, the more ominous it seemed. The even stranger and more ominous-seeming fact about all of this is that the spark plugs were also being replaced faster than our engineers could replace them. In tandem with this activity, certain parts of electrical circuitry would go missing. Often this would not be discovered until our planes were in the air. Then they would immediately return to base, and before the engineers could create replacements these parts were replaced too. Then parts related to top-secret projects started to go missing and be replaced. Stuff to do with radio-controlled flights. Every new item that went missing and went on being replaced brought a greater intensity of ominous silence around the base. The more that was carried on out of sight the less would be discussed within range. Within us all an unfathomable feeling of unease took hold. Among us all a clear idea of the new threat was communicated. I am a test pilot on the radio-control programme. We are to pilot old bombers fitted with explosives to a safe altitude and then parachute out, after which the planes will be remotely piloted to target. That plane in that moor is one of our test planes. We have her stripped of non-essential equipment and fitted with a fake payload. The radio equipment lies mainly under the cowling. While in the air the week before last I noticed the cowling lift. In flight, gentlemen, there is a phenomenon whereby fast-moving air appears to take on a black edge. You see this black air when it hits the solid mass of your airplane, running over its surfaces. But where the black air should have flowed smoothly into and over the raised panel of cowling, it rose well before this, up and around an invisible human-like form. I could make this human-like form out, you see, by the black air flowing around it. I could see it pulling the cowling further away. I had no option then but to quickly down the plane. Once it was on the moor, my priority was to hide the plane as best I could. Evidently your son and I, Mister Dotsy, failed to hide it well: this afternoon I discovered that the mud over the plane was undisturbed but that the plane itself was completely hollowed out of all its internal equipment.'

The officers and Mister Dotsy, who was fascinated by stories about technology, listened to Joe's story intently. Silence remained for a few moments after Joe had finished.

Then Rory, the taller officer, said, 'For many centuries the sheeha or deenie ooshla were known in this district for the fixing of wheels. They have a control over the working of things. The fixing of wheels was a way in which they would do you a favour, but sometimes they would spoil things for mischief. They have an understanding of materials but they never use it for real harm. They are pitiable beings. They are like prisoners of our world. They are pitiable for their needs and often they find their needs in us. They have adapted to the world of men and changed with it through all of its ages. If what you say is true then what we could be seeing is a new phase.'

'A new phase,' said Joe quietly. 'Well, I sensed that.'

After they had finished their stout Joe was given his still-filthy clothes from the laundry sack and brought away by Marky and Rory. He did not return again to the Dotsys' house, but his name was heard once more, years later, after the war, when news came back that some time during the war, probably after the Dotsys had encountered him, he had been killed when the aeroplane he was piloting exploded over the Blyth estuary, GB.

Some time again then after the war, when Jean was a grown-up schoolgirl, a creature known as Petticoat Loose went about the district and surrounds taking medical paraphernalia off children. Twelve boys had their calipers taken. One day Jean was walking home along a lane with a friend when the friend was grabbed by Petticoat Loose and spun around in a bush. In the course of it the friend's electrical hearing aid was removed. In the end anyhow Petticoat Loose was banished by unseen forces to the mouth of the Red Sea where she spent her time overturning ships.

9

Denny Kennedy-Logan stirred from a deep afternoon sleep. For one phantastic moment he thought he was on a foreign holiday, before a dull but disoriented wakefulness settled in him. He lifted his arms either side, studying them, blinking … He was in a chair, not a bed. The chair was in a windowless room; designed with only function in mind. The walls were of rough brick, painted a stark white, with a violet tint. In front of him was a mirror, with no softening bulbs around it (though there were flowers on the table – lots of lilies).

He leaned forward to his reflection. He looked ghastly, gaslit. His eyes were seeping sea anemones, and from them his face dripped in ghoulish green phosphorescent rings. He leaned closer. His chair zipped back on its castors an inch from under him, making him gasp and grasp the table. The smell of lilies almost choked him, and their cold rubbery touch caused him to shiver.

'Where am I?' he shouted, slapping the wall.

How did he get here?

He had been embraced and swept in one movement from some point he could not remember with any ... great deal of sharpness.

Who embraced him?

Where were the others?

His shirt was damp through.

Why was his shirt damp through?

'Where is my jacket?! Where is my cummerbund?! You cannot take a man's dignity like this!'

Bit!

Let me change this light bulb, he said. But how am I meant to safely pull this off? The chair was on castors. He reached in his trouser pockets. And where am I meant to get a bulb? But that ghastly light from that ghastly tube! No, there has to be a way to do it. And if I were to hold my nerve so that the poles of the tube did not touch any metal along the way. Poles of a tube! A riddle: how can a tube have poles? When it is a light bulb. Or a telescope. And how many tenors does it take to change a light bulb? But I still do not have this light bulb. And that chair is still on castors. How am I meant to do this? I only care so much for puzzles, you know!

A door opened. A woman entered. Red haired, with ringlets, and a burst of red spices for a mouth.

'Bored yet?' she said. 'When do your friends arrive?'

She poured from a jug and handed him a huge glass of water. He took a sip, gingerly, keeping his eyes on her. Thimbles of ice and slices of cucumber piled up at his nose, and his throat and heart and lungs contracted in pain.

'I believe we're both going the same way home later. We should share a cab. You'll enjoy the people on before you. The show-tunes girl is a darling. Can you wait a few more minutes? I have a little more house-keeping to do.'

'Excuse me,' he said after the closed door. 'Where are the others? Excuse me,' he said. 'I am a man and I have my dignity! I said, I am a man! And I have my dignity!'

He stood in silence for some moments.

Then he took another gulp of the ice-cold water and slowly sat back in his seat.

* * *

'Well now, Clive. Did you envisage, when I proposed the idea for the White-Headed Boys, dressing rooms such as this?'

'Oh I did.'

'As large as this?'

'Oh I did.'

'With a picture of Franklin W Roosevelt on the wall?'

'With a picture of Franklin D Roosevelt on the wall.'

'Is that FDR?' said Rickard, getting up from his seat, and peering closely at the framed newspaper clipping.

'A great man for second chances,' said Denny. 'And now ...'

He cupped his ear to the closed door.

'Oh, she's good, she's good,' he said, about the soprano who was on the bill before them.

'What are these words again to the second verse of "Letters from France"?' said Clive. 'Do we agree to go as far as the second verse?'

Denny pulled his chair out from under the table.

'Who's been smoking shag tobacco?' he said, brushing his elbows.

Rickard was carefully reading the framed newspaper clipping. Jeremiah was playing Grieg in quacking tones on his machine.

'"The Hall of the Mountain King" is right. Damn freezing in here.'

'You shouldn't have removed your cummerbund,' said Clive.

'What I need is a fur hat … Do you remember how the pigeons had a taste for Sweet Afton?'

'Which pigeons?'

'"Which pigeons?"! The pigeons in old Dovelin! But only the blue ones round Beggar's Bush, mind you.'

Then he began shadow-boxing, throwing left-hand jabs and right-hand uppercuts millimetres from Clive's face.

Pit! A left-hand jab connected with Clive's face.

'Agh! Gotcha!'

Clive coughed out a laugh, but his eyes brimmed with tears.

'And that's my weaker hand too! Should have got 'em to build you a bigger chin, old girl!'

He turned to Rickard and Jeremiah, absorbed in their own activities.

'They should have used his hip bone instead of his ear bone!'

* * *

Now they stood before the curtain. Denny in the middle, Clive and Rickard to the left and right. Cummerbund in place; it was lined with canvas, and compressed his abdomen, pushing his diaphragm into his chest space.

Jeremiah secreted.

In the wings, the goblin man wiped his hand on his trouser leg. With the same hand, he rubbed the machine's cladding.

Denny gave him 'the thumbs up'.

In Denny's mouth, the taste of blood, pus, and something similar to sparking flint. A more pronounced sensation of clutter than he had experienced before from the sound sampler. A sensation like the one he had had as a child when he contracted brucellosis from watercress and he tried to put every marble he owned in his 'pucus', or 'buccus', as his mother corrected.

The device cut into the bracket that rooted his tongue. Something made enquiries at the back of his nose. The fronds? What were the fronds doing at the back of his nose?

Saliva overflowed from the corners of his lips. He drew his sleeve across his mouth.

A hush descended the other side of the curtain. Outbreaks of 'Shhhh'. The curtains fluttered at the split.

'Thank you, everybody,' came the voice of the woman with the spicy mouth. 'Yes, thank you, please. Didn't our soprano Miss Herschel sing like an angel for you?'

Static panning in and out: applause.

'And so we've come to our final performance tonight, our last act. I feel I've known these men – these wonderful Irish tenors, the Whiteboys – all my life. I've never met them before. I've never set foot in Ireland either, but when I listen to these men sing I feel like I've been transported on a rainbow to a great pine forest and that I've drunk from the cleanest Irish spring. And when you hear them too, I think you'll say to me, "Aye, lass, 'tis true." Harh, harh, me hearties, are you ready, boys? I think that they are. Curtain, please!'

A rattle and a whoosh and a wind on his face. And then ... And then ...

He stood, squinting.

Lights and darkness. The one and the other.

Mostly lights. Hot, burning lights.

Below the lights, the darkness.

He twitched his head inquisitively.

A movement: glasses, glinting.

Drawn back to the lights: white and yellow. The heat seared into his eyes. He closed his eyes. Pulsing red. He looked to the darkness again. A blob of white flashed and faded – to blue, to nothing. Leaving a blacker arid nothing.

And there he stood, squinting.

The void was hot. Now he remembered. He had forgotten how it felt, that it could be felt, that it was hot – it excited him in a way he hadn't felt in years. For this he used to live and on this he used to thrive.

To project, Maestro Tosi had said, was to propel goodness into the dragon's mouth. If you do not believe in monsters, let it be nothing and the thing to fill it with is your soul. But for me, I am a Crusader of Palermo and what I have to give is Christian goodness.

So let it be nothing. This was how he derived his energy. From being on the edge of nothing. This was his element. Nothing. This was his challenge. To give something to nothing. Ringed by lights, inside the ring: nothing. He leaned into nothing.

To his surprise, nothing answered. From the middle of nothing a small light shone. Whiter than the white lights above, but cold, fixed in the dark like a star, but not like a star, stable in the light it threw out. He could sense its coldness from a distance, but not a great distance, no. All that he felt in his body told him he was looking down at the light, not across. The dark gave him no mooring, no reference, nothing to tell him that he was not looking down. But his chin was held high and his ribs were well spaced; how could he be looking down and not across? And what was this now? A rope, dangling from the stage, wrapped around his ankle, dropping off, out – down through the dark. It was made of a very long piece of grey woollen fabric and had a thousand knots in it. It waved, arced greatly in the dark, seeming to summon him, like a beckoning finger. Was this how he was to feed the void? To give himself, all of himself? It was time.

He had no say in the matter. Gravity ploughed him forward, the rope tightened around his ankle, and he was yanked upside down. The jerk and the snap broke the tension in his body, whipping his spine, but instilled a kind of suppleness. He fought against his harness, thrashing spasmically, spinning zanily, and making the rope bounce and the bind stab at his ankle. He knew by the pain that his show of defiance was futile, and he stopped, but a vestigial electricity fought on. Stop now, he urged his muscles. His body relaxed, and the physical laws took over. He rocked through a gentle torque. The rhythm of it was calming, slowing all the time. His arms hung limp, and he felt an odd sort of bliss. He was both constricted and free – his arms were like strings of blood sausages, or the necks of pheasants in a poulterer's, or the ends of mammy's mink scarf, or daddy's shirt on mammy's line – and he could have stayed like this for a long time. But then, having the urge to invigorate his fibres, he took the rope in his hands and twisted with a new stripling strength, and his ankle was liberated from the rope's bind, and he flipped the right way up, and he slipped an inch, and then he carefully descended, taking knot by knot with his hands and feet. Only when he got to the end of the rope, dangling by his hands from the last knot, and his feet kicking in the dark, did he permit himself a look down.

He saw there Aisling, bright as a pearl, fathoms from him. He said, I want to reach you, lovey, but I am afraid of letting myself go in the dark. He pulled at the rope in his frustration and the last knot disappeared – he felt a thump as he dropped the three inches. He looked above him, at the rope tapering into the darkness, at the many knots he had let through his hands, at the many bound inches, and he started back up, snapping at every knot along the way, lengthening the rope by many more inches. When he had got half the way up the rope he thought that he might have added enough length to it to enable him to reach Aisling. But descending to the bottom again he saw that she was still a good distance from him. And so he went at it once more, shinnying past halfway, snapping out the rest of the knots as he met them. It was tiring work, and he felt the child in him disappear, and the stripling too, and he felt again like the old man that aeons ago he knew that he was. He twisted some of the rope around his wrist and his ankle and he rested. The rope smelt like rotten mutton, and it was clammy.

Then a lifeline came down for him: a white cable with a metal clamp on the end. It required no gymnastic effort to get across to the cable; it hung side by side with the rope. He threw his legs over the clamp and sat on it like a jack on a swing, intending to rest some more and build up his energy. His head was slumped forward and the cable was at his shoulder and he drifted into a semi-sleep, but he became alert again when torpidly he noticed the remaining knots in the rope trickle by, trickle by – the cable was being drawn up! It reeled him all the way back to the stage, dematerialising above him, and finally dematerialised in his hands, leaving him suspended for a moment in the air before he thudded to the boards. Immediately he was on the stage floor he scrambled around like some crippled vagrant thrown in a gaol cell. And he no longer sensed, as he looked into the dark, that he was looking down; when he looked up he felt that he was facing up, that up was up and down was down and across was across again.

Aisling hovered above him, almost within reach. She was wrapped in the grey wool of the rope. No pietà Madonna could have looked so sad. The cloth was wrapped around her head as a mourning shawl and wound about her body. The weave was caulked with thick body liquids. She chewed and sucked one loose end.

He sprang up. He sang:

'If I die in this prison you will know before long,
But they give me no word of you.'

She began to unfasten the cloth. It unwound and broke down to a dust. The dust built up below her feet, making a picture. The picture built up around her until she was the figure in a medallion. The scene in

the medallion was of a land barely green and the grey
and black clouds that roofed it. The underclothes that
she wore were the same colour as these clouds and the
land that took on the colour of the clouds. They melted
into and came of these clouds, even as her feet touched
her little piece of earth, which seemed so cold and
lonely.

White-Headed Boy:

'Do not lose heart my Emerald Maiden –
For your friends are many in number!
Call to the lands where they bow to the ring,
They will raise in arms Peter's great crozier!'

The clouds came down, enveloping entirely the
scene in the medallion. She floated among them. The
clouds parted but the undergarments of cloud
remained. She stood aside in her medallion to a plat-
form of grey rock and swept her arm to indicate a new
scene. The sky was black and starless but held a faint
faraway moon. Far below the grey rocky platform was
a sea lough. There was no water in the sea lough except
for a sluggish trickle. Did this water once meet the sea
as an equal? Did the sea keep its distance because the
moon was feeble? Was the sea as black as the dark,
blacker still, devouring the moon in its stolid tarry
waters? On both sides of the river's weakly black course
lay great flats of grey estuarine silt. No French longboat
would reach this far, nor the row-barges of a relieving
Spanish fleet. Her face carried the sad expression of

the feeble moon, saying, I am fallen to an unconquerable conqueror, I am condemned to my destiny.

White-Headed Boy:

'Though the clouds they have gathered to darken your
skies
And tears fall to black earth from your smoke-stung green
eyes,
And the bite of the crow and cut of the chain
Draws out the Royal blood from your faint-beating veins,
It must be remembered
'Twas not always thus!
This eternal December,
This sepulchral dust!
In your gilded past glory
No burden you bore!
This once was your story
And will be once more!'

The medallion enlarged and changed shape. It made now a lozenge, and came low enough so that he could enter. He did so, and she backed away across the hillside as he did. She stood among the ashes of weeds. He kicked the ground beneath him and saw that it was as black. The edge of the plateau marked the drop to the sea lough but he could not see the lough over the lip. Nor could he see far in any direction – only darkness, and the waveforms of intertwining bands of mist. He was frightened at having entered the scene, but then this was his country too. But it was hard to imagine that it was ever a place of wealth, or of hope, and hard to imagine that she was not lonely here.

White-Headed Boy:

'The light will shine on you again!'

But the moon was gone and it was so monstrously dark. Even the dark above was like the light shut out by the cap of a cistern.

White-Headed Boy:

'There is a harp with strings of sunbeam;
To play it and to sing the name:
Ireland! Ireland!
Will summon light oh once again
And bring that name back to a gleam!'

She clutched at her left breast with both hands to form the shape of a heart. The fingers dug and clawed. Her fingers were withered to relics and the place of her heart was the reliquary she sought to reach. From that place leapt a rainbow. The rainbow was composed of different shades of grey and one shade of black. It leapt like a leaping fish – slow near the top of its arc. When it hit the ground it made the thud of a landed fish. He saw something writhe in the ash and went to it. He found a dead pike that was already half pus. The pike curled up its head and hissed through its dreadful lips and teeth, 'The borders of countries of the place whence you came have no meaning here. Even the border of that country you mention which is so fixed by nature has no meaning here where nature has no meaning.'

White-Headed Boy:

'Is not Erin that place of which you speak?
Is not Erin that place o'er which you weep?
Is not Erin –'

Some light appeared as a greenish grain in the air. Distantly amid this disturbance, across the abysmal territorium, he saw a city emerge. He peered hard at the city. The dead pike hissed up at him, 'It is built to an order you have never known. Columns are thin and twisted and carved with a uniform pattern of gnarls. These end in gigantic capitals carved in the design of a bouquet of frayed nerves. The columns support gigantic rhomboid pediments one to each column and each set on a column on one of its acutest points. Across the opposite acute points of the pediments balances the entablature. The architrave of every entablature is carved in an arrangement of various inverted mammalian nipples. The frieze of every entablature is carved in an arrangement of various mammalian anuses. The cornice of every entablature is carved in an arrangement of shards of various mammalian bones broken the better that the entire body will pass again into the matrix of origin. The city also abounds in finials carved as stacks of hairballs as extracted from mammalian stomachs, rostrums carved

206

pressure lying all across his face as if a sheet of glass were against it. It was most severe at the bridge of his nose, which, he suspected, had been flattened altogether along with the rest of his facial topography. It was as if he had woken from an operation in which his face had been shattered with a mallet. Through the glass he observed a new scene. It was a more intimate and homely and familiar scene than before. A wall to his left was plastered in the floral wallpaper of the living room of the flat he and Aisling had shared in Rathmines, Dublin. On it hung that gaudy picture of a weeping owl-eyed Spanish peasant girl. The wall to his right was plastered in the same wallpaper. And there was their old Lambert range. The furniture was theirs too, along with its horrid antimacassars (a wedding gift from Aisling's mother), but it was all moved to the sides to make space at the centre of the floor. On the floor was their reproduction antique Chinese rug, a tribute to the orientalist Lafcadio Hearn, whose family had long ago lived in that very house. The floor was otherwise wooden boards. The plan followed approximately the same rectangular layout of their living room. But there was no wall opposite. The room opened out to darkness. Above, on that side, stage lights were suspended. He realised now that he was viewing this space from the perspective of a framed picture of the young John McCormack, a print of a painting in which the tenor had a dreamlike saintlike appearance. He had often stood with his back to the picture and sung, and he knew this perspective. Around and around the Chinese rug trundled a Friesian cow. It was not an actual Friesian cow, but a pantomime Friesian cow. Its bagginess, and its wellington boots, made it look very preposterous. One of the black markings on its pied flanks was a crude map of Ireland. Aisling herself occupied the front of the cow. He could identify her because she did not wear a cow's head. The effect of a cow's face was generated with the use of black and white face paint, pink paint on the nose, long false golden eyelashes, and gold hooped earrings. The cow appeared to have been delivered bad news. The around-and-around motion suggested perplexity and distress, though the face did not give much away, because Aisling was a bad actor. Adding to its distress now was the fact that its back half had come off. Yes – the back of the cow now lay on the floor, moaning. With no surprise he could identify himself poking out of the open end. He wore a pair of woman's tights on his head and the way these pressed up his eyelashes made him look womanly. But he looked punch drunk too, which partly restored his manliness. 'Oh what will I do now my four beautiful stomachs are taken from me?' said the front half of the cow, stiffly, looking down at the detached back half. She stood arms akimbo staring into the dark, grinding her pelvis around to test the unexpected adjustment to her mechanism. With a sudden spiritedness then she kicked off her wellington boots to reveal balleri- na's plimsolls. She turned round to the back half of the cow and, with one of those delicate plimsolls,

He waited for an age for the pressure on his face to ease. Finally something cracked. He stumbled forward on to the boards. The fourth wall was now in place, and light flooded in from Prince Albert Terrace through the window. 'You look perfectly ridiculous,' she said, albeit with tenderness. She added: 'But at least not awfully ridiculous.' He opened his mouth to bark something back, and felt a lump in his throat and his jaw unhinge, and heard a crackle right through his head like burning cellophane. The lump pushed up through his throat, widening it all the way. His head bloated to an enormous extent to accommodate the lump, opening along the fissures of his broken skull. The head only returned to something near its normal shape when at last the lump had fully extruded and revealed itself to be the half-pus pike, now slathered in mucus and bile too. The pike flipped about the floorboards, as surprised as anyone in the room, looking for a hiding place. Then it divided into a dozen eels, which searched for cover too. Each eel split into a thousand earthworms, which each became a thousand white parasites of the gut, which all crawled through the spaces between the floorboards. 'Where is he?!' barked Denny, pushing about the newspaper kindling in the range. 'Where is he?!' he barked, marching into the bedroom and opening the wardrobe, and looking under the bed. 'Where is who?' answered Aisling, as equably as she could pretend. 'The pike! The pike! You know who! That rotten bastard roe!' said Denny. 'And who is this?' he said, each other against the umbrella stand. The umbrella stand was circular, representing eternity. Romance was yuck unless you could put it in, or on, a box, he thought. He looked out a window. It was like a loophole in a citadel. Hell was a skyscraper in danger of flaking, from the heat at its core versus the ice on its skin. Hell was hoping. Heaven was seventy Stain Devils at the grocery store, and finding one for black ink.

White-Headed Boy:

> *'Hark! Listen to the voice of my heart!*
> *Listen to my cry of love!'*

'Explain Limbo to me,' she said. 'It's a very confusing part of the doctrine. And I think they deliberately confuse it, because they don't know themselves. Well I'm ready to throw the whole lot out.' 'Limbo,' he said, hating his own tone, but going on, as he'd committed himself anyhow, even *if* her question was rhetorical, 'is different from Heaven or Hell, in that spatial time passes. One is given the confusion of the world there, and one is given a test to find the purest form of oneself there, but one knows one will be released once one finds it.' (What was all this 'one' pomposity? Damn it, man.) 'No, no,' she said, 'what you've explained there is Purgatory. Isn't Limbo for babies?'

White-Headed Boy:

The line of Denny's shoulders lay more or less flush with the edge of the stage. Beyond it the first rows of audience members sat splattered in Denny's blood and brains. Many among them were lacerated by splinters of Denny's skull.

Immediately Denny's head exploded some in the audience jumped from their seats with a curious readiness. Rickard retained just enough of his senses – like Clive, he had cramped in shock – to notice that those who sprang into action had all been seated at the ends of rows. They fell into line behind one another – five in one side aisle, five in the other – and ran up the steps flanking the stage. By the time Rickard had limbered back to some measure of mobility and turned around, the stage was empty, save for Jeremiah and a dark gritty track of blood that led into the wings and out through the stage door.

A pity, the whole episode, because up to that point the concert had gone exceptionally well.

Back in Denny's apartment – Jeremiah let them in with the master key – they complimented each other on their individual performances: Clive had sung high and sharp like a piccolo, Rickard's vibrato had been so rich and resonant that it was felt through the boards of the stage, and Jeremiah had manipulated Denny's voice with deftness and virtually perfect timing.

* * *

Clive made tea, putting eight spoons of sugar directly in the pot, and they sat in silence sipping the astringently sweet beverage. When, after some time, the noise of their slurping was joined by Bit's purring, Jeremiah called the dog over with a click of his fingers, rubbed it on the chin, and said:

'So, then. Splat.'

'Mmmh,' said Clive. 'It was a stroke, I fear. He can get very wound up.'

'I could see that about him all right,' said Jeremiah.

'A curse, they are. One day you're yourself, the next you're not quite. But he's in the best hands. I suppose we should think about ringing around the emergency rooms.'

Rickard absently eyed Bit, then fixed on the animal. He whistled and tapped his ankle, but the dog would not move from Jeremiah's caress. He became aware once more, by a deep ambient silence, of the absence of Denny's clock, the one that had been cleared out to the skip; and then conscious again of the sound only of slurping, and of the satisfied grunting (and mellow flutings) of a snub-nosed dog, and of the distant cacophony of a New York night.

He remembered the girl in the Puffball Store, with the wolfish grey eyes, and that one of the people who had taken Denny's body away was this girl. He remembered how the halogen light in the store had caught her name tag and flared.

He got up out of his seat, electrified by a revelation, and made a new pot of tea, unaware that that was what he had done. He saw the thing he would do. He would go to this girl, Fondler, as if she were a white sacrificial slab, or a dark jagged reef, and offer his own self up, fling his own self down, and be obliterated, foundered.

A blood sacrifice.

The others were looking at him.

He tried to describe the girl but struggled for precise enough words.

'She sounds delicious,' said Clive.

Three minutes later, after trying to describe her better, and telling them how he had seen her a little while before – and how the image of her from that first time and the image of her from hours earlier had moved one over the other and matched like two of the same bloody fingerprint – he had convinced the others that he was smitten.

'She sounds like the kind of female that a male would know by instinct was beautiful,' said Jeremiah.

'Really very beautiful,' said Clive.

'You should have courted her.'

'You should have taken the chance.'

'You should have heard you there.'

'Our man is in love.'

Rickard was aghast.

'But I've only seen her twice – briefly.'

'Briefly is all it takes,' said Clive.

'You should have let your heart do the talking,' said Jeremiah. 'You should have said to this female there in that Armory concert hall, "X.X., we were put here together at this time for a reason." Because that is Denny's message – yes, Clive? Allow the feeling to fill your sails.'

'Oh yes. Denny is a great believer in acting on impulse.'

'Go with the life force, that's what he says. It's the cord –'

'The filament –'

'– that runs through us all. Do not resist. Love's sweet ways are all that count. Love's accretions mount and mount. But love's too shy to show its face. And when it does, it is too late. You must find its hiding place.'

'Well done, Jeremiah,' said Clive.

'These are very stupid songs. They are not philosophies,' said Rickard.

'But in them all, taken together – layered, serried, racked – is the truth,' said Jeremiah.

'Rickard, you must never let guilt hamper you,' said Clive. 'Was it guilt that got in the way last night?'

'Well – yes, actually.'

'Rickard, Rickard. Don't let guilt ruin your life. Guilt is a terrible thing.'

'And it's dishonest,' said Jeremiah.

'It is,' said Clive. 'It's dishonest. When we feel guilt we are hiding.'

'Guilt is false. It's a false emotion, that's what Denny says. So you must be honest always – he says that too.'

'He's all about the honesty. As a singer. As a man.'

'We could all be more honest, and it would bring pain, but there'd be less pain in the long run, that's what you'll find, that's what he says,' said Jeremiah. 'He says where honesty meets danger, that's love. But we get asphyxiated in all sorts of whores' front-bottom farts. He didn't say whores' front-bottom farts. This is what I'm saying, all of it.'

'But he says that too,' said Clive.

'And … yes, *carpe diem*. He learnt that in Italy.'

'Italy,' said Clive.

'Desperate,' said Jeremiah.

'Don't talk to me,' said Clive.

'All those young females he met over there.'

'Oh no, the young females came later,' said Clive. 'Remember, Aisling was after Italy.'

'All those young females he met after Aisling.'

'He never got divorced from her, that's the thing,' said Clive. 'That's where your guilt comes in.'

'But even if he could have got divorced, he says it wouldn't have mattered. He always feels … or *felt* … I suppose he's a little past the point now –'

'Oh, there'll be life in the old dog, you'll see, once he comes around from this stroke.'

'He always feels that he needs Aisling's blessing. Have I got that right?'

'That's what he's been telling me too. He should have moved on. And everyone saying she was the great love of his life. That was false too. Listening to all that, in his head, that's what held him back.'

'When he should have listened to his heart.'

'Yes! At all times.'

'So.'

'There's a message for us all there.'

'So go after this female!' said Jeremiah, cracking a fist into his palm.

Rickard could hold back no longer.

'Gentlemen! It just wouldn't do! It would not do to ask a girl out at a murder scene! Especially if the girl in question is complicit in the murder!'

'Who's talking about murder?' said Jeremiah.

'Murder?' said Clive.

* * *

The next morning Rickard lay in his bed, his bladder a balloon of moiling brown bog water, thinking about this girl, and thinking about his coming end. He imagined the words of his death notice – the 'loved by his many cousins', and the telling absence of Toni – and the sentimental music that would play at his funeral, and he imagined also how the goo of that sentiment would remain to sicken and spite some, but calcify in time to inspire others. He was never surer that an enemy was ranging against him and his kind, but the only way he wanted to belong to his side now was as a symbol, a talisman, a totem, as some kind of idol that could be held on a bier in battle. He recognised, as a witness to the nefarious act of the night before, and as one who understood its implications, the great solemnity of a calling: as if Justice, with her gold scales, hovered in the roundel of the porthole; or Hibernia, with her gold spear, stood in the grotto of the wardrobe. He could, of course, have willed to his flesh the point of Hibernia's spear, but that would have been inglorious and meaningless. A more effective use of himself would be as he had first conceived – to force from the enemy the very worst kind of outcome. He would predecease his parents. At any rate, he would force an outcome. He got up and finally went to the bathroom.

Later that evening – he had fallen back to sleep and dozed for hours, terrorised by horribly vivid dreams – he returned to Denny's building in Morningside Heights and found Jeremiah in the basement. The unmistakable popcorn smell of Bit infused the fuggy air. The dog, now taken into the care of Jeremiah and his brothers, had the run of the place.

'This is a very serious situation,' said Rickard.

Jeremiah entered the main part of the basement from a side room.

'What are you doing here?' he said. He was grimy from work, and wearing a jersey of the Gaelic Athletic Association county of New York.

'Your brother directed me.'

'Oh did he now? Well isn't he very clever. Would you like a cup of this?' He held out a mug. 'It's buttered coffee what all the youth are drinking. Healthy, they say. And they say only Irish butter will do for it.'

Rickard took one look at the lacquery black liquid with the shining globules on its surface and waved it away.

'Jeremiah, we must examine this music machine. We must open it up.'

Jeremiah scratched behind his ear, making a scouring sound. 'And what would you hope to find?'

'It's not what I'd hope, it's what I'd dread.'

'Would that make it any closer to your understanding?'

'I'm merely looking for evidence. I feel there's a link between that machine and what we all witnessed happened to Denny last night. What do you think?'

'I don't know. I think he went out like a watermelon, that's what I think. He wouldn't have suffered a bit. Now,' – he took a loud slurp of his coffee – 'if you don't mind, I'm in the middle of work.'

'Oh, and Jeremiah – this girl that I talked about.'

'Yes.'

'I want someone to know. I'm going to go to her. To these Puffball people.'

'And do what?'

'I'll have to think about my words carefully. I want to really put it to her. The thing is – I know exactly what it is that I want to put to her, but –'

'And that is what?'

Rickard described his vision of a future war – the Sharks, the Owls.

Jeremiah swilled and inspected his coffee. 'I know nothing about women. But what you say there does not seem, any of it, the wise and fructifying thing to be telling them.'

'Yes, you're right, you're right, that's the wrong approach. The thing … The thing is – I know what I want to do, I know what I want to represent, I know the outcome I want. I think.'

'Maybe you think too much.'

'I must inveigle myself.'

'Let what happens happen.'

'And be damned.'

'A man can be thinking too much. Actually,' – Jeremiah clunked his mug down on a shelf – 'can I come and observe?'

'No, Jeremiah. No. But if you'd remember please this exchange, and my motives.'

* * *

By eleven o'clock most of the tourists were gone from the plaza. A light spring rain had fallen and the granite surfacing gleamed. Not a droplet of water clung to the Puffball dome and its green laser spider. Rickard had worked his way down to the bottom pretzel in a stack of five. The foil was opened in his hand like a tawdry moonflower. He was on his third paper cup of coffee, and his heart was bouncing.

The girl came to the door of the building, stopped, and zipped up a black leather jacket. He was certain it was his girl, though her hair was different this time – tied up at the back. She looked straight in his direction. He dipped his head to the centre of his flower. All he had to do was let her know – soon, but not now, and somewhere private – and his martyrdom would be assured.

He came to the back of the store, on to 39th Street, and looked right, then left. He spotted her across the road, a hundred metres away. He was happy to leave this gap: it was narrow enough so that he could keep an eye on her, wide enough so that if she turned around he could sidestep, duck his head, become just another head in the crowd.

She led him down through the old business heart of Manhattan, under the bulk of the Empire State Building and the other mud-coloured ziggurats. Something about the area always made him shiver and speed along. Half of it was lost to the night – hardly a light was on above, the mud of those ziggurats dissolving in the oily dark – but on the streets was madness contained. Steam hissed from the ground; magnesium sparked in grilles and catch basins. Many times in the past he had strolled these unfaltering streets without any purpose at all. How had he kept going? Walking in Manhattan without purpose was boring and exhausting. Only romance had kept him going: songs about this or some other avenue and cross-street, *The Severe Dalliance* and the hope of that dream in his head and this in reality converging.

Occasionally the girl was lost in the clusters, reappearing with a zing of bright yellow – her jacket had a lemon stripe across the shoulders. His eye was tricked more than once: tiger stripes rippling through the backlit vapour; dazzle-ship taxis with their chequered flashes. It became a game of keeping pace: taking ninety seconds to reach the end of a block, running a light when he could. How before now had he not thrown himself under a bus with boredom?

On to Broadway, then the strange lonely Bowery, with its pot-and-pan shops, its procession of domestic dioramas. A clatter of windblown litter brought echoes of skid row. At a window she halted. Catching up, he noted a fan of spatulas, knives on a magnetised strip, sharpening rods. On she led him; left again on to Houston Street and southwards; eastwards. Was this Alphabet City? East again of Alphabet City?

As the streets condensed so he had let the gap narrow. Now only fifty metres separated them, with no one else this side of the empty street. She stopped again and turned around.

'Hey!' he shouted.

She went on, quickening her pace.

Into a courtyard in the middle of a squat housing project, each building just five storeys high. Two rusty basketball hoops craned at either end of the space from chipped, rotting backboards. Many windows in the buildings were broken, the walls sprayed here and there with graffiti. From the windows in one block soot streaked up the brickwork. Behind him a fire escape rattled.

He turned to see a line of ... six, seven, eight people emerge from high in the building. They spread out along a horizontal gantry, spaced themselves evenly apart, and leaned by their elbows on a handrail, taciturnly observing him. Below them, on another gantry, a further eight people appeared and arranged themselves in an identical pattern. On the steps between the gantries others sat and slouched and eyed him also. They were all the same; that was, the same age: young, in their early twenties. And all were clothed identically, he saw now: in grey scruffy one-piece boiler-type suits, with concertina sleeves and red piping around the shoulders, elbows, waists and knees. Every one of them, boys and girls, wore his or her hair in messy spikes, and every face was lightly sponged with smut.

'Hey, yo!' he heard from behind. He turned back around.

Fondler was standing in the courtyard. She was still dressed in her black Puffball uniform and leather jacket. Her hands sat defiantly on her hips and her feet were planted in obdurate firmness and widely apart, in a puddle.

A voice called from a gantry:

'Who's your friend, Fondler girl? He one of the newbies at work?'

'I don't know who he is. But I know his face.'

'Ooh là là!' somebody else called. 'I want to hear that face speak! Let me see that face again!'

He turned to look back at the gantries.

'Speak, Proteus Boy!' called a boy with bright blond hair.

'Speak!' called a girl with lurid red hair.

'Speak!' screamed somebody else.

'Speak! Speak! Speak! Speak! Speak!' came the chorus, at once harsh and deep and high and shrill, getting louder and louder, as upwards of twenty pairs of arms banged the scaffold in perfect time.

Then suddenly, on one of the beats, the noise cut out, leaving the ring of resonant metal in the air.

In unison, eight legs were slung over the handrail of the bottom gantry, and eight legs over the top gantry, as the youths on the stairs began to twist downwards through the helix of metal like jungle cats in the branches of a jacaranda. Then the second in each pair of legs came flying over the handrail, and the two troupes of eight each dropped gantry by gantry to the courtyard. In less than a minute he was encircled, the dead centre of an anticlockwise-moving formation. All eyes were on him. Each left arm in its concertina sleeve quivered like a rattlesnake, the hand open, the fingers splayed.

'Hisssssss!' went every mouth. 'Hisssssss, hisssssss', and then –

'ssssssssssssssssStop!'

Fondler, outside the circle.

It broke to allow her in, then split at the opposite side so that now two straight chorus lines were formed.

Rickard stood facing his erstwhile quarry in a silent stand-off.

'Who is he, Fondler?'

'Yes, who is he?'

'Why has he come?'

'What is he doing here?'

'Pray, tell!'

Fondler remained silent, and kept her gaze fastened on Rickard. He detected a minute trembling of her sockets, a tic of the pupils. Yes, she must have recognised him; he had been on stage, under bright lights, for nearly an hour the night before.

'Come out with it now! Give us the truth!' came twenty-four sing-song voices all together.

Now the open left hands, which had never stopped quivering, were joined by twenty-four quivering right hands, and each pair of quivering hands rose from its owner's side to chest height and became jazz hands.

'Stop goofin' around! We need to know:
Why has he come here among us?
Did Townsend send him to snuff out our plans
To smash up the smooth white fungus?'

The chorus lines swapped sides, slicing through each other in cartwheels.

Rickard grabbed at his heart. He felt light-headed. He felt himself slipping away.

* * *

Fairy lights and candlelight were the first to meet his sight before his eyes adjusted to a room gutted to the bare brick. But the occupants had made the most of it: the candles gave off a smell of sandalwood, red and orange Moroccan floor mats hung on the walls, and toy spaceships from the merchandising line for the eighties film *Privateers of Orion* dangled by fishing thread from hooks in the ceiling.

'The heat rising from the candles makes them spin,' said the boy in the chair. 'Cool, huh?'

'What am I doing here?' said Rickard. 'Who are my captors?'

'You nearly hit your head on the ground. One of us caught you.'

'Did you use the power of embarrassment to try and kill me?'

'No. We used a blowpipe, and a dart dipped in mescaline. But only to disable you. My name's Slipper. Those are my ships. I tied them up for you. Sorry for calling you Proteus Boy earlier. It's just that your head reminded me of Proteus, Neptune's irregular-shaped satellite.'

'We like asymmetry here,' came another voice – Fondler, standing in the doorway. She was wearing one of the grey outfits and her hair was now in spikes.

'Where is here?' said Rickard.

'We like old stuff too,' said Slipper. 'We bought a VCR last week. It took us a long time to find one. We don't buy things online. Maybe you know how to work a VCR?'

'I share this room with Slipper,' said Fondler. (There was one single bed in the room. Rickard lay on a sofa that smelt strongly of body odour.) 'Let me show you around.'

She brought him into a tight dark corridor and pointed towards rooms – none of which had doors in their doorways – where other gang members slept. The lower floors were much the same: corridors of crumbling plasterboard or bare brick with doorless rooms off them. The only illumination in the corridors came from garlands of fairy lights, gaffer-taped to the walls and ceilings. In every corridor at least a couple of the grey-suited youths loitered, some of them smoking. All of them cheerfully acknowledged him.

'I've explained to them who you are – that you were in the singing group with Denny Kennedy-Logan, and that you once came to the Bryant Square store and appeared very confused about the machines,' said Fondler.

She seemed a leader among the people here; they took care to nod back to her. From her body language – by where she stood and in the way she stood squarely to him – he was never in any doubt that he could not go up any of the corridors to look in the rooms, and her manner suggested she was not simply keeping to house rules. He found her certainty and her power, and the subtlety with which she wielded it, an attractive quality. She was so subtle with her power, and so certain and so brave, that he felt her manipulate the space between them. It was only then that he noticed again the dense black eyes, and also her pert figure that still managed to assert itself under her loose grey boiler suit. He felt helpless and acquiescent despite the conviction that she was using her allure to break him down.

Taking him by his limp hand she led him into a large basement. This, it was clear, was the main communal area in the building. Walls had been knocked down to make the space open plan, and iron girders were wedged vertically under sections of ceiling that had lost their support. Beanbags were thrown about the floor, and a long and shabby sofa curved with one of the corners. The area was filled with junk – on battered, mismatched tables, on rickety shelves, and on any space that could contain it. There were many commonplace items from the recent past: naked dolls and other children's toys, office toys with steel balls and blobs of coloured oil in them, a broken 'ghetto blaster', scuffed ice-hockey sticks. There were also older items: brass deep-sea diving paraphernalia, a phrenology bust, wooden crutches and prosthetic legs, a stuffed baby warthog. And there was a framed picture, executed largely in airbrushed paints, of a naked black man and a naked black woman fornicating under a full moon and a bolt of fork lightning in front of a waterfall with a black panther stalking the upper rocks. Rickard, awed, felt a compulsion to comment, but did not say a word. To speak, he feared, would have been to disturb and complicate something delicate; delicate and already complicated.

There were three others in the basement – two girls on the sofa and a boy on a beanbag. They were smoking. The windows were all shut; Rickard tried to swallow a cough. He stood awkwardly among them, then was bidden to take a beanbag, as Fondler went to a kitchen area and fetched him a beer. The bottle was welcome coolness in his hands.

'So I can tell you,' she addressed her fellow gang members, 'that he's no threat to us. He may well even be on our side.'

She already knew his name: she'd picked it up from the bill poster for the concert.

'I take it' – now she was addressing him – 'that you followed me here because you assumed I was on *their* side.'

'Yes, yes,' he whispered tragically and wonderingly from his supine position.

'Well you assumed wrong. I may be on the payroll of Puffball but I'm actively working against Puffball. From the inside.'

She went on to describe how all the members of the gang – they called themselves the 'Fungicides' – were disgruntled employees of Puffball who worked across the company's ten retail branches in New York City. The initial cause of their discontent had been their low wages and long hours, but all of them had developed a loathing of the company's workplace culture and political aims. Its workplace culture, Fondler explained, was a kind of slavery obscured by a language that took from Zen Buddhism, Sufism, white witchcraft, the idealism of the kibbutzim movement, and lifestyles associated with sixties rock music. Its political aims were domination of the world via the accumulation of a vast proportion of its wealth and replacement of all of the world's machines with its own technologies and the control of the content that flowed through and among these technologies, and ultimately the control of all people's minds. Again, to achieve its political aims, it spoke a language to the world that drew from movements and religions whose main concern was with universal welfare and happiness.

Before she had finished explaining this Rickard had sat up with excitement from his beanbag thinking of how it all corresponded with his own ideas. He wanted to tell Fondler and her friends everything he had thought about but found the ideas jamming in his throat at once, and he became breathless.

Fondler slammed her beer on a table, bent down to him on her haunches and said, 'Let's talk outside.'

He followed her up some steps and out to the courtyard. She turned to him suddenly, and stated:

'You want to make love to me.'

'Yes! Yes!' he whispered pitifully.

She pursed her lips and looked to the ground. He stared at hints of her scalp at the base of her spikes.

'I'm sorry,' she said, 'about the bluntness of my language. I've become very plain speaking. It comes from having to talk mumbo jumbo all day at work.'

Rickard, trembling, managed: 'Tell me what I need to hear.'

She leaned back on the concrete pier beside the steps to the basement and began smoking a cigarette, tucking her free hand in her armpit. She had a habit of pronouncing her esses as ess haitches and she spoke with a stern crease in the brow.

'Well, look, it's like this: the more fully we integrate with Puffball, take their crappy little wages and do what they ask us to do, the better placed we are to bring them down, you must understand. Last night I was told that I was needed to help carry your friend away. There was a risk he was going to pass out, they said – always a risk. I didn't know he was going to die. I think *they* knew he was going to die. I think he was programmed to die. They'd set the machine in his mouth to explode. But not before it had gathered all the information they needed. I don't know where that information is now. I know that Denny Kennedy-Logan's body is with Puffball, though. They're going to use his remains and all the information they've gathered from him for some kind of secret development. Your friend has become Townsend Thoresen's last great project, some vital component in that. The guy behind me on the gurney last night said, "This one's Townsend's baby." I suspect it's to do with the power struggle. You've heard about Townsend Thoresen, that he's dying? Yeah, he's really sick. He's going to die really soon. The board already have a new CEO lined up: John Thomas. Thoresen and Thomas hate each other. I mean, they're talking, prepping for the handover, but Thoresen knows Thomas has different ideas. Thoresen operates from the right side of the brain and he doesn't trust Thomas, he thinks he's a left-side-of-the-brain person. So whatever this thing is that Thoresen has your friend for, it's going to be this seismic happening to keep Puffball in line with what he wants. That's what I suspect.'

Rickard, who thought of himself momentarily as 'Velily', and thought of a former atmospheric railway in the old country where he used to play, that stood between breeze-block walls between gardens and constituted a very real no man's land, where cypress trees used to overhang and insects became trapped in their resin, and the tracks no longer remained, and where he had hidden once with the girl next door, and had attempted his first kiss but failed to open his mouth, but from which mistake he had learnt when finally – finally – he got to kiss Toni, forgot what he wanted to think about.

'How was our concert for you?' he said. 'Were we very very good? Did you enjoy our singing?'

Fondler, who was reaching behind her to stamp out the butt on the top of the pier, paused in mid-stub as if trying to catch some faraway sound.

After a moment she said, 'Yeah,' and nodded, creasing her brow in even sterner furrows, but smiling. 'Yeah, you know, you guys were great. That's just the kind of shit we're into right now.'

The doors at the bottom of the steps swung open, with Slipper between them. Golden light flooded from within. 'Can you try and fix this VCR now, Rickard?'

11

Clive bought a cup of tea with milk in it from a *horchata* vendor on Verdi Square. The vendor had to be told to put milk in his tea, and that the tea he wanted was not *maté*, but –

'English breakfast tea?' the vendor said, pulling a sachet from a box she'd discovered in the hold of her trolley.

He took the tea back to the bench. He'd not tarried here before, Verdi Square, but it was a pleasant spot, open to the late afternoon sun. Noisy, though. He lifted his face to the heat.

With his eyes closed, he tried to imagine an email. Did they roll in the air like coloured scraps of paper? Did they come in colours? Did they fall off trees and plop into dark pools? The man Quicklime's card had an email address on it. He tried to imagine a fairy with an email and could not even imagine an email. When he opened his eyes he was looking at Giuseppe Verdi himself's greening white head and the milk in his tea was cooling to a little ghost. Once, the Virgin Mary decided to show the Protestants in America that she was divine by turning a river into tea. But this river of tea had milk in it and the Americans had never before seen milk in tea and thought the river was polluted from a part of a mine that had been closed off. Jean Dotsy had liked that the Americans thought like that. Magic did not enter their minds. She had longed to go there – the fortunate isle.

In a mad fit she had even once suggested to Veronica, her best friend and colleague, that they run away to America together. She was more than half serious. When Veronica, who was otherwise dumbfounded, managed to get out, 'And do what there?', Jean proved that she was serious. 'We'll become freedom fighters,' she said, and she showed her a booklet, *In Defence of a National Imaginaire*, that she had taken from an event at an old guildhall in the Liberties in the forgotten heart of Dublin and that was written by a group that called themselves the Davy Langans. The addresses at the back were a catalogue of some of the most exciting places in the world. 'We'll go to New York,' she said. But Veronica ran off in a tizzy, and things were not the same again between them.

So she came here on her own and it was a young and modern and man-made country as she had hoped and dreams were made with rivets and documents and wishing wells were oil wells and what have you and so forth. She had hope for a while and to look at the young now gave hope. You are *wonderful*, he thought at a boy passing. *You* are wonderful, he thought at a girl passing. The young, in this young time, seemed so in control of their souls, as she had not been in an older time. It was the young people's time and the young people's country, and he wondered if he was better off out of both. For a while this was what he had been thinking. Since he had met with Quicklime, or perhaps that had crystallised what he had been thinking. He could talk to Quicklime about this. He could at least talk to him. There was no one here in America to say that his body should be disposed of in this or that way. He would be found, a heap in a room, and he would be buried around the back of a clapboard hall in sand and chalk dust.

(Look at Denny, he thought. Gone. *Whoof.* And the body taken before even the devil knew.)

It lifted his heart now, the idea of finally being the master of his body and of his soul, of wrestling her to the ground with the body she had made, and of freeing that soul. And it would be a ground of his choosing: he would be buried in Ireland, as Jean Dotsy, and have a place where someone could leave a flower. A decent church burial would put paid to the hoodoos and the good hungry soil would put his body beyond use for ever more.

But there was the greater problem, he thought – the problem of what might happen to his body was not so great, or pressing. The problem of what to be done in the dying days was the one that needed, now, to be taken head on. A man or woman could not stay still in these days. It was beholden on every person to have his affairs in order. You could not beat the decline but you could still win, it was all still there to be won.

Earlier that day he had left his apartment in Stuyvesant Town and since then had been walking and mooching and jumping on trains. He had borne west (actually plumb north) with Broadway and come north (actually east) with it and had passed through that part of town that once was the Puerto Rican barrio and now was a great campus dedicated to the higher arts. And even after not-so-many years that district was changing again. And now early afternoon had found him here under the statue of Verdi. The ground in front of him was covered in hard round seed for the pigeons. If he stepped on the seed he would roll and would fall flat, feet over ass, and the homeless men on the benches would erupt in laughter. Ha! he thought. There we have it. If you kept your nose out in front of you you would be fine.

So if he just talked to Quicklime, anyone, a professional. Veronica. Someone who would listen. Veronica had been a good listener, though the running-away-to-America business was the closest Jean Dotsy had ever come to telling her anything that mattered. My God though, she used to come out with it. Veronica was not a bright girl, thinking back. She used to tell Jean these very stupid things. Details of unspecified successes. Or successes Jean never paid any attention to the details of. And then the words of reassurance. 'I feel certain it will happen for you! I think it happens for everybody, at some time! The way it has happened for

244

me, I can't imagine my life having turned out any other way! Now doesn't that sound silly! But nobody's life is truly bad! It just looks like some people's lives are bad! It's an illusion! It looks that way to give us balance! But all those people whose lives look bad are living completely different lives to the ones we think they're living! The lives that those people live are actually happy and successful, or will be soon!' This with the ring of white gold on her finger, and the rock on it.

But, she didn't mind. He just didn't have the energy to laugh about it now. But no, Jean didn't mind, he didn't think. She was happy just to listen to Veronica's voice, whatever she came out with. They used to go to a tearoom on the Terenure Road for their lunch. They used to go there and Jean just liked to listen to her voice, the sound of it, and to stare in her eyes and for Veronica to hold her hands in hers, and they rolled their eyes at the same time when the radio in the tearoom announced '*Pleasant Hour*, sponsored by Eir-Lite', feeling there could be no escape from work. And Jean rolled her hands over the tops of Veronica's so as to capture them again when they became loose. Just the sound of her voice, with that music. Sometimes Jean's attention drifted to all those strange arrangements and the gusto or the leadenness or the pum-pum-pum of the singer and the strange words about beautiful Ireland with its fallen-away forts and shattered cathedrals, and the air that was very ... blue, in that tearoom. And other times her attention went back to Veronica. Veronica's speaking voice was like her

'There are no conditions. No contracts. Whatever it is you want from us we'll do it, one hundred per cent. Tailored your way.'

'And you'll look after all the administrative hassle, you say? Tie up all the loose and frayed ends on this side?'

'Loose ends will be tied. Frayed ends will be burnt. You should have no worries about any of that. We will do everything, from arranging shipping of your goods to physically boxing your goods. And the legals. It's all part of the service, and all absolutely gratis.'

'I have a lot of stuff in that apartment. I ... I don't want to be getting in anybody's way ...'

'You'll be getting in nobody's way. The day of departure, you just leave your apartment as you would on any normal day and we'll take care of the rest. You'll be safely on the boat, steaming ahead for Ireland, before a single item is moved.'

'Boat?'

'Yes, we use our own transport. But it's a very comfortable boat, with stabilisers, a jacuzzi and television. And plenty of space to move about in.'

'And that's free too?'

'It's all free. We're sponsored by the President of Ireland. Just leave it with me, and I'll get back to you with a departure date, which pier to go to, etcetera. Should be sorted out in the next few days.'

The waitress tidied the counter in front of them, and Quicklime paid for both their lunches, and ordered two teas and whatever cookies they had in the house. He stretched himself, puffing his chest forward, and looked at himself in the strip of mirror facing them. He was wearing the mould-blue sweater he'd had on the first day their paths had intersected.

'I realise,' said Clive, 'that I'm not in much of a position to make extra demands, it being a free service –'

'Clive, Clive. It's all on the state. You tell me what you need and I'll ensure you get it, no questions asked.'

'– but there is one thing, one thing that I'll need to know, straight up, that you can provide, otherwise I won't be able to go ahead with any of this. I'll need some security. Protection. I'll need the strongest men you can find. They'll need to be armed. And I'll need a cleric. A priest. And someone versed in the dark arts. A witch, or an augur, or whoever you can get.'

The waitress put two cups in front of the men, and the pot of tea.

'And milk too, ma'am,' said Quicklime.

He poured Clive's cup, then his own. He tipped the spilt tea from his saucer back into his cup. Then he poured in his milk, and stirred it slowly with his spoon. Clive could see his taxed expression in the mirror.

'None of that, of course, will be any problem,' he said. 'We'll have all of them to meet you off the boat, or be on the boat with you to escort you to land, and to stay with you at all other times.'

'It's all to do, you see, with, you know – this thing I tried to tell you about the last time.'

Quicklime chuckled. 'All this transgender business? Don't you worry now, we'll get you some very beefy fellows to look after you!'

'Oh no, Mister Quicklime. No, no, it's, it's … You'll remember I mentioned the fairies the last time …?'

But now his companion appeared distracted, his attention directed towards the front window, as if something passing had caught his eye. He got up from his seat and stood at the window, looking down the street.

'Mister Quicklime, please, if you wouldn't mind hearing me out, now that I have you here –'

'Can you hold it a moment? Just one moment,' he said, bustling back across the floor. 'I'm just going to the loo.' He grabbed his rolled-up trench coat from his seat. 'If anyone comes in and asks after my whereabouts, don't tell them where I am. I get embarrassed. I have a bowel condition. Best tell them nothing. None of their business.'

After twenty minutes, Quicklime had still not emerged from the bathroom. The only people to have come into the coffee shop in all that time were a couple of Hispanic construction workers.

Clive followed the sign to the conveniences. It took him into the kitchen. The door to the loo cubicle was ajar.

'Did you see a man come in and out of here in the last twenty minutes?' he said to a man flipping French toast in a pan. 'A little shorter than me, pudgy, bald on top, with light ginger hair? He has a bowel condition.'

'Oh yeah,' said the cook. 'He didn't go to the bathroom. He just went straight through the back.'

* * *

On a chisel-blade corner in Greenwich Village was a business that announced itself, in a red neon cursive and stencilled letters in silver sticky tape, with:

CASEY BYRD, THERAPIST, A.N.A.C., S.U.T.
'I'M ALL EARS'

The corner was mainly glass, blocked out with sheets of paper except to let the neon sign show. The door opened on to a first-floor reception area. In the same wedge-shaped space were a chair and a chaise longue. The city lights made will o' the wisps through the sheets of paper, and the neon sign hummed irritably like a fly trying to push through the glass. In the sharp corner of the room sat a late-middle-aged woman with a heavy tan, short parrot-blue hair under an astrakhan cossack hat, and tattoos all the way up her bare arms. Sweat and hair dye streamed down her face. She also wore safari shorts and knee-length flight socks.

'I saw the sign from outside,' said Clive. 'I'd like to talk with Casey Byrd.'

'You're talking to her. Do you have an appointment?'

'No …'

'That's okay. Normally I'd close up now, but I've had a quiet day. Lucky for both of us.'

250

'Yes. I'd just like to say, straight off the bat, as you might say, that I was born a woman.'

'Please – to the couch.'

'No, I'd rather get this part out – and out of the way – right now, standing here, otherwise it will become a distraction. I was born Jean Dotsy, in the Irish Free State, seventy-four years ago. I became a man, not entirely of my own free will, some forty years ago. The transition was drawn out and not completed. The treatments were rudimentary. They were able to fashion a tube of sorts for me but it has only ever effectively operated as a run-off pipe, never a penis, and I never could grow a beard for all the pills that I took and oils that I applied. Anyone who is close to me, which is one person, recently departed, knows this about me.'

The woman took off her cossack hat and patted her forehead with a handkerchief.

'So – your secret died with this person who's just died?'

'No, not quite. No – lately I've become rather uncomfortable in my skin and have made no great secret of who I was formerly. Many, many people probably know.'

'And this uncomfortable feeling ...'

'No, that's not the problem I've come here about. I mean, that was easily dealt with. People have listened to me on that one, they've heard me out, or at least it hasn't seemed to bother them.'

'The problem is then that you, well – you say that you didn't undergo this transformation willingly?'

'Again, no, that's not my problem. Not in the way that you think it is.'

'But it is a problem?'

'Not the one I've come here to *talk* to you about!'

'Okay. So your problem is that not enough people take you seriously as a man?'

'What?! Yes, but … no! That's not it!'

'But you don't want to be taken seriously as a man, because you didn't become one willingly?'

'No! No! I did want to become one! I mean, I must have, even before my hand was forced.'

'Your hand was forced …? What kind of *cruel* society …? Ireland, you say …?'

'But it was my decision, ultimately! That's to say – it didn't take much pushing. I mean, I was *pushed* – there were other forces, and it was necessary to take drastic action, and I didn't come from a culture and a time where I could make such big decisions of my own free will, and these forces *forced* me to put my body finally beyond *use*, but … I grew into my new skin. I was happy to have that skin, you know, when I did have it. But this is all … No, I'm not here for help in that way. This was all after the important change.'

'I see. I understand.'

She invited him again to take the chaise longue, and he stretched himself out this time.

'The important change. Okay. So – your acceptance of yourself as essentially a man?'

'No! I never did *think* that I wanted to be a man. There was no light that flicked on, no moment of "Ah, eureka!" before I did become a man. I didn't very much like men. I wouldn't have wanted to become a man, it wouldn't have entered my simple mind.'

'A-ha!'

'I hated them. No, that's too strong a word. No – I hated them, I did! The last time I spoke to Veronica, in that tearoom on the Terenure Road –'

'Woah, woah, pull up –'

'– just the day before, I'd been to the doctor about my fainting fits. I was fainting a lot around then. I'd fainted that time after trying to make myself pee standing up. But there was a germ in there, you see, and that was the cause of the fainting. I'd let a germ in. But the doctor, do you know what he said to me? "You need a husband", and, as I got up to leave, "Smile, Jean, just smile." If there'd been anything I could have done to take the smile off his face I would have done it, let me tell you. And the next day, over lunch, Veronica looked over my shoulder and she said to me, "That Indian medical student has been staring at you the whole time", and I knew that she was trying too hard, and I knew that she was troubled, and I said to Veronica, "How do you know he's a medical student?", and she said, "What else could a handsome Indian man in Dublin be but a medical student?", and I said, "You've obviously not read about the recent murder case in Dublin in which a handsome Indian cook beat his Irish girlfriend to death with a pestle and hung her on a meat hook to drain and cut her into small pieces with a cleaver and put her in a pot of mince and served her to the guests in his restaurant." And later, later the same day, after I drove all the way out to Dunleary and parked my car, a little Ford Anglia, by the coal pier, there was a man with a cap pulled low on his head carrying a bale of something wrapped in waxed butcher's paper – paper which, now that I think about it, he probably used to masturbate with – and he startled me by peering in at my window and rapping on the glass with a penny, and I could see the yellow boiled sweet he was sucking, there in his mouth, and I drove further down the road to a place near the baths where in any case there was a view of the open sea. He was the last man I saw while I was alive for the first time. Can you imagine? But my problem now is not *men*, or how I *feel* about being one, or how and when I came to the *decision* to become one.'

'While you were "alive for the first time"? Do you mean –'

'I'm a ghost, you see, as well as anything else. Well, I'm technically not a ghost.'

'No. You are technically not a ghost.'

'No, I am a sort of reincarnated spirit.'

'Yes, I can see how you might see yourself as a reincarnated spirit.'

'I am a reincarnation of my own spirit. And the body that I occupy is my own.'

'Interesting way of putting it.'

'That was where I expired in the last life. In Dunleary, in my Ford Anglia, by the baths looking out to sea. I was young, but I had warnings, and the warnings did not alarm me. Just that morning, as I've told you, I'd had another collapse. Standing above my toilet with a bare foot on each arm of the mat. "To hell with it," I used to say. "To hell with it", like an American person. I would take it upon me – take off my black fashion pants, then my knickers. Sometimes I would feel that the angle was not right and I would have to bring my feet forward until my knees touched the freezing cistern and I would put my hands on the ceramic top and I would look at the window. It was not a window you could do much else with but look at – you could not look through the window. The wavy surface of the glass I would think of as the wavy surface of the tide. The mould that clung there was seaweed drawn in the churn. I would feel for a moment a calmness, like I was part of something, a natural flow, that I never had to think or worry. I would think of water, how it sounded and moved, and I would listen to the sighs from inside the walls. My legs would quiver and they would not stop quivering. I would move my hands to the backs of my knees and I would be tense there, like metal traps. I would wait and I would push. I would wait for some command. I would get confused and I would wait for – I didn't know – a feeling, something – waited and pushed and commanded it myself. I would say, "There must be some valve", and then I would collapse. But because I had an explanation for these collapses – I had a germ inside me – and because I would always come round from them they did not panic me unduly. If I was standing when I felt a fit one of these rotations, perhaps the third or fourth, I noted sadly – although maybe I am just recalling it with sadness – that my body had fallen over to the side, so that the head was on the passenger seat, and the face was set in the weirdest leer. Everything began to change. "Began" is the wrong word. "Everything" is the wrong word. There was no beginning, no linear or planar arrangement of time, and there were no "things" in this new place, and "place" is the wrong word too in this context, clearly. Although I did at some point perceive sweetly scented soft domes in suspension which became stone and which I gnawed on and which caused some hidden teeth to break through my gums, gums which I had seemed to retain, or perhaps develop, for my journey, although "journey" is perhaps not the right word either. And I felt a ridge like the rib of a vault although I was not high up as under the vaulting of a roof but very low down as under the vaulting of a crypt, and I was pressing upwards, against this rib, and this pressure rolled me upwards with the rib towards a point where it and other ribs converged. A grinding sensation, or a grinding noise, gave way to a conversing sensation, that is, a conversation, between a greatly divided form of me or separately existing mes, and many others, all of whom I could easily occupy or assume, whose consciousnesses I could take on, who, in this everywhen, could say this and think that while another said this and thought this, and – was a button pressed? Yes, a button was pressed, revealing sections of governing code: obelus up-tack and large but neat black eyebrows. He had yellow teeth, each edged with brown streaks of caries. He occasionally prodded the dashboard as he spoke. His fingers were peculiarly thick and long and smoothened. They had just left the county of Dublin, via some back road at the foot of the mountains. The stranger had a very particular idea of a route they would take.

'At Edenderry then we will turn north.'

'Where is Edenderry?' said Jean.

'It's not for a while yet.'

'I don't have enough petrol to get back to Donegal.'

'You will have enough petrol.'

'I will need to stop at a garage.'

'You will not stop at a garage.'

'Will I die?'

'You have already died.'

'Will I die again?'

'Not while you are of use.'

'Am I alive now?'

'Yes you are.'

'Have I you to thank?'

'Yes you do.'

'Thank you.'

'Thank ye, you mean. You can thank us all when you arrive.'

'What do they want me for?'

'You will wet-nurse a child. You will be put to proper and natural use. You were no use to anyone with your interests lying the way that they did. And you will perform your duty because you have been given another chance. Be grateful that you have been returned. Be grateful that your body was not replaced with a changeling, as is the normal routine of these things, and then you would have had nothing to return to.'

'What is a changeling?'

'A shambles put in the place of someone who has been called to better use.'

'You have called me to another use and have not even left a shambles for my family to mourn over?'

'We have not. As far as your family are concerned you have disappeared on them.'

'How have I anything to be grateful for?'

'Because you have been returned.'

'How can you be sure that I will produce milk?'

'You are a woman so you will produce milk.'

'My fingers are very cold,' said Jean. She could not feel them on the wheel. 'I do not feel alive.' Only the fear, she felt, was animating her.

'Carry on now.' He tapped the windscreen and she noticed he was wearing a garnet ring.

They had entered the plain of the Curragh. There was no hedge or wall or fence to hem the road in and on either side the grass stretched away into the distance. The clouds hung low, lobed and frowning. A squall blew up across the grasslands, buffeting the car from the side, carrying with it a riddle of hail. The air became a fizz of white and black speckles, like on a television screen; soon there was no black at all, it all was white. The rattle on the metal and glass brought her back, temporarily, her head among the typewriters in the central secretariat going like crazy and the windows fogging up from the heat of bodies; a scene such as she had escaped that morning in her car to go to Dunleary; and she had an urge come over her to have her vitality confirmed, to feel the little shots of ice pummel and pinch her skin. She leaned to her right and put her cheek on the window, to feel the cold and the movement of the engine. Then she stretched her left arm to bring the engine up to fourth; she could not reach, and in a moment's panic her foot, by instinct, stamped down on the brake. The seat belt suddenly tightened at her neck and she was pressed hard against the door from the centrifuge as the car spun on the road. Miraculously, when it came to rest it appeared to be still on the road. And then, as suddenly as it had descended, the squall blew over and away, beyond, to Wicklow; to Wicklow, she knew, because that was the way her car was pointed, towards the mountains.

The clouds separated and became the most beautiful white and sublime things and the sun and the blue shone through. She thought of the Assumption. The stranger in the passenger seat was gone.

In the same direction as Wicklow was Dublin, and Dunleary, whence she had come. She looked at the little white balls strewn all over the tarmac and as far as she could see back up the road. Some poor sheep was collapsed on its front knees. She looked around her at the exposed plain. She thought she would go

12

15

Rickard enjoyed the most magical few hours of his life. It was a day he hoped wouldn't end, and indeed thought would go on into the night, until Fondler told him that she had to work an evening shift. By that moment he knew, anyway, that they were sweeties. The day began with a breakfast of vegetables at a former stevedores' hut on the East River, one of the last of its kind in the city. He found the food largely indigestible, but the radio gave them endless terrible music to joke about and he was able, easy enough, to leave most of his food to one side on the pretext that he was laughing too much. At the end of their meal Rickard thought that they might part ways; that awkward moment came when knives and forks were left neatly on plates and throats were cleared. He suggested that they go for a walk so that she could burn off her food. She looked at him with a deadly serious avidness; ambitious, from deep behind her eyebrows. He noticed a tint to those darkest black eyes now: a golden sparkle, like the flash of quartz in the deepest pool.

But soon he felt completely relaxed in her company, and sensed that she was in his, and he allowed himself to believe that she was not so at ease with everyone she met. They sauntered here and there, with no route or destination in mind. He walked with his hands behind his back; she with hers swinging freely, or gesticulating energetically. She did most of the talking, and he was happy to listen. He learnt to his surprise that she was from Canada, and that her surname, which he forgot immediately, had a Q in it. She had threatened to throw herself in the Saint Lawrence Seaway numerous times over various Don Juans she'd been barred from seeing. She liked dogs and cats, and would like a house in the country. She had only taken up smoking recently, and would never smoke in her own house. Ideally, she would like one of those cute barn-like houses, with land, near the sea.

They stopped at a home-décor store and his thoughts raced out from him, but not at such a pace that he began to fret; they flowed one into the next, like little bubbles of dawn, dreamlike and pleasant; they were of barns, animals, pumpkins, straw, roof beams, gingham, snow, the Amish, handshakes, threshing machines, a brood of children. When she handled two small dried scented mandarin oranges and made suggestive remarks he surprised himself again by not becoming embarrassed. They laughed, in fact, both of them – so loudly in the middle of the shop that others joined in. By now they were able to laugh at anything:

resolved to find the statue of John McCormack he had heard was in the park. He had no idea where exactly it might be; they asked questions, were met with bemused faces or replies ('John Mac Cortlandt?'), and pushed on regardless, Rickard determining that they would find it by chance or be led there by a celestial finger. They never found it; but during their criss-crossing of the lower park he told her about this great singing count they were searching for, and many other things. Of McCormack, he pretended that he was more of an admirer than he really was, and that his interest in the singer was lifelong. He made up a life story for him too, or filled with fiction the yawning gaps between the few facts that he knew. He sang her lines from songs. The wind in the wall it is whistling your name/ And giving a sound to the cause of your fame. She asked him if he spoke the Gaelic tongue. Ah, the language of the bards and poets! – of course I do, he said, although in truth he only had a smattering of the language. She asked him what the Gaelic for Central Park was. Fortuitously he knew – Phairc Láir, he told her. She said to him that that sounded like 'folklore' – and did he know much about the folklore of Ireland? Oh, Fondler, Fondler, he said, taking her in a one-armed bear hug across the shoulders and spinning her so that they were facing the opulent apartment buildings of Fifth Avenue that overlooked this eastern edge of the park. And would you give up your dream, please, he said to her, of an upstate barn-house for something a little grander, somewhere where you might have room to store a forest of fur coats and a thicket of evening gowns and a whole clerestory of perfume bottles, so that we might be nearer the centre of things, the centre of where all the great and wonderful things will happen when the dust has settled and all is resolved and the good and right are standing?

She was looking at her watch.

'Damn it,' she said. 'I have to go.'

* * *

('Listen to me,' he said.

'Rickard, come on, I don't have time. What is it now? What? Car horns? A gunfight?'

'No. Listen to me.'

'Pfff.'

'Listening?'

'I'm listening.'

> *Honey, you think that rye is high,*
> *Well you ain't known nothin' till you've scraped the sky,*
> *And you ain't tasted nothin' like a Lalo's pie,*
> *But betcha don't know what they do for sport.*
> *Sugar, you think your world's enough,*
> *Well you ain't thought nothin' 'bout tons of other stuff*
> *Till you've come and seen these people huff and then puff,*
> *But betcha don't know what they do for sport.*
> *Baby, how's Redcomb and how's li'l Suze?*
> *Well they ain't seen nothin' like tomorrow's news,*
> *'Cos the days go by here in their twos,*
> *But betcha don't know what they do for sport.*

269

Bunny, you're as sunny as a sheaf of wheat,
And there ain't no sunshine in these grey streets,
So how's about sellin' up and comin' out east?
And I'll show you exactly what they do for sport.'

His throat was soldered together like poor Denny's had been and his voice sounded like gravel and water in a cement mixer.

'That was lovely,' said Toni. 'Genuinely.'

Rickard heard her blow her nose.

'Toni, I know I'm a disappointment to you. You've never heard me sing before, and I said I was a singer, and you've just heard me, and I was terrible.'

'Stop that now.'

'And I know I've been consistently disappointing. The thing is ... I've been thinking, and I've had an idea, and – beginner's luck you'll say, but ... Yes, I've been thinking about the times when you said you had a crushing feeling of disappointment about me. Like when we made jigsaws and you said it wasn't enough. Or when we gave out about the neighbours and you said it wasn't enough. Or when we went to Zumba classes together and you said it wasn't enough. I know I never said it to you at the time – it was my pride, probably – but, remembering those occasions, I can tell you that those moments weren't enough for me either. Yes, really. But, now – isn't it uncanny that we felt disappointed exactly simultaneously?'

'Hmm.'

'I believe in the concept of soulmates. That when

people have that rare, precious, metaphysical connection they feel the same highs and lows, and they feel them as waves in that connection. Even when their bodies are separate, and their conscious selves are separate, they still share that connection. You know, Toni, honestly, I have this awful, doomy feeling about New York. It's been coming down on me almost since I got here. Like … I don't know, it's like the opposite of romance. It's like reality, but super-reality. Like, people are as hard as in the real world – harder – and they're not real. They're super-hard. And they're not romantic because everything they do starts from without. It's as if there's no spirit there. And I know – I know – that in parallel with that feeling, that place that you work in has only seemed greyer and more synthetic and more spiritless. How has it seemed to you? Greyer? More synthetic?'

'Yeah, look, you're worrying me with this talk. What about this "doomy feeling"?'

'I feel there's going to be a war. Between humans and … zombies.'

'Zombies?'

'Yeah. Sort-of zombies.'

'Pfff. That's just typical.'

'What is?'

'Well, stereotypical. Guys. It's always zombies, cyborgs and androids with guys. Just like it's always fairies and the occult of northern and eastern Europe with girls. I see it a lot in fan fiction.'

'You know I'm not stereotypical.'

271

'Yeah, but then there you go with your zombies. It's so disappointing. It's not Mars versus Venus with men and women. It's zombies/cyborgs/androids/aliens versus fairies/witches/vampires/necromancers.'

'You're not stereotypical either. You don't go in for fairies. Do you?'

'Pfff. Well. You know. I suppose a part of me does. Pfff. Yeah, it's so disappointing.'

Silence.

'My friend's head exploded the other night at a concert.'

'Rickard, I think you should come home.'

He sighed. 'You sound more American than the people here. Your accent is different.'

'I mean it. I think you should come home.'

'Will you be there?'

'I've told you before, I'm not going anywhere.'

'So you will be there?'

'I'll be in Dublin, yes.'

'Well stay safe.')

* * *

Rickard and Fondler met a couple of evenings later at a diner of her suggestion. When he got there she was already seated at a table at the low central partition. She gave him a tepid smile across the floor. Her hands were clasped, palms upward, in front of her on the table, and he dared to touch them as he took his seat. They were cold, and damp, like a mound of potato peel. Her hair tonight was messily tied up in ribbons, like a prayer bush aflutter with rags. There was something obscurely wrong with her, just as there was something obscurely wrong with him.

He remained silent, for he sensed that he had already communicated his discomposure, and he did not want to blunder. He looked around him: over the low partition; back at Fondler. Something further seemed to deflate from her; she looked down at her conjoined hands, at the upturned fingers stiffening, like slow-growing tendrils in speeded-up time. It was a glimpse of disappointment – the first glimpse of disappointment – after all the magic and glitter of the last day. He could not safely locate this disappointment; he was sure it was in both of them. He privately reproached himself. He looked down at his trousers, in case his flies were undone.

Finally she said:

'My name got drawn out in the lottery. Please come to Minnesota with me. Observe a moment in time.'

* * *

He had never been further west than Riverside Drive, and he had never been at a Viking funeral before.

On the stroke of midnight, after three hours of propitious faintness (so far from city lights, there was a sherbet tinge to the sky; later, some said it was the dust churned up by the Valkyrie; another said it resembled 'a screen the moment before hibernation'), a blast of a horn, reminiscent of a note of whale song, swept through the pines and the still Midwestern air and over the palisades. The door of every cabin down the slope stood open and silhouettes of figures waited, framed by the light behind them, each as if for the command of another to lead them on to the stake-paved path and down to the forest road. The smell of turf drifted from the open doorways, and then a movement of grey figures at the bottom of the slope pulled everyone into its tide. The portent was false: the mood of the mourners was not dour; it was jocular, even, although the chat and laughter did not rise above a whisper. Ahead, a flaming torch led the line. Here and there electronic devices were held aloft for added light, their soft blue screens bobbing in the darkness like luminous moths.

The forest road opened to a plain of even and dry though spongy ground. Far off to the left and right the dark treeline continued against the faintly glowing night. From all directions, from many paths in the forest, hordes of mourners pooled on to the plain. Flaming facias on long poles were skewered into the ground, spaced regularly apart. The crowds settled into a crescent formation around the head of a lake, or to the point that the rushy ground would allow. The lake stretched away into the darkness, more like a sea. The surface was silver glass and held the picture of the moon without any degradation of the satellite's power. A black tuft, like a brush head, poked out of the water around where the silver became darkness. A flame could just about be seen flickering in the tuft. The mourners waited, all eyes on the island. A small dark blip appeared in the clear silver; only when it was near the shoreline could the shape of a small Viking galley be made out, sitting high in the water, its prow cresting to a carving of a cat's head with mouth set in a wrinkled and pained cartouche. A team of men waded through the soggy littoral ground and into the water, either side of a wooden track. The boat hit the track underwater with a crunch. The oarsmen threw ropes to the team of men, who dragged the craft into a flat-bottomed stabilising frame half in the water. The boat was left in this position for several minutes, the team of men having to dig their heels into the bog to keep the ropes taut. They waited like this until, one on each side of the boat, two rafts had caught up. One carried Guru Mahseer Chaudhuri, wearing robes of pink and beads of white and blue; Guru Chaudhuri had been Townsend Thoresen's spiritual adviser since, as an eighteen-year-old, Thoresen had run away to India. This raft also carried the rock star Rainy Fairmount, who was shaking and wearing a life jacket. On the other raft was a tall blond local Scandinavian man, who wore dark woollen robes secured around the waist with vines of ivy. Once the raft passengers were on land, the boat, in its stabilising frame, was hauled on to the track's rollers and fully out of the water and on to the plain, and lugged in time with the slow pace of Guru Chaudhuri and Rainy Fairmount on one side and the Scandinavian man on the other. The track ran out at the top of a low flat-topped mound. Here the boat was left to rest. The oarsmen laid their oars

13

13

The body was delivered in a glossy white casket, brought upright in the service elevator, and rested across a trestle table borrowed, by the Mac An Fincashel brothers, from a caterer. There were no Christian or any other religious symbols on the lid of the casket; only a yellow sticker that said BIODEGRADABLE. The lid was attached by suction or a snug fitting; certainly not by weight: Jeremiah and Rickard were surprised by how light it felt ('like polystyrene,' said Rickard) as it came off.

'He looks only beautiful,' said Denny's seventy-eight-year-old sister, Geraldine, who had flown over from Ireland the day before. It was Geraldine's first time in America, and the first time she had seen her older brother since the early sixties, which was the last time Denny had visited Ireland. She had arrived at the apartment directly from Appledorn's enormous New Jersey outlet, with her fifty-two-year-old daughter, Karen, the both of them laden with bags of shopping. The chairs in the apartment were draped with new coats, dresses and handbags and the door handles were hung with frocks. Ladies' shoes and balls of tissue paper littered the floor. Geraldine and Karen were tipsy at this stage: the Mac An Fincashel brothers had set out the wake table with cans of beer and bottles of spirits for the evening's spree. Karen, who wore a sequined top that revealed almost the entirety of her deep pink prickled bosom, kept lifting her knee into Emmet's behind.

But Denny did not look beautiful. Clive and Rickard knew it – Rickard's face was warped in terror. Rickard was grey. But then Rickard had not looked right since his return from his trip out west.

It could have been worse: there might have been no head there. There might have been some botched attempt to cauterise the hole in the middle of the shoulders. But it was horrible all the same. It was not easy to look at. In place of Denny's head was a bung of white wax. No effort had been made to shape the bung into the form of a normal human head; and there was no neck, as such. It was all neck: round in its girth, and a foot long, and tapering suddenly at the top to a chiselled end, like a lipstick. Two pockmarks for eyes and a simple blip for a nose and a zigzag frown made a hideous mockery of the hominid face.

'He aged very well, it must be said, God bless him,' said Geraldine, surprising Clive again with her pronounced Dublin accent. 'That's over fifty years now since I last seen Denis, and he hasn't changed, not much at all. He always had a great complexion. I was jealous of him, Karen, I was. He had this gorgeous creamy white complexion, it was like a girl's, and the smoothest most flawless skin, not a line or a wart on him. He could have modelled for a Parisian make-up house. And that awful bitch, Aisling, God forgive me for using language like that in the presence of the dead, but she couldn't appreciate what she had. If he's beautiful now, a dead man of eighty-three, can you imagine how he looked in his twenties?'

Jeremiah held Bit upside down over its master's body, gripping it by its soft belly and delicate hind legs; its little leather triangular ears flapped about and its front paws paddled the air in panic. He gently let the animal on to the corpse's chest whereupon it took one sniff of the wax column of a head and flinched. Whimpering, it turned itself in the tight space and examined the hand; the whimper levelled to a low, distressed oboe-note, and rose to a grumble. It began to gnaw at the knuckles and fingers. Jeremiah scooped it away.

'I suppose,' he said, 'in its grief, all it can think to do is eat him.'

Or in its hunger, thought Clive – *in its hunger*. He put his own hand to Denny's. As he'd suspected: cold, cold, colder than cold, and not firm enough for a human, living or dead, compressing to beyond the point where the bone should have been. Like putty. Protein. Meat.

This was not Denny, but a gimcrack, fobbed off on them – a shambles left in his place. A changeling, yes. The real Denny was being put to use somewhere, somewhere still, on this earth here.

A changeling, he thought, touching his face. This could have been for me. (His face was as cold as the meat; his flesh thin and numb against the cheekbone.) It was true. Or am I the changeling, he thought – left behind? What is my status now, in the sweep of this and the parallel life? In life, such as I have been given and stolen more of for myself?

He slowly lowered himself into a chair, into the rustle of a crispy fabric.

'Mind that feckin' dress,' said Geraldine.

'Hey, Mam,' said Karen. 'These lads have another brother. Emmet was saying there's a fella called Breffny down in the basement. Says he works out and that he has the best arse of the lot of them. Get him up here, Emmet!'

'Yeah! Get him up here!' said Geraldine. 'And bring an extra one for me!'

'Would you like me to invite the other super we've got?' said Emmet.

'Yes!' said Karen. 'Call Superman, call Limahl Ataturk, call Don Bon Johnson. Bring them all up here and tell them they must be six foot eight and ripped and we'll have a proper Irish wake.'

Breffny came to the door, his eyes propped wide open in pretend sexual agitation, and sputum pouring over his stiff bottom lip and down his Punchinello chin. He was banging a handheld brass Eastern gong, much to the amusement of Emmet. Emmet had also brought with him Denny's record player and a box of LPs that had been gifted to Jeremiah after the clear-out.

'In remembrance of the old man,' said Emmet, dropping the needle on a Richard Tauber record.

'Oh get that off!' said Karen, not a minute into the first song. 'So bleedin' miserable. This is a wake, for Jesus' sake.'

She began twiddling with the MP3 player that Denny had bought to replace his record player.

'He never got around to loading that up,' said Jeremiah, and so Karen planted her own portable MP3 player in the stand, and the sound of the ubiquitous 'Sexy Taxi' by Much Ass Gracias feat. Luzette vroomed into the room, completely drowning out Tauber.

By late in the evening several of Denny's neighbours had joined the party. The room filled with peaty-smelling cigar smoke and the sweet smoke of fried bacon. The music turned mellow; Jeremiah had swapped his own machine for Karen's, and now McCormack came from the speakers. And Karen hadn't the energy to object having danced herself silly, and her mother was more or less passed out, lying over the back of a chair into an empty bookshelf, while Breffny mimed the movement of a horse jockey behind her bottom.

'McCormack?' said Clive to Jeremiah.

'Yes. Denny's favourite.'

He was singing a Chauncey Challoner song – 'We Will Leave This Vale of Tears One Day'. And from the other room came another Challoner song.

'Mister Franco down the hallway has brought the record player inside,' said Jeremiah.

'And is that still the Tauber record?'

'Yes, I think so.'

Tauber was singing 'Wild, Wide, Uncrossed', and the two songs together – discordant, words falling on and between words – were a memory bank gushing empty to the sound of a punctured accordion and made the rhythm of a heart, it was like, or a wheel, buckled, with one vane, beating through smoke, that compelled a person to rest.

'Whoo,' said Clive. 'It'll put me in the mood to sing myself before too long.'

'Yes!' said Jeremiah. 'Sing for us!'

'Jeremiah,' he said, leaning forward on his knees. 'Do you know what my name, Clive Sullis, means in the Gaelic language? It means "sword of light". Don't you think it's strange that a man's complete name would translate to something? Almost as if he made it up himself?'

'I knew what it meant all right.'

Jeremiah gave a great yawn.

'Jeremiah – now. Now. The time has come, I think. We must tell our stories. This is a wake. We must tell our stories about Denny.'

'Sing first!'

'No. There's a great elephant in the room, as they say, and we're ignoring him and we must talk about him. He is why we're here, let's remember.'

Clive got up, and in this movement quieted the room. And as he was standing, looking into the casket, he remembered again with horror that the elephant in the room was a different one to the one he thought it had been a moment before, and that it was one that did not bear talking about. In horror he sat down again.

'Yes indeed,' said Jeremiah, standing up himself, and loudly cupping his hands together, while he had everybody's attention. 'Who is the person that we have gathered here to remember? Well, I'll tell you who.'

But *where* is this person we have gathered to remember? That is the question.

Thought Clive, staring at the blank white side of the casket from his seat: Where is he, Jeremiah?

Where are you, Denny?

As Jeremiah went at his brothers fists and feet flying and the room exploded in a burst of broken bottles and the casket was knocked off its stand and the Turkish curtains were ripped from the rail.

* * *

Oh blessed mother undoer of knots what was this? Blessed mother daughter of Ephesus elected intercessor and buffer of wrath give me strength.

He gazed at his watch until the blood drained from his arm by the power of gravity. His arm collapsed anaesthetised. It was five o'clock. *Was* five o'clock. He looked at his watch again. Ten past. Dark already. The only light – and he was outside, because he was cold to the bone, and a dog, a slimy black docker or a butcher's dog, was sniffing around his feet – came from a bulb on a bracket, attached to a wall, opposite.

The underarm of the bracket was wrought into a delicate shamrock sprig.

He thought: My home, my prison, my emerald in the hospital waste, here by my Anna Livia Pleurisy.

Wasn't it wonderful even in the murk of Hell to find such a detail? Butler Yeats's stated wish to exist eternally as a golden bird upon a bough came to mind and he thought that it would not be a bad thing to be a wrought-iron shamrock on a lamp bracket, being shone on all the time, and expressing so succinctly what one was about.

He was at least supported: his back was against the wall. Someone in his anger could find it in him despite it all to be merciful. Wasn't that wonderful too? He stood up, turned around, and studied the soot-black terroristic brickwork. For a whole minute. And took one step to the side. There was a door and he tried it. To his surprise it opened and he found himself, by and by, in a brightly lit showroom for gas-powered household appliances.

A little old man dressed as a gendarme came skating towards him. Ladies in headscarves eyed him askance and aghast.

'Ah, it's all right, I know where I am now,' he said.

The gendarme came up close. 'Mister, if you've any respect for yourself you'll remove yourself from these premises, go home if you have one, and clean yourself up.'

'I know where I am now,' he repeated, 'and if you'll just allow me back the way I came in, I'll be out of your way.'

'You'll go out the front door.'

'Can I use your bathroom?'

'You'll go out the front door now.'

'Can I dry my knees in one of your gas-powered monstrances?'

'You skedaddle out of here fast and stop scaring the customers.'

He stood for a moment on D'Olier Street, turned right, and right again back into the dripping worm-hole of Leinster Market, and came through on to Hawkins Street where he paused and looked up at the Theatre Royal, itself resembling a fancy gas-fire surround. Two young girls in raincoats ran by.

'My great-grandfather saw Pauline Viardot in *Don Giovanni* in that place,' he shouted after them, then blunderbussed into the grubbiest rugby-club ditty he could think of, holding up, as he spun in the middle of the street, a *Press* lorry on its way to or from Burgh Quay:

> *'John Clancy's sister bends and picks*
> *The coal up from the road.*
> *The fuel van's not the only thing*
> *That easy sheds its load!'*

... and continued to the opening of Poolbeg Street, and carried on to Mulligan's Bar, feeling aglow in himself again.

'No hard feelings,' said big Vincent Fennelly, who had turned around on his stool. His two bigger pals either side of him looked at Denny with amused contempt. 'You've swollen up worse than I'd thought,' said Vincent. 'You wouldn't want to get a second concussion.'

His seat, on the bench at the corner table, was still free. Billy Sperrin – who hadn't a tooth in his head after taking a kick in the mouth from his own out half, and proudly on nights like this left his gnashers in his pocket – and Beast Features McHale – that very out half, who had never pretended that he had missed the ball by accident – greeted him, with a large amount of irony, like a returning hero.

But Denny's mood was apt to darken suddenly at this time and, after the way Fennelly and his fellow scrummagers had looked at him, bringing back the memory of the afternoon's events, he was in no mood now for jollity.

'They've no respect for their elders, Fennelly and that Saint Mary's crew,' he said, swatting at the hands of his companions, who were prodding his bruised temple in mock awe.

'They were only two years behind us,' said Beast Features.

'And are twice our size,' said Billy.

'If they weren't in our Senior Cup year then they're our juniors, and we're their elders,' said Denny.

'You were beyond the bounds there in every way, Denny,' said Beast Features. 'And asking for it.'

'Frankly, it was about time – both Beastie and I agreed,' said Billy.

288

'Now,' said Denny – he semaphored the barman for another glass of malt; Billy and Beast Features glanced at each other with bowed heads, and Beastie looked at Denny disapprovingly. Both B&B were on the lemonade.

'Well, he's given me the wake-up call at least,' he said. He pressed his contusion, rather enjoying the fizzle of the pain between fingers and bone.

'Good for him, and for you. I hope you realise now that you're a stupid bollocks. You're lucky he didn't garryowen you all the way to Belfast.'

'Ha! You said it, Beastie!' said Billy.

'What I realise …' he said, having to break off to allow the guffawing and table-slapping to die down, 'What I realise, chaps – what Mister Fennelly has woken me *up* to – is that the time has come for drastic action.' He paused for effect. 'Fellows, I've made up my mind.'

'Go on,' said Billy. 'You're about to deliver something dramatic, I can see.'

'I've finally given up on this country. I've made up my mind that I'm going to America.'

'Settle yourself down there, Denny,' said Beast Features.

'Listen to him!' said Billy. 'America! You're a mammy's boy, Denny! You didn't even last six weeks in Italy! You came running home for mammy's milk!'

The barman pushed his way through to them and, with a deliberate bang on the table, put a glass full of ice, and only ice, in front of Denny. To Beast Features he said, with a wagging finger, 'Not a drop more for him.'

'Good on you, Mick!' said Beast Features. 'That's the way. You see, Denny, even Mick is taking Vincent Fennelly's side on this one. You've become an awful arse, it's obvious to everybody.'

'America!' said Billy again, shaking his head.

'Pay no heed to him,' said Beast Features. 'He's always been a home bird.'

'I was a home bird, Beastie, that's true, and I still am, to a degree.' He twirled the ice in his glass, and hiccupped. 'That degree being the point at which the Ireland that could have been changes to the Ireland that is now. That first is the Ireland I'm tied to for ever – the Ireland I carried in my kit bag to Italy and sang to Maestro Tosi about.'

'Who dismissed it as claptrap!' said Beast Features. 'As anybody with any taste would and does. Sentimental crud, manufactured in the main by Englishmen and Americans and West Britons!'

'Ah, Beastie now,' Denny protested. 'Those Thomas Moores and Chauncey Challoners – they had great antennae for the Irish soul.'

'If it's from such as your own that that rubbish was divined then your soul is as shaky and artificial as the corner turrets on the Irish House Bar.'

'And I'll tell you what,' said Denny, 'at least those ballads have more of a connection with this land than the rock and the roll and the doo wop that's rife about the place now.'

'Oh, not this again! Jealous of youth! Jealous of youth!'

'Why would I be jealous of youth? Get out of that!'

'Jealous of youth!' said Beast Features. 'Because the good discerning people of this country didn't care much for your music anymore –'

'Ah, easy now, Beastie,' said Billy.

'– and now these rock and rollers have come along, and the folks are lapping it up. And you can't bear it seeing Pádraigín Cruise (what's he calling himself now? Pádraigín O'Clock?), you can't bear it seeing Pádraigín getting in on it. The girls falling at his feet!'

'Beastie, Beastie. Janey, man,' said Billy. 'You'll finish poor Denny off.'

'Sure it's not making a dint on him,' said Beast Features. 'Look at him. His head down like bloody Dropjohn. He's a heap. The man is a shambles. You're a shambles, Denny, at thirty-one years of age. I'm telling him this for his own good. It's a tragedy. Had a fine young voice, took a wrong turn with it, and too proud to admit he had. Rejected, not the pride nor the strength of character to regroup, try something different, move on from his stupid romantic notions. He could be a minor operatic star by now, if only he'd stuck it out in Italy. Or be doo-wopping and fingerclicking Pádraigín off the stage. But he's not. He's a drunk. A flailing and bilious drunk. And he's shredded his voice with that poison. No – that won't ever come back.'

Denny listened to every word, and Beast Features was right – not one of them made a scratch, because they amounted to nothing he didn't know himself. But still in his dampened and sedated state he could rouse himself to spar. He lifted his head.

'Well, you don't understand me and the force that animates me. I was born a long time ago. Oh but that is how I feel. Have you heard about this idea from other religions of the transmigration of souls? This is how I inherited mine. And my soul is as green as the essential green chlorophyll of Ireland.'

'The only thing green in you is the bile in your gullet,' said Beast Features. 'And what cod! It's painful to listen to you. You claim to know yourself, but do you have any idea how you appear and sound to others? Is this what poor Aisling has to put up with at home?'

Aisling! The word cut through his toxic shield. Aisling! These things – they were the kinds of things that Aisling herself would say to him. Like when he would try to tell her that she was beautiful, and she would tell him to please be himself, to stop with his film-star talk.

'I am bilious, it's true, Beastie. I am bitter. What's happened to Ireland these last few years … at least it gave me hope that the youth would clear out. Till only recently I used to will them to the boats. Be gone and good riddance, I used to say. I hoped for a cull. I hoped the poverty would ossify the country. I hoped that every pregnant young girl would queue up outside of Mamie Cadden's abortionarium. I thought: Leave the place to the old and old in spirit now! Because the youth were ruining the country with their alien ideas.

Still are. I passed the statue of Lord Ardilaun on the Green this morning' – he looked at a bottle of stout on the adjacent table – 'and I cursed him, I did, for ever having given confidence to the primitive, because we're seeing the fruits of that now in the swagger and slouch of these wild apes with their rock-and-roll music and their sex mania.'

'You're only a scut yourself, Denny, give it up!' said Beast Features. 'And if it wasn't for Ardilaun and his likes you'd still be in the jungle. Didn't you need a scholarship to get into school? Another tragedy – you got to your airy little niche by talent alone, and only talent was going to keep you there. The rest of us bob along nicely on daddy's largesse no matter the damage we do to ourselves.'

They fell into silence for a moment, before Billy said, 'So, America, Denny. You're not serious about this?'

'Of course he's not serious,' said Beast Features. 'But he'll say that he's serious, watch him.'

'I am serious,' said Denny. 'The country's gone to ruin and there's no going back. The rot has set right in deep now.'

'And you're off to the land of modernity and rock and roll itself?' said Billy.

'A point well made, Billy!' said Beast Features.

'America's the shining light of the world,' said Denny, 'even more so now than before; too big to be tarnished by the rubbings and scrapings of a few skiffle musicians.'

293

'A hopeless romantic! Beastie's right about you,' said Billy.

'Would you call the Jews who built a country out of the dry rocks of Palestine hopeless? Would you call the Germans who took the dream of Deutschland to south-west Africa and made it real hopeless?'

'Steady on with that talk,' said Beast Features.

'You're going to build a new Ireland in the Mojave Desert, are you?' said Billy, sniggering.

'First things first. I'll land in New York, same place that McCormack made his name.'

'You'll find a few dewy-eyed descendants might indulge you there for a while all right!' said Billy.

'Good enough for him!' said Beast Features. 'And does Aisling have a say in any of this?'

'She does. She can say that she'll come with me.'

'Or say that she won't?'

'Indeed.'

'You'll put her up to it?'

'If you like. But she's my wife, and she'll come.'

'She's had enough of your pipe dreams. She won't budge, and so neither will you.'

'She has every reason to come. She could have a career in singing herself.'

'She would have had it by now if she'd really wanted it. Denny, she lives in the modern and real world – what she wants is for you to settle down and do what husbands do.'

'I think you misinterpret my attitude to modernity. I don't accept what's become of the world, but I am a

294

modern man! I am a modern man! Just because I take from the past doesn't mean that I'm not a modern man.'

'You take from no past that's ever happened! You take from the dream world!'

'Well there you have it! The mark of a modern man is someone who wants to change things by the force of his dreaming, and to lead by his own example!'

'The most you'll do in the way of action is walk as far in the direction of America as the James's Street fountain, take a gulp of water to sober up, and turn around for home again, stopping in every pub along the route.'

'We should open a book on it,' said Billy. 'Five pounds that he'll make it as far as Saint Patrick's loo-lah hospital!'

'So you'll land, anyhow, in New York,' said Beast Features, 'helped down the gangplank by Marlon Brando, and you'll be straight into making the big bucks at the Met Opera House, this Great Bard of Ireland, Denny Logan, with Aisling dangling off your arm, and you'll be living it up in grand style on Fifth Avenue?'

'Well, no, not exactly.'

'No, I shouldn't have thought so.'

'The plan is, that I will go ahead on my own for a while to test the waters. There'll be some hardship, of course there will, initially.'

'And you'll tough it out in some dosshouse or the YMCA, will you?'

'No. I've joined a club. An uncle of mine down in Waterford has some connections in that way, and I've joined a club. And I'll write to their members in New York, and they'll take me in. The Davy Langans, they're called. Men and women after my own heart.'

'The Davy Whatkins?'

'Langans. True cultural and political revolutionaries. Or rather, half-revolutionaries. Revolutionaries come right the way back around to where they started from. The Davy Langans seek to flip the world one hundred and eighty degrees.'

'It gets better, Billy!'

'I'll go over, Beastie, and I'm telling you, a year from now you'll be calling me a visionary.'

'A double visionary!'

'Hoo hoo!' went Billy, nearly slipping under the table.

'A year from now the rock and roll will be shown to have been a passing craze,' said Denny, 'and we'll be back on with the real stuff. I'm going, fellows, this isn't waffle, I'm going to America, and that's it, just you see.'

'You'd better run!' said Billy. 'Your ship is sailing!'

'I'm going to go, I will!' said Denny. 'Unless ...'

Beast Features lifted his hand to stay Billy's hooting, and, needing to take a deep breath himself, said, 'Unless, Denny?'

'There's another thing I might do. That we might do. A proposal, if you like. I don't know how this sounds, but ... Perhaps, well ... I was thinking: a tenor trio. Me. You, Beastie. You, Billy. The three of us. I even have a name: the White-Headed Boys.'

The laughter must have been heard all the way back up Leinster Market.

'Have you even flippin' heard Billy sing before?! Have you heard me sing?! The White-Headed Boys! Oh boy, indeed! Lennox bloody Robinson's already kicking in his grave, I can hear him! Will you go off to America now! Go off and stop stinking up the air with your horse manure! And don't forget to swing by the Gaiety along the way, because you've a ticket to see *Otello* this evening.'

'Lennox Robinson doesn't have copyright on that name! And I have heard Billy sing, and he has a voice of very great potential! And I'm offering you both greatness and glory! And … yes. You'll go away and think about that now! And … oof! Both of you – to Hell and to Hecate with you!'

Otello! He patted his breast pockets.

'You'd forgotten, you drunk! Go up there and watch Paolo Silveri and see how a real singer should conduct himself! "White-Headed Boys"! Go on, piss off!'

* * *

He should have gone home to Rathmines for a wash and a change of clothing, but he didn't. Instead he spent the time left before the performance wandering the streets, about the Green mainly; four or five circuits of the perimeter, past Ardilaun again, the horse trough, Loreto, the College of Surgeons. He opened another button on his shirt, sucked the air hard to feed off its freshness. But all that he tasted was on the turn: something rotten from the York Street tenements, the muck of the leaves on the ground. He had once told Aisling that he knew Silveri; or at least that Silveri had, like himself, received tuition from Tosi. At any rate, Silveri, a regular performer in Dublin in those days, would have heard enough about the Maestro's Irish charge that he'd welcome him always into his dressing room. And he had reminded Aisling of this again, before he came out.

The walk had not had the effect he'd wanted. By the time he entered the theatre foyer he was tired; his goose-pimpled skin shivered in the heat; he felt fluey, pooey; in that awful between-state place. Opera evenings in Dublin were democratic gatherings: women bossed their men around and told them what to do for them and what to think of this and that aspect of this or another production. He mooched in a corner. He himself lived in rooms in the former childhood home of orientalist Lafcadio Hearn in Rathmines; he wanted to tell someone, because someone was talking about *The Mikado*.

He kept slipping off into sleep during the show. All that booze and all of that air made it sleepy time for his body, and his body was being a brat. From the dark of the circle the image of the stage was soft and vibrant like the projection of a loose slide. Twice or four times he woke gulping air and feeling as if he were falling. Gravity surged through him in a crook shape: down, then through his stomach. Once he opened his eyes and there was Silveri, murdering his part. Silveri was a baritone; someone had had the terrible idea of moving him up to tenor. He died there with Silveri, back into sleep with the steep pitch of the balcony.

With a clunk and a clatter he was let out through the fire doors. He felt better now, although a smell of heated felt and gloss paint and burning electrics lingered in his damned nostrils. He came out of Tangier Lane into Grafton Street, splashing through puddles of milk and oil. He looked left and right, and up he started into the foothills.

He came out the other side of sickness, feeling bright even, but sad. Over the hump of the canal bridge at the end of Richmond Street rose the mint-green dome of the church of the township. In the dark it was especially vivid. He experienced a deep sadness for all he was to leave. His father's side going back generations had been Dublin people. His mother's father's people too. Soldiers stumbled away from the cricket club with their heads on the shoulders of women they'd only just met. University students ran in coursing packs. These were the transient. Then there were the lonely. It was the township of both these types. The passing-through, and the people worse than himself that lived in cornered-off spaces on sagging boards. They wrote letters to sisters saying they were not so bad now. Anyhow. He was not so bad. He'd had his revelation and his mind was made up.

He'd go in to Aisling and tell her he loved her and damn her if she didn't believe him.

He leaned against the railings outside the house. Downstairs' cat Tiddles was on the little patch of green by the basement, arched and on the defensive. It was a lovely little cat. 'Tiddles,' he called to it. He went down on one knee and stretched his arm in through the bars.

He washed his face in the sink that all the flats shared. The light was weak, yellow and cold. He ran the tap and let the basin fill almost to the brim. There was no stopper in the plughole, and he watched the water very slowly drain away, thinking of what it would be like to be sick in a foreign country, to fight and fend, to freeze in a vest.

On evenings she wasn't working she liked to light the fire, because there was one in the room, and it was romantic. She loved the fire, and she'd got permission from the landlord to paint the iron surround white, and while she'd been at it she also painted the detailing, the finicky flowers and ferns, so that now the surround was more green and red than white. They'd read all about Lafcadio Hearn, and they liked to think his spirit was still in the room, of course. He, too, had gone to America.

The fire was not low in the grate as it usually would have been at this time. Aisling too looked fresh and alive: she was sitting high in the bed with his pillows and her own propping her up. She was waiting for him with a warm smile, and the book she'd been reading was turned down on the blanket over her tummy.

Her face looked soft and glossy under beauty cream, and her hair was tied back out of it. The smile dissolved as she saw the bruise on his head.

'Ah. Don't worry about that. I was out with the boys.'

'Come here to me.'

He sloped over to the bed and sat down.

'Come here!'

He threw his feet up. She rummaged about his hair with her fingers.

'We were only acting the maggot. Ouch!'

He tittered.

He said, 'You're lucky you didn't know me in my rugby-playing days.'

'You and your boys,' she said, her voice now full of relief and tenderness, and her fingers too, full of tenderness and affection.

'What's the book?' he said. He could see what the book was: it was a motoring guide to Ireland.

'I'm planning some weekends and day trips.'

'And who'll drive us?'

'It'll have to be me, won't it?'

'It might yet be me.'

'That'll be the day.'

She began humming a rock-and-roll tune.

He rested his head fully back on the mattress. His coat and shoes were still on him.

'What did you do tonight?' he said.

'I was over at Jim and Sheila's. We played cards. And then Jim went off to his parents and then me and Sheila talked about nonsense.'

Her nightdress was made of linen, gathered at the top, with a kind of primitivist motif embroidered down its front. It was like a cross between an old farmer's smock and a kimono – Aisling delighted in the Lafcadio Hearn connection as much as he did. She looked very virginal and very pagan in it.

'I wish you'd come to the concert,' he said.

'You need your time with the boys.'

'But I was at the concert on my own. I wish you'd come.'

'I couldn't go to a concert. It'd make me feel down.'

'How do you think it should make me feel?'

Gently she said, 'It doesn't seem to bother you. Why would it bother you? You bought the ticket so it mustn't bother you. And it shouldn't bother you. But seeing these people ... It bothers me.'

She picked her book back up.

'It shouldn't bother you. Deep down you should know that.'

'Deep down where?'

'Where your voice is hiding.'

She went 'tssk' as if to say he was silly.

'It doesn't bother me because I don't see myself as an operatic tenor any more,' he said. And then, after a pause: 'If it's any consolation, Silveri was abominable. He can't sing tenor. Would it bother you now if I sang?'

'It's not the singing that bothers me, or Silveri. It's the people that come to these things, all the not-so-grandees. And all the people on the make. They make me feel ... Ah, look. Let's not.'

'"Not-so-grandees". I like it,' he said, and proceeded to sing 'Niun mi Tema' from *Otello*. His body was so at ease, so forgotten, that he thought he had never sung so well. He opened his eyes to the cornicing. The ceiling was the colour of peaches, and throbbed softly, and he felt secure, but remembered his sadness.

'Did you meet him?'

'Who?'

'Paolo Silveri?'

'Why would he want anything to do with a scut like me?'

'You still sing opera beautifully.'

He turned to face her, making a pillow with his elbow. She looked down at him from her book, her chin resting on her shoulder. There was virtually no gap between her top lip and her nose, and she looked like a cornflour rabbit.

'My boy,' she said.

'Do you know what is great about you? I can tell you things that I don't tell myself.'

'Like that you love me?'

'Like that I'm a scut. But sure I know I love you.'

'How do you know?'

'Don't I say it?'

'To who?'

'To you.'

'You do.'

'I've proven it.'

'How?'

'"How?"'

'I'm codding.'

'I know it. I'll say it now: I love you. You're my wife. And that's to me I'm saying it.'

She laughed and went back to her book. 'What do you think of "Paolo" for a name?'

'I don't like it.'

'I think it would go well with Logan, though. If we ever have a boy I think Paolo Logan would be a fine name, because if he got too big and manly for his boots, he'd always have "lolo" in the middle of his name to make him feel like a girl.'

'So what sort of nonsense were you talking about with Sheila?'

Well, said Jeremiah Mac An Fincashel to a thirsty buck – as water finds its level so the wanderer finds his too, and usually where there is water. It was all very still. He turned around to the sound of the crunch of stones. The Hudson River heaved by quietly beneath the glide of its surface but nonetheless washed unexpectedly and in unpredictable patterns against the shore. Thorny seed casings and old rope and rusted rail-plates were scattered among the stones, and the stones were sharp as if freshly broken. These surfaces and textures he enjoyed against his thin shoe soles. He followed the wooded valley until the smell of the air changed from rusty to flower-like. He found that he had drops of salt water collected on the fine hairs around his mouth, as if his mouth itself were a flower. He turned left, and walked on narrow country roads alongside wooden fences that buckled inwards and then went towards righting themselves outwards so that what he appeared to be following now were long helixes that stretched away out of sight before a full revolution was made. He forgot to look out for the completion of these revolutions before the wooden fences gave way to recognisably picket fences and the picket fences became chain-link fences.

Having assumed that the commanders of all trucks across the American continent were male, Jeremiah was shaken to discover that the commander of the vehicle that pulled over for him near the Indiana state line was a female.

He would have run away across the field only he had already flung the sports bag containing his belongings into the vehicle's cabin. It had landed with a sludgy rubbly crunch.

'It's funny,' said the woman on seeing him in the seat beside her. She wore glasses with bright red frames and lenses so large they almost covered her cheeks and in those cheeks he was certain he was identifying the lost bloom of maidenhood. 'You look tiny on the road, tiny in the movies, but normal-sized in real life. Is that all trick photography or something?'

'I feel you must be mistaking me for somebody else,' he said. He grappled about him because he had the sense that if he touched things, these things would disappear. His arm went through the hollow centre of a triangular tubular calendar with a nude woman on it that sat on the dashboard. The inside of the cabin was covered with postcards with nude women on them.

'You're British?' she said.

'No I'm not,' he said in his best General American accent.

'On the run?' she said.

'Where are we now?' he said after a couple of hours.

'We're still in what used to be called the Old West and is now commonly known as the Midwest, heading west.'

'Can I get out now?' he said.

'Have we established where you're going?'

'Not yet.'

'So what's in the bag?'

He croaked like a mechanical crocodile.

'Do you know what eternity is?' she said. And then: 'It's the condition of being an electronic seabird.'

Later he said:

'Do you know any of these people?' He pulled each postcard slightly on the dab of chewing gum that held it. For each one he touched she replied:

'No.'

The cabin filled with the smell of mint disturbed from the chewing gum.

'Do you know what elasticity is?' she said. 'It's the condition of living as a seabird electronically.'

Presently she said:

'Would you like to go to a casino? There'll be women at it. And private rooms.'

'Where would I put my bag?'

'Will you stop worrying about your bag? There'll be a changing room. You're right to be making plans for tomorrow, that's what my ol' momma used to say. My mother was stupid. Jesus Christ lived only for the moment, and he hated the stupid. You know who said that?' Oscar Wilde. And you know what Jesus Christ said? Have faith in me alone, not in laws or morals written down. And the only way to know Christ is in yourself. It's all there in the Bible.'

'Would I be invited?'

'I'm inviting you. Nobody else will see you. It starts off dark and only then the lights slowly come on.'

Some time later, observing black bushes sweeping by across an endless plain in a dim blue light, he said:

'Maybe between here and there will be the Crack of Doom, and I won't need to worry about my bag. I intend to throw my bag in the Crack of Doom.'

'What the hell is in your bag that you need to be throwing into some crack of doom?'

'Do you know the Crack of Doom?'

'Never heard of it. Is it like Brig o' doom?'

'My brothers tell me about it. They'll regret it. If it's possible that there'll be a future in which they exist to regret it. They said to me, "Off you go now so, off you go to the Crack of Doom." They don't realise that I'll carry through with my threat.'

'You guys had a fight or something?'

'A terrible fight. A terrible, terrible fight. They said, "Here you go now. Here are the spark plugs from the server. Go off now and throw them in the Crack of Doom." Do you think that was terrible of me to have pushed them like that? But they were laughing as I left.'

'See – I knew you were a fugitive.' She poked him playfully in the ribs.

She left him off in a strange landscape that was as arid and cold as the moon. He came in from the road in case she came back. He dropped to his knees behind a collapsed termite mound. Soon after dawn it became very hot. He walked through the day. His eyebrows would be almost blond now. He began to miss the woman. No, he said, he was missing the foam that she offered. He imagined with self-tormenting pleasure the pop in his mouth of bubbles, the most perfect things that there were. He looked in his bag for food, though he knew there was no food there. A giant moth had got in. He quickly zipped his bag closed. It was to be hoped that the heat would kill it, and then he could eat it later.

He had his moth that night and the effort of chewing made him even more desperately thirsty than he was. He needed now to dig for water. With a sweep of his foot he cleared some of the loose stones off a patch of desert. As a result of his thirst, and of the cold, he could not summon even a drop of urine to soften the ground. He got down on his belly and started to lick it instead. This worsened everything. The effort would kill him before he got to the water, but he was going to die anyway, he said. Ignorance kept him going. He had some idea not his own that he had come out here with his brothers before, and that they had dug up and then filled in again the soil beneath this very patch of ground. In his delirium he thought repeatedly of bubbles, the beauty of them, and that they were a whipped soul.

Lo, he had been at this spot before. At least that's what the Indian told him. The Indian helped him out of the hole, and he hauled out the Indian. They flicked the clay and dust off themselves. The Indian wore only a leather loin covering, and his skin was as brown as the desert, which was to say (which Jeremiah didn't), not very. With ceremonial emphasis Jeremiah slung his bag into the hole.

'I made you,' he said.

'And all of my works,' said the Indian. 'Now come with me.'

Their little caravan travelled through the night. As the sun rose in the sky so the Indian's skin became darker. He led Jeremiah to a land of greater variety. They followed a dry river bed, smooth and scaled, until it became filled with pebbles, and continued along its course into the higher ground. For water they drank from a fistful of clay that the Indian had taken at the last minute from the hole. They rested when they reached the top of the height. The Indian wrung the last drop of water into Jeremiah's mouth and then moulded the clay with the palms of his hands into a perfect shiny ball. Standing up again he beckoned Jeremiah to the edge of a cliff. Hundreds of metres down on the floor of the plain was a vast sward of rich lime green. The Indian allowed Jeremiah to observe it for some minutes.

'What am I looking at?' said Jeremiah.

'A multi-leaved clover,' replied the Indian. 'You must pluck the clover from the desert and hold it up to man and woman. What it means is outrageous and everlasting luck, and what it stands for is the Multinity. To God, the Son and the Holy Spirit, we must now add every man and woman.'

'But how am I meant to hold something so large?'

'In all beauty there is some strangeness of proportion.'

Jeremiah reached out his hand, holding the clover in the C of his finger and thumb, but felt only the breeze.

'I said proportion, not perspective,' said the Indian.

Jeremiah made his way down the cliff face through a vertical fault. Dead skunks littered the route along the horizontal. Ahead was a thin strip of green and, seeming to hover above it, an iridescent pall. Closer to the clover he heard the pulsing hissing chorus of a million snakes. A car whizzed by in front of him. He saw a sign that said:

WELCOME TO PALM SPRINGS!
A DIFFERENT GOLF COURSE FOR EVERY DAY
OF THE YEAR

From the open top of a converted Routemaster double-decker bus he saw that the golf courses connected up into one enormous piece of landscaping. He mashed around his mouth the salty paste of disappointment, and imagined the sweet taste of water in the hissing, life-giving sprinklers.

'There's nothing to see in Palm Springs,' said the Mexican in the seat beside him. He wore small pink binoculars on a string around his neck. 'But you might find something you like in this.' He handed Jeremiah a leaflet. The front of it read:

THINGS TO SEE IN PALM SPRINGS

Jeremiah slid down the banister rail of the bus.

'Can you take me to the Clover Bowl, please?' he said to the driver.

The driver dropped him off three-quarters of a kilometre from the Clover Bowl and gave him good instructions on how to get there. On arrival he did indeed find a bowl, an upturned one, though it could also have been a shield resting on its concave side or an empty turtle shell. The bowl reminded him too of the monument at Newgrange and, while he was thinking of that cruel trick played on antiquarians, he thought also of an upturned coracle. Atop, supported by scaffolding, was an idealised shee, beside his crock of gold. By the front door a child was having a disco in a coin-operated Spanish galleon with flashing bulbs. He walked the perimeter of the bowl, through a car park and then a backlot strewn with litter, dead palm fronds and full-to-bursting dumpsters, to see if the rear of the building made a clover shape, but it was elliptical all the way around. He supposed that a multi-leaved clover would, in fact, be elliptical.

The inside of the Clover Bowl was blessedly cool, owing to an absence of natural light. The walls were made of rough-hewn granite held together with a tar-like pointing. Where the walls were not like this they were panelled, mirrored, plastered, or obscured by partition walls that sectioned off rooms. One of these rooms had a sign beside the door that said:

HAVE YOUR PARTY HERE

He peeped in the door and saw a room that was very well fenestrated and full of natural light. A man had come to his shoulder and he asked the man:

'Do you ever have foam parties here?'

One half of the Clover Bowl was taken up with bowling lanes and a range of clattering traps. Above the clattering traps ran a facia that depicted a scene of green hills among which jigged and jiggled many more idealised shee.

'A-ah,' said the man at his shoulder. 'You can't go down there without the right shoes.'

Jeremiah minced to his designated seat in the right shoes. They looked tiny and shiny on his feet, and felt tiny too. The sounds of the Clover Bowl resembled nothing so much as the drippings inside of sewer pipes greatly amplified with the use of software. Other than that, the William Tell Overture blared over the speakers. Beside him was a rack of bowling balls. They connected one with the next with a pleasing clonk. He tried all the balls for size and found that his thumb,

which was as thick as a cucumber as a result of callous-
ing from hard endless work, would only fit in the
thumb-hole of one of them. This ball was brown and,
funnily enough, but maybe not so, had a clover on it.

His thumb felt as tight in the hole as his feet did in
the shoes. He flung the ball into the lane almost glad
to be rid of it, and stumbling as he did. It thumped on
to the greased wood, screwed immediately into the
trough, and rolled slowly towards and then into the
trap. The gang of undisturbed white skittles at the end
of the lane seemed to laugh at him.

Back in his seat he realised that his thumb was gone.
It didn't pain him one bit, and hadn't when it came off,
otherwise he would have noticed that he'd lost it when
he did. All he could do now was wait for his ball to
reappear through the chute. Perhaps five minutes
went by and still it had not returned. He did a test: he
hefted all the other balls out of the rack and rolled
them down the trough and watched them fall into the
trap. One by one, and with a suck, they returned. But
his brown ball never did.

'What happens to the balls when they don't come
back?' he asked a passing cleaning woman in pink and
white overalls.

By now his blood was everywhere.

'Shee-it,' said the woman. She ran.

He looked up at the digital screen that showed his
points tally and was sure he saw there his brothers.
Breffny was holding the brown ball with Jeremiah's
thumb in it and he would lift the ball between his face

and Emmet's and they would kiss it through their laughter. In this vision the image was drained of colour, not quite monochrome, but almost, and of low contrast.

The gang of white skittles still seemed to be laughing and the William Tell Overture continued to blare over the speakers.

Jeremiah sprinted down the lane, the sound of his feet like thunder, gathering speed all the while until, two-thirds of the way, he launched himself like a bullet at the lead skittle. The moment he hit the wood he came to a painful stop, resulting in a loud squeak and a friction burn to his chin.

15

Clive baled out of a nightmare and into something far worse. In his head – his nightmare – his head had exploded. Outside his head – reality – his head was about to explode. He ripped every drawer from his bureau. The floor became a mess – of papers, coins, scapulars, books, lighters, video tapes, medicines, batteries, broken machinery, broken wood. He searched frantically for the document that he needed. By now, critical moments had elapsed.

He dialled 911.

'I'm afraid to report,' he said, 'that I don't have to hand my healthcare plan, so it's with regret that I'll have to cancel the ambulance.'

'Wait a minute, madam. You don't have to cancel an ambulance because you can't find your healthcare plan.'

'Yes, but you don't understand. The only place that can help me is Saint Charles's Anglican Hospital Head Trauma Unit and that would require a journey by ambulance of a distance my insurer may not be prepared to pay for. Unfortunately, I would need to check the terms of my plan to see whether or not this is so. Also, being nominally Roman Catholic, I would prefer to know for sure whether or not my insurer will pay for treatment in an Anglican hospital.'

'If it's an emergency you'll be treated in the nearest hospital. What is the complaint, madam?'

'I'm having a stroke.'

'Your nearest hospital will deal with that, madam. Why do you feel you need to go to Saint Charles's, madam?'

'Because I've seen the ads, and it's the only place. They're specialists.'

'Madam, try to remain calm. What's your address?'

'1202, The Birches, Stuyvesant Town.'

'Aw, madam, there's no record of an ambulance having been dispatched to that address. Would you like me to send an ambulance?'

'How much will it cost me?'

'Madam, I'm going to send an ambulance around.'

'No, please. Don't.'

'Madam, let me take care of this. Madam ...?'

He quietly put down the phone whereupon further critical moments elapsed. He stood in the dark of his hallway with his hand on the receiver and looked out through the panel of green glass beside his door. He was hungry. No he was not hungry. Yes – he was hungry. Nom, nom, he went. He fancied a cup of coffee. And pancakes. Maybe some Japanese food. Umami, he said. He put on a sweater, trousers and shoes, turned off all the lights in his apartment, pulled all the blinds, and went for a walk.

322

He summoned Quicklime later that day. They arranged to meet in a branch of Offal Cabin. Quicklime was already there when Clive arrived. It was a tight squeeze – they were in a tiny cubicle. Quicklime looked anxious. He seemed sweatier and puffier and altogether more pitted and vermiculated than he had before. Simple-faced characters from the Offal Cabin advertising universe were joined hand to hand in a paper entrail whose nadir dangled inches from his head. He had already ordered. Pleasantries ensued. Clive ordered. Perhaps Quicklime was right to be anxious. Then Quicklime said:

'So, my friend. This business?' His eyes trembled with suspicion, and his fingers compressed his Guinea Patty, wringing the grease on to the table.

Clive went to speak. Then shied.

'Mister Quicklime ...'

He unconsciously toyed with his sweetbreads.

'Clive, leave that alone. You brought me here to tell me something.'

'Yes ...'

'Clive?'

'I can't go back to Ireland. I'm sorry to have to tell you that I've changed my mind, and that I want –'

'Oh, the boat is booked. The boat is leaving next Saturday week, like we agreed.'

'Let the boat leave without me then.'

Quicklime took a bite of his patty, dipped his head and shook it. 'You can't do this. The Office of the President of Ireland would lose a lot of money.'

'I've made up my mind.'

'You'll remake it. The President will sue. And who is more powerful relative to you, a member of the Irish diaspora, than the President of Ireland, who controls all his subjects, and all the diaspora? There's a new law on the statute books.'

'I can't explain, Mister Quicklime.'

'The President lights a candle every night for the likes of you. Indeed, he has taken a personal interest in your – Clive Sullis's – case.'

'Mister Quicklime, if I go back to Ireland, I will die. I had it all wrong, you see. When I came back to you, it was to organise my affairs, and I thought it was a prelude to death. It was an acceptance of death. But I realise that I don't want to organise my affairs. I want them to remain as they are. I want them to remain as they are, and I want to remain here, in America. I will deny death. I will live on and again, and on and again. I've done it once, and I'll –'

'No, the paperwork is already filled out' – he flung his half-eaten patty down – 'and my team have come over from Ireland. They're all set to start on your apartment. There's no going back. The process is in train. We agreed all of this.'

'With the greatest respect, I haven't signed off on any agreement yet.'

Quicklime sighed, wiped his hands on a napkin, and sat back. 'No. That's true. You haven't signed anything. *Mea culpa* for that.' He closed his eyes and rubbed his brow. 'So,' – he sighed again, rolling his napkin into a ball – 'what we'll need to do now is get your cancellation on a firmer legal footing.'

'If you say so, yes, all right.'

'No, it shouldn't be too much of a problem. But we must sign some papers now, cement this. Time is of the essence.'

'Yes, yes.'

Quicklime stood up from his seat, drawing his trench coat over his shoulders.

'Right now?' said Clive.

'Yes. Come with me. I have some pro-forma documentation back in the flat. We can change the wording a bit. Maybe devise something more suitable to your situation.'

A taxi took them on a three-minute ride to a door beside a launderette. They went inside, up two flights of stairs to a second-floor apartment in the back of the building. The rooms were mainly grey in colour; in the living area the bare floorboards were coated in a grey undercoat. A single chair faced the window.

'Make yourself at home while I put on some coffee,' said Quicklime. 'I have the documentation here in the kitchen.'

As he waited in the chair, his knees almost touching the windowsill, Clive realised that he was looking straight through an empty lot and down to the entrance of the Cha Bum Kun clubhouse.

'Ah!' he called. 'You might have seen me come and go on occasion!'

The words had only left his mouth when a jangle of terror ran through him.

He spun around.

Quicklime was standing the other side of the chair with a large Waterford Crystal paperweight in his hand.

'You *are* a fairy!' cried Clive.

Bof!

His last thought before he blacked out was: Yes, the nose of a pugilist, that'll complete me!

* * *

He came to in the same turbid scene of grey. A blind was down on the window and a powerful desk lamp was sitting on the floor, switched on. He could feel its warmth on his face. His hands and feet were bound. The only movement he could muster was a flip on to his back. The pain from his nose, warming also, pulsed the full way to the back of his skull.

He heard footsteps on the wooden floor. The clack of a chair being put in position. A parp.

'You will be getting that boat on Saturday week,' went the placating Ulster voice. 'But you won't be getting it to Ireland. Once you're safely out of this jurisdiction you'll be thrown into the ocean. Dead. You'll be thrown, dead, into the ocean, and be eaten by eels. Ha ha ha ha!'

The laughter gave way to a cough, which took some time to settle. 'Sorry,' said Quicklime, wheezing.

Clive stared, deadly, at the ceiling. *'Dead'* … *'Eels'* … It was all so unreal. Like an out-of-body experience.

His shoulders and back and hands – and arms and legs, limbs always so ungainly – were numb now from pressing on the hard floor. Hearing of his fate like this, of events catching up … of meeting them halfway …

The floor seemed to take his shape, and a deep comforting melancholia set in.

'And you won't be going anywhere between now and then, oh no you will not. You'll stay right here, trussed like you are now. I may even look into getting some croquet hoops, and spreadeagle you, and nail you down. You bitch. You wriggled about free for long enough. But you can only run for so long from the Davy Langans. Yes – there's a name for you! You thought we were gone, didn't you, having brought down the whole American operation? Well the Langans are still around, and we've some scores to settle. We've been on your trail forty years, Jean Dotsy. I'd finish you off here and now, you thieving traitor, you treacherous slut, only I don't want to be banged up in Sing Sing.'

The words 'Jean Dotsy', spoken by another, and this talk of thieving, brought her wallop back into her body. She lay in it, freezing. In her fear, she thought. In all her fear she'd forgotten. Taken her eye off it. Didn't even think of it. She tried to sit up. *If they'd had any idea*. If they could only have understood how desperate she was. That she needed the money, fast, to get rid of her diddies. To have this thing done.

'Although, to be honest, between yourself and myself, and seeing as it makes no odds as you're going to die anyway, it doesn't matter a jot to me if you're out of the way or not. But there are some of the older folk in the movement bear a terrible bitterness. I'm just the middleman in all of this, you'll understand. And I thank you, Jean Dotsy, for a wonderful adventure these last few weeks. I've greatly enjoyed myself here in New York. What a fabulous city. Magical. Exactly as it is in the movies. Now, if you'll excuse me, I've developed rather a taste for surveillance, and there's a sale on telescopes, periscopes and night-vision goggles down at M&D that I want to check out.'

A door shut. The light phased out the other side of the blind. He slammed his head back down on the floor so hard that he might have lost consciousness again.

* * *

She lifted her head and she was still here. For a moment she had forgotten herself. Took the din in with her. Had allowed it to retreat and surround. Like under the swell where she was weightless. But something had pulled her back. A kind-faced cousin had a smooth hand on hers.

'Time will heal, Jean, my girl,' he said.

She returned a smile and watched him walk back to the bar with a kind of kink to his walk as if those sympathetic words had meant nothing. Goodness knows how long she had been like this, sitting with her eyes closed underneath the trophy display. Patrick's twin girls sat in the seats either side of her. She put her hand on little Sarah's knee and smiled at her too. Sarah looked at her peculiarly through one eye, dragging on an unlit cigarette. Jean got up from her seat, yawning and stretching. She staggered as she walked towards the long table with all the sandwiches laid out on it, though she had not been drinking. Earlier her mother had asked her if she was all right, as had Patrick. She had not seemed to them as upset as they were about her father's death, and Patrick looked at her even now as if her behaviour were inappropriate. She had no reason not to grieve as they were grieving, because she loved her father dearly. But even coming up in the car from Dublin she had said to herself that she would do things in the way that she felt was natural.

And now for some reason the atmosphere in the room did not seem sad enough. The back door was open to the patio. Outside she went, into the cool bright afternoon and the invisible rain. She stepped over the white chain on to the golf course and stood for a while on the soft fairway observing the rings of wilder grass that had overcome the greens. Patrick called her in and asked her to stay on at the house for the weekend. She stayed until the next Tuesday. All the time her mother worried about her, making her meals when her mother should have been looking after herself. Somehow she managed to get her mother's new cooker and hob working. There were other jobs to do: she ran errands in her car down to the town. On the morning of the day she was due to go back to Dublin she decided she neither wanted to be in Dublin nor to be here. She stood in front of her house wakening her back with one of her father's golf clubs pressed across her shoulders like Patrick did sometimes. Again, she thought that if her mother saw this she might have thought that she was grieving for her father. She went over the stile at the back fence and through the McGeevers' farm in as straight a line as the hedgerows would allow. This brought her to the brow of the low broad hill that was known as Mazzard Hill. It was said often enough that it had a magic character because the sheep would not stay long there. She sat in the weeds and laughed to herself thinking of her Dublin life. She had felt the need to change many times and never had changed and had called for guidance to show her what needed to be changed and had never received it. Now she knocked the ground quietly with the knuckles of both hands while still laughing quietly to herself. I want to change, she said. She watched two very different wasps. One floated about in a random and slow rubbing motion as if it were bad with its nerves. The other stayed very still and then darted sideways in a straight line like a space machine. Suddenly a hare broke out of a bush and came as quickly to a stop. It seemed to inspect Jean from afar with its twitching Y-shaped nostril before it ran on again making quite a disturbance. It would be nice to be an animal, she thought. Honestly, she said, lying flat down on the ground now and thinking of the fairies, I need to change.

* * *

she was not in control of her feelings any more and to get any sort of handle on them she would have to change as a person. What sort of feelings, what sort of change? asked Veronica. She would not answer the first question, and to the second she could only say, 'I am not sure, and I am not sure either if I have the power within me to bring whatever it is about.' Divine intervention is what you're looking for so, said Veronica with some frustration in her voice. She had a cold, and it sounded as if she had said 'divined intervention'. This immediately had Jean thinking of hazel rods and the opposite to divine intervention. She thought too of how she had sat on Mazzard Hill and called for help, and how apt Veronica's words as they sounded were.

Passing along Burgh Quay one evening she heard a drunkard singing. This was not unusual on the streets of this city but what caught Jean's attention was how the singer made the terrible noise he was making into a virtue, as if in singing 'The Lock Hospital' he actually acted the part of a man whose brain was riddled with syphilis. Also, he was not just wailing in the street at random passers-by like a normal drunkard but seemed to direct his singing at a window of an upper floor of a building on the quay. Also, she saw some slum boys carefully remove the man's belt without the man seeming to mind or even to notice, and he now continued with his performance oblivious to the fact that his trousers were bundled around his ankles.

What most caught her attention though was that he was young, perhaps only a few years older than she was, herself, and that he was on his own. Usually when she saw a young man drunk and loud in the street he was showing off to other young drunks in his company; only older men got drunk on their own and shouted in the street. She had never seen such unselfconsciousness in a person; that someone of that age could become paralytic to the point of appearing syphilitic hugely impressed her. As she studied him, she supposed she could recognise that the man was handsome enough, though the feeling he really brought out in her was envy that she could not lose herself as he could.

The belt was a good one because it was stiff and kept the shape of a circle; Jean picked it up from the flagstones and approached the man. He did not seem in a particularly angry mood like one of those out-of-control drunks, so she felt it was safe to tap him on the arm. All the same, if the man had eaten her head off like a lion she wouldn't have minded. She stood there with the man and the evening pedestrian traffic flowing around them. Her, she stood in a pair of white nylon size thirty-four sailor's trousers she had just walked out of Guiney's wearing. Her coat was unbuttoned to the river breeze.

The man took the belt from Jean, showing no surprise at all. Without too much fluster he bent down to reinstate his trousers, muttering something about 'a copy taker above' as he buckled himself up. Then he resumed his straight but slightly unsteady posture and returned his attention to the window.

'I have beautiful girls taking my breeches off in the street now, Aisling! And if you don't come down to me in ten seconds I'm going off with her. Right – I'm gone!'

He pressed his finger to Jean's chest and told her to speed along. She turned to walk beside him. He walked with his head stooped, giving just the one glance back at the upper-storey window. Only when they had reached the corner with D'Olier Street did he look up at Jean. And he did have to look up at Jean: she was a good three inches taller than him.

'You're a big girl all the same,' he said.

'Where are we going?'

'That depends on whether you're happy to come along.'

'I am.'

'You know who I am, then, yes?'

'I don't.'

'Just as well. Will you come and have a drink with me?'

'Yes.'

'I'm up at Jury's. This is my last night in Dublin.'

She went in with him to the grand old hotel on Dame Street, where a cheerier and more civilised hubbub prevailed than out on the street. He ordered her a gin and tonic at the bar and, for himself, a glass of milk.

'The ruination of the singer's voice, milk,' he said. 'But I've done enough for the day.' Then, shooting out a hand, he introduced himself as: 'Denny Kennedy-Logan.'

'Jean Dotsy,' Jean replied.

'Do you know who I am now?'

Jean hesitated.

'Denny Logan?' said the man.

'Denny Logan ...'

'I suppose you're all very taken with the rock and roll?' said Denny.

'No,' said Jean. 'No, I don't really care for that kind of music.'

'What do you like?'

'Emmm,' said Jean, thinking. 'I like ... I just like a good song, sung well. I like more of the old-time stuff. John McCormack would have been a favourite in our house.'

'Ah well then you will have heard of me. Think about it now.'

Jean rolled her eyes to the floor to make like she was searching her memory. In truth, a tiny bell did tinkle.

'Yes, I have heard of you, I think,' she said.

He wiped away a milk moustache. 'There you are.'

'And you say this is your last night in Dublin. Are you emigrating tomorrow?'

'No, I'm heading off home tomorrow. I'm only on a visit to Dublin. But I don't intend to ever come back. No sirree, this is the last time,' he said, banging his glass down on the counter. 'Shall we go somewhere more comfortable?'

They took two soft low seats at a table. This left them some feet apart. It was more effort to talk over the clamour so they contented themselves with resting in their chairs. Not that Jean could ever rest very much. 'At rest' she was a ball of wire – people had pointed this out to her; at her Christmas drinks she remained with her shoulders hunched up around her neck as if she was still at her desk. She was aware that her shoulders were like this now, and she slowly let them down, and stiffly reclined into her chair. In contrast the man seemed at ease in his own body, and with his chair. From the crazed blackguard who had made a show of himself on the street he had now transformed into a 'cool'-looking sophisticate. Each pose, in its way, showed equal indifference to what people thought. Slumped almost sideways with his legs crossed, he was smoking a cigarette with steely relish. The brown suit he wore was woollen of a very fine grade. She knew from looking at him that the country he had come from and the country he would return to tomorrow was America.

As meanly as he had been enjoying his cigarette he was eyeing her now, she noticed.

'Will you have another drink?' he said.

'I will.'

He went to the bar, and came back with a gin and tonic, and another glass of milk for himself.

'You are very disciplined,' she said.

'How do you mean?'

'When you said earlier that you'd done enough for the day, you clearly meant it.'

He looked at his glass of milk and laughed. 'Oh no. I meant I'd done enough singing. Sure I haven't drunk a drop of alcohol in over two years.' He looked quickly about the bar. 'Do you know,' he said, and with a little impatience, 'we have awful trouble hearing one another in this place. Let's go to my room where it's quieter.'

She rose from her seat, inhaling deeply. As she stood beside him again, he seemed to tighten slightly, like a slug. His face showed uncertainty, and his skin turned pink. 'This way,' he said, ushering her with his hand. It was as if he'd forgotten and now was reminded of the height difference between them. She became conscious, as she so often did, of her own ungainliness. He slipped a couple of paces behind her on the stairs. 'This way,' he said again on the landing on his floor. His room was a single-bed, very small, with a low ceiling. She had expected something bigger and smarter. Even the tartan-patterned curtains showed tobacco staining.

He pulled out the seat under the desk; she sat at the end of his bed. Taking the shape of the stiff wooden chair, he seemed to regain his composure, and studied her silently again. She folded her hands on her lap and mainly looked at his feet. She slid one foot out of her shoe, and slid it back in. She asked herself if she felt anything. Genuinely she did not. She didn't know what she was doing. She had vowed to herself earlier in the week that she would not think any more about her actions, and would allow herself to be guided by events and impulses until something happened to her. Well, these were events, at least; but impulses – she did not feel any of those.

'America,' she said. 'Tell me about it. I have always wanted to go there.'

'Mm-hmm,' he hummed into his cigarette, then ripped it from his mouth, blowing out the smoke. 'America, yes, great country.'

'Is it just like it is in the pictures?'

'The thing about America,' he said, and he returned the cigarette to his lips, and savoured a slow drag, 'the thing about it is, the reason it's the best country in the world, is that it takes the best of all times. It takes the best of the past, and thinks only of the best sort of future, and in that way it makes for itself the best kind of present. You take this country – it seems fixated on only the dankest aspects of its history. And the future! Well, there is no future on this earth, that's what they tell you in Ireland! And what's the point in earthly ambition when there's no future!'

Jean nodded. 'The best of the past. It's a nice way to go about it.'

'Do you know when you think back on your childhood, and you remember sunshine and ball games and ice cream, and you edit out the wet stockings and the fits and the fevers? A similar process happens to you when you arrive in America. All these people come from every part of the world, many fleeing hardship, and it's as if, at the gates of New York and Boston, they shed the memories of war and famine, and they

338

bring with them into the heartland the most beloved aspects of their histories and cultures, and make them into something again.'

'And it's full of millionaires, they say. And anyone can make millions.'

'What they say is true. It's true! You're looking at a living example of it.'

'A millionaire?!'

'Well. Let's just say I've made enough money in the couple of years I've been in America not to have to worry very much about work again.'

'My goodness! How did you make your fortune?'

'Sales. I was a travelling salesman.'

'Did you see much of the desert? And the prairies?'

'Yes. Both. But cities and prairies mostly.'

'What are the prairies like?'

'Lots of cattle and great big farms.'

'And the desert?'

'Buffalos and escarpments.'

'What did you sell?'

'I sold sheet music. Books of songs. I picked up some work with a music publisher, PD Decker, of Broadway. They were one of the last of their kind in New York. Specialised in all the very old Irish ballads.'

'I would not have thought there was much money in that kind of thing any more.'

The man sank down in his chair, and joined his hands on his chest. He looked dead centre at the bed between Jean's legs. 'I was told I had a very narrow window of opportunity. When I set off, there were still people who bought songs in that form. There were many pianos still in front parlours. But I knew, anyhow, that within the souls of a great many of the American people was a latent affection for this sort of music. Americans love the emotion of these songs. It speaks to that side of them that yearns for their ancient homelands. So, it was a matter for me then, as a salesman, of trying to appeal to that side.'

'And how did you do that?'

'By using picturesque folk costume and through performance. I found it all very easy. I didn't think I'd take to it as well as I did, but I did. Well, I suppose I am a performer by training. But I collected so many orders. I sold sheet music to people with not a trace of Irish ancestry – Russians, Armenians, Swedes, you name it. I sold sheet music to households with no pianos in them. The American people delighted me. They say this country here is the land of a thousand welcomes. Well, you should come to America. A stranger is often treated like a hero. A stranger is valued.'

Jean repeated the words: 'A stranger is valued.'

'The frontiersman and the moneymaker. They're the two model heroes of America. The travelling salesman is the both of those in one. The motor car is his steed. You're nothing without the motor car over there.' He stretched his legs in front of him, touching the valance with his feet between Jean's own. 'Ah, it's a good life for those with the gift for it. Full of adventure. Sometimes I would feel quite lost, an Irishman out in those big open spaces. But curiously it was rarely a lonely job, though people think that it is. There was a good camaraderie among those of us that did it. You met some interesting people on the road. Selling all sorts of wares. I owe a lot of my success to one man that I met. Though he was a rival to begin. That's how I saw him. I used to see him ahead of me on the road, his car ahead of mine, all the time. I got to memorise his number plate. Every pit stop along the way his car would be there. Often I would be walking up a drive to a house and I would see his head and shoulders over the fence in the property next door. It was getting to be a bit of a joke. One day he turned around to me on a quiet suburban road in Chicago. He used to wear a suit of all-white. He turned around to me and he said, "Okay." We went and had lunch. He was selling a religion. That was his product. That is another one of the great freedoms permitted in America. Anyone can be a prophet. Some can even be a messiah. I admire those people. They're in business like any other. This man was preparing the world for the coming of a new god. It was the god of technology. An actual god – he was not speaking in figurative terms about technology itself. Like the god of cereal, or the god of the sea, this was the god of technology. This was what he believed, or had invented. It was all in his bible, or manual as he referred to it. To prepare for the coming of the god of technology, man had to make certain technological changes. People

She went away with her admiration for the man deepened. He had great purpose of movement and manner, and great control over atmosphere, and yet there was a pitiable quality about him that would make him a fine job for some wife some day, she thought. She went away too with his call for her to become an animal resounding in her head, remembering how she herself had called out to be transformed into an animal on Mazzard Hill the previous weekend. In the days after, it was those words, and the pleading delivery, that most stayed with her from her encounter with the man, his cry reinforcing her earlier thought. From a bench in Mount Argus she took keen notice of a ruck of pigeons making a meal of the crusts of her sandwich, crusts that lay on the dirty ground and that in any event were covered in large human germs from her lips, and she thought of the pigeons' tiny fast-beating hearts and wondered how they survived. On another day in Rathgar she saw a dog sniff and then lick and then eat its own filth: and this was not a street dog but a small and clearly well-looked-after animal that was as clean and well groomed as its owner. She decided that it would not be a bad idea to test her own system out by being careless about food cleanliness. She began by deliberately dropping a couple of slices of apple on her floor, waiting for them to go brown, and then picking them up and eating them. Then she tried a pinch of cold potato from the plughole of her sink. Over the next week she ate whatever she could find in public waste bins. By the end of that week she

16

The Filipina lady, Rosa, came in and tossed some logs from the basket into the grate. She watched for a minute until the wood caught flame, and sighed along with the hissing. The drawing room filled with a churchy smell. She scolded them for letting the fire go so low. 'You can't let it look like a picture of the fire I take for my children,' she said. 'Even when the fire is angry, when I take a picture of it for my children it doesn't look angry. And when I come in the room I was not looking at a picture of it for my children and it didn't look angry.'

Without quite knowing what she was talking about everybody in the room felt the scorn in her words. They all looked glumly at the flame-wrapped logs. Each man – there were seven of them – turned in his seat towards the fire even if it put a crick in his neck. They stared straight in at the flames with shamed expressions and dared not look Rosa in the eye. The room was quiet tonight because a monthly board meeting was on and all the most boisterous and go-ahead club members were upstairs in attendance, or where they usually were: inside, playing cards.

Rosa put her hand on the shining soapstone chimney breast and leaned against it and shouted at them like some fat southern housemaid from the bad old times. 'You're like babies, all of you. I leave you alone for an hour and you're like babies.'

Normally Rosa was not in such bristly form. But sometimes when she felt she had a nice group of them like this on their own she let them have it. It was almost as if she were punishing them for being the weaker ones. When she left the room every man turned back to face the way that was most comfortable for him. Then the heavy oak door burst open with unseemly force, and a club member called Lancelot, a normally elegant and sullen grey-bearded black man, charged into the room with pursed lips, bowed head and excitement in his eyes.

'Evening, Lancelot,' muttered the men in staggered unison.

Lancelot went to the middle of the room and sat on the wooden chest there, knocking over a pile of golf magazines. Nobody had sat on the three-hundred-year-old chest before. It groaned under Lancelot's huge weight. He crossed his legs. The logs snapped in the grate. The only other sound was of Lancelot's breath.

'Gentlemen,' he said. 'Some news from the board.'

He paused another moment.

'Perhaps this circular that we've just drafted will best explain it.'

He gave each man a letter. It began:

The Finance Committee and Long-Range Planning Committee, in consultation with the House Committee, with reference to the Articles of Incorporation and Bylaws set down by the Temporal Founders of C.B.K. Lodge 8, New York City, U.S.A., under the guidance of Our Always-Smiling Founder, Cha Bum Kun, in The Year of Our Lord, 1886 A.D., and in consultation with the Father Lodge in Pusan …

The men, nonplussed, scrunched their eyes to comprehend the text, or at the import of it, the papers shaking in their hands.

'Look,' said Lancelot, 'in summary, we've provisionally agreed to sell the building for one billion dollars.'

He licked his lips in expectation of the reaction.

'When do they want us out?' howled one of the men.

'As soon as possible, Gilbert. And we're ready to sign. We've been talking to the boys in Pusan, and it's all okay by them, and we are ready – if you guys are – to sign.'

'So we'll be homeless?' said Gilbert.

'For a while, perhaps. Until we find someplace new. That's if you even want to continue.'

The men croaked and grumbled like a pond of angry frogs.

'I *said*, that's if you want to continue, because from now on we'll all be busy with our turbo-powered golf carts, or our luxury yachts, or our space rockets to the moon, or our moon rockets to space. There are two hundred and sixty-three members of this lodge, and by the rules of the club all proceeds from the sale of property must be disbursed among members. So what's one billion dollars divided by two hundred and sixty-three?'

Somebody piped up – Rude, the Dutchman: 'How much is a billion these days?'

Someone else answered, 'Just the thousand million.'

'Oh,' said Rude. 'Still.'

A sherry glass fell to the floor, smashing.

'I propose,' said Lancelot, 'that we all retire to the saloon for whiskey and wine and gin, and to consider this offer for all of one billionth of a second.'

Six of the men rose from their chairs, doubled over, hobbled- and hocused-seeming. They found their balance, and the room emptied. The sound of whooping was heard from the direction of the stair hall, and then the heavy oak door creaked closed of its own accord.

* * *

Rickard Velily started out through the back end of Murray Hill, unusually alert to its sights. He took in every mud-brown detail in this mundane section of town, every machine-brick new-build. He let the smut linger in his eye. He took it all in for he knew that these would be among his last glimpses of the city. His mind was made up: he would leave New York – soon, tomorrow, whenever he could arrange it. It was not sentiment or a creeping nostalgia that made him so keen to the details, but an urgency to record, to make an imprint of the place on his senses, so that he could tell the story of the bright city on the hill and the particular unstable quality of light within it. Maybe later would come the time for sentiment – regret, for sure. Regret, for he had come here with dreams: the dream of the Chrysler Building, of Tin Pan Alley, and of *The Severe Dalliance*; the dream of the city of his and of others' imaginations; the dream to 'make it big'. He hoped not to have to go back to Dublin, for he still had dreams of going west.

If he were to go back to Dublin he would tell Fondler that their little bit of tomfoolery had been the highlight of his time here and was just the tonic, but that it had to come to an end. No – he would not use the word tomfoolery. He would say to her that their affair had meant the world to him.

And if he were not to go back to Dublin he would take Fondler with him on his adventure west. No – he would not go west. He would go north.

He was certain that the Q in Fondler's surname (which he still could not recall) had been part of a French name. He felt that she was in denial of this element of herself, and the very element of her Canadianness. He would go north with Fondler and they would become fur trappers. They would bludgeon

351

seals and shoot moose, and start a fur-trading company. He believed that the Canadian Shield and Hudson Bay area was the forgotten wild frontier. He became convinced that if the French had been the dominant European influence in the early centuries of new-world colonisation, then the Canadian fur trapper rather than the cowboy would be the great hero of North American folklore.

The travel agency was closed, and appeared to have been for a long time; its windows were streaked with furrows of paint and its inner windowsills thick with dust.

A few doors up from the travel agency was a shop selling fishing and hunting equipment. Along one wall was a glass display case packed with rifles, pistols and machine guns. In the centre of the floor was a horizontal display case containing antique weapons – flintlocks, swords and a variety of spiked paraphernalia. He asked the man in the shop about trying out a machine gun. He was asked for his licence, told the man he had left it at home, and then was asked which machine gun he'd like to try. 'Something for about three hundred dollars,' he said. The man laughed in his face, needing to suck back a string of brown phlegm that had escaped from his mouth. 'Only weapon you're going to get for three hundred dollars is an air rifle,' he said. 'What's the most powerful air rifle you have?' he asked the man. 'The most powerful one we have,' said the man, 'doesn't fire on air, it fires on super-compressed gas canisters.' Rickard asked if it could kill, or slow, a bear.

'Sure,' said the man. Rickard offered him five hundred dollars, plus the morning star that belonged to the clubhouse that he had recently taken to carrying around with him for self-defence purposes. 'Deal,' said the man, after some hesitation, examining the antique.

Back in his room, Rickard went about assembling the weapon. Six pieces locked together, quite beautifully, to make a long, heavy rifle. He loaded a gas canister into a compartment near the butt, and clicked a magazine of pellets into place. He had never had anything like it in his hands before. He patted his left hand to the grip underneath the barrel, and was overcome with the urge to experience immediately the awesome destructive power coiled and packed into this satisfyingly solid hunk of metal and plastic.

He flipped open his porthole window and rested the end of the gun in the window frame. The terrace across the street had a huge gap in it, as if the building that once stood there had been blasted to atoms. He squinted through the gun-sight and turned the weapon back and forth through an arc of a hundred degrees, making explosion noises with his mouth. Several moments elapsed before he realised that his gun-sight was not in focus. Twisting the milled dial, he watched a hazy grey image sharpen until the grain and twinkling mica of the masonry of the building the other side of the gap came brightly into view. He thought of taking a pot shot at a hanging basket, but resisted. He slowly panned the gun to his right again, across a window.

A man was standing at the window, smoking a cigar. Rickard knew this man, had spoken to him: a near-bald pudgy man, with a collar of sandy hair round his head. It was the strange, crazed, north-of-Ireland man, the man who had followed him to Bryant Square.

The man had the window open, and every so often turned his head from his fat cigar to talk to someone in the room, someone lower than himself, seated, or very small. So sharp was the focus of his gun-sight that Rickard was able to observe, in the crosshairs, the droplets of sweat nestled in the pores of the man's scalp. How very strange and bizarre that he should be looking at this man again, thought Rickard, the butt of the rifle thumping into his shoulder, as almost instantaneously a red hole opened in the man's forehead. How very strange. Image and sensation were disconnected for a second, in which Rickard pondered: What is he doing? What's happening now? Then the chill realisation broke, and in disbelief he peeled his eye from the rubber socket of the gun-sight and looked at his finger squeezed on the trigger.

He pressed his eye back to the gun-sight and watched, as his horror increased, the man stagger backwards, deeper into the room, his entire head a ball of rippling, glistening red, like a peeled tomato.

Now he shrank from the porthole on jellied legs, throwing out his hand to steady himself. He dropped the gun with a clunk, and fell against the bed, sinking to the floor, and hugged his knees to his chest. For a long time he remained like this, numb.

Numbly he thought of the weeks ahead. Of what he would do, of the duties and tasks to be taken on. He thought of his parents. His poor mother and father. His responsibilities to them – yes, he could be a sort of herald, of a sort of danger. Inside his head a broken flap of magnetic tape spun furiously on a reel, slapping and slapping the same processes of his skull through each rotation.

#ne7äž¾çq9ù±†ËÛÚ[yä8Æõãn:à`s·=³ž¿y©5p4m. neÕ$žçOòÃc...ÝÞ¸ÛÀÎqœzàrpÉRY£ŽÃÍuá[¸‰‡ryÀ ŒŽ8ëÐ 'Êò@š´e- ™ÆçÎðÜŒp PÄíeËìç^'-dʃ-

All he had to show his parents for seven months in New York was a gift. All he had bought for his parents was a plastic slide-show machine, a sort of blind-ending binoculars in which could be viewed touristic images of New York – the 'Lipstick' Building, the Ulysses Grant Memorial, and others. His mother would find many hours of distraction in this toy. He should have bought more for his mother, but he had thought he would have more time. He would buy more for her now, but he was afraid to leave the clubhouse. Would he try to win back Toni? Yes he would. Yes he would. He would try to win back Toni. How? With a cock-and-bull story about his time in New York. He would fill it with romance and heroism. Perhaps he would tell her about Fondler, and draw out her inner alley cat. And for money? He would approach Robert again about getting back his old job at Verbiage, for the short term anyhow. Yes he had unlearned everything, but he would learn it all again. It would come back to him. He would expose himself once more to the information.

ç‚Ïl· ö;‚â° '¹ÞXm ŽsÓ§#®0 é£´éY°H^¡£Œnùö‚Ø# 'ß9'ø· CNÂÌó¥¬¬© *É¨«ùÜr™ÁÏ¨{ñÇÌ2®kã ä!„XÙ ÎB, ì9êO^ÄçøšµÍð*Ë^Ùa ù£î `&µ'd½Ž YÚHÙñ+á Ød°è3ŽIç Õ‰å°*³F÷ ê^çË| p¤ Öòïž,·'äq¼c "z£ ëýü Ae àü@·Ë i';åŸ iUl ò s£ é¨ñ »³Ôæ¹'Ætû! $xÊ´'et% ‚`, ò@ !k"×U Þ!påŒ ²(â^ÝK x9ÎO!±¬ ‡„~Î ™T Ìhµ;p 8™TÄ5ØŽxä `}Á k¬Q°±'Ùç æ&TeÂ B äu'¿lÿ ‚|¥˜ žH8ã åx +k)uf ‰N;...Žb÷âçq rF...£Üv· û§Ž9ç''z†É tá #8'U òJ›}Ž w|Êø # í=1 £ÅF O©·Ÿg, Ò¡wU... w®øòçŒ ã ¹ùŽIÏa× !D z ]œ¢U •„rÆ¨>Ðv ð¬{ ~¹É Ýr"Õ^·ÚF²¬ x·$±í• œ à ~‚ã...'Ÿ"l £§Q¥' ·W! œ• Ü×M„·kmvûó 9*GÞ#° œ`Ÿâ9Î Yf'd 'ãí "'q6e' É=G ü± Œà nnqÉè "òNF0 2W ûÆ,ø ¢tœ ‹S–I ÆìX vg ã * ?Ø ^M~Öâ u{hŒ gÈ\¤·Ÿ(œääóž 8 !EH µ; ;³$çj"#l ·Á!¨‡çð ?0~Oñ

Damn, he thought. Damn! Damn!

He was staring at a spent dark-green cartridge on the floor, the remains of a pellet. And beyond the cartridge was the gun. Yes, he said, collecting himself, slinking towards the weapon. His only responsibility now was to himself. He had a duty to make it safely to an airport. He would bring the gun with him, dump it in a bush as close as possible to the airport, and make it to an aeroplane.

He stood up, over the gun, bent down to pick it up, and then – BOOM!

He spun around. Two pistols were pointed at him, easing into the room, and behind them two police officers. Between the police officers was the face of Club President Paulus.

'This is the room that corresponds with the window, all right,' said Paulus, who then retreated.

'Okay, kiddywinkles, hands in the air!' said one of the officers, a tiny man. 'Where is it?'

'We've had reports of a firearm discharging from the window of this room,' said the other officer, who was barely bigger than his partner.

Both policemen were limescale-furred, rhubarb-coloured, typical Irish cops, though diminutive versions. Their badges said 'Donnelly' (the tiny one) and 'McBrearty' (the small one). And both were Irish, properly so: each had a marked brogue.

'Ah,' said the bigger one, spotting the gun on the floor. Inspecting it, he said, 'It's only some class of air rifle, Marky.'

'Oh?' said Marky, disappointment in his voice. With pistol and manic eyes still trained on Rickard, he said, 'Are you sure, Rory? Looks like the real deal from where I'm standing.'

'Nah, it's an air rifle. Nothing illegal about that.' To Rickard, Rory said, 'Sorry about all the fuss then, sir.'

'Wait! Wait!' said Marky, waggling his pistol. To Rickard: 'Let me see your ID card. And keep your hands up!'

'I ... ID card?' said Rickard. 'I'm not an American, officer.'

Marky's face suddenly divested itself of tension and his arms relaxed, bringing down his pistol. 'You're from the old country?' He looked to his partner. 'He's from the old country, Rory!'

'I can hear it, Marky, I can hear it! Whereabouts in the old country are you from, sir? The midlands?'

'I'm from Dublin,' said Rickard.

'Dublin!' said Marky.

'And where in Dublin? Drumcondra?' said Rory.

'No, I'm from the coast.'

'I had an aunt owned a guesthouse in Drumcondra. The both of us are Donegal men,' said Rory.

The officers slid their guns back in their holsters.

'Well who'd have thought it?' said Marky.

'Well isn't it a great place to be Irish all the same, New York, haven't you found?' said Rory.

'Listen,' said Marky, 'I'll have to ask you for identification of some description. Federal law, you understand. Have you got a passport?'

Rickard fetched his passport from the drawer in his bedside locker, which he had not disturbed since he put it there all those months before.

'Ah yes, "Éire",' said Rory, taking the document. Then, holding it sideways, and after bringing it to the light of the porthole, a vexed expression crossed his face. 'Do you realise you were only on a three-month holiday visa? And that it's expired nearly four months?'

Rickard was bewildered. 'Eh ... "holiday" visa? Um ...'

'Oh-oh,' said Marky, taking the passport from his partner. 'Do you know what this means, now?'

Rickard didn't answer.

'Deportation,' said Rory.

'Deportation?' said Rickard.

'We're afraid so. Next flight home,' said Marky. 'But ...' He looked to Rory, pursing his lips.

'But ...' said Rory.

'Yes,' said Marky.

'If you don't say anything –' said Rory.

'We won't either,' said Marky.

They stood side by side now, both of them with their eyebrows – which in Marky's case were drawn on in brown-red pencil – held to their highest extent in a gesture of encouragement and self-congratulation.

'We're very involved, the two of us,' said Rory, finally, 'in the campaign to improve the status of the undocumented Irish in New York.'

'So you have our full, if clandestine, support,' said Marky.

'And now,' said Rory, as the men gathered themselves, 'we must be on our way. But if you're not doing anything tonight, there's a session on in the Donegal and Derry County Club in Flatbush. Always a great evening.'

They left the room. Rickard remained unmoving for several moments, unsure of how he should have responded to what had just taken place.

Eventually he stirred himself to chase the men down the corridor.

'Excuse me now! Excuse me! I *will* say something about this! You officers are turning a blind eye to a breach in federal law! You must deport me! You'll escort me to an airport immediately!'

Rory and Marky stopped, looked at each other, and turned around, waiting for Rickard to catch up.

'Do you not know what's good for you?' said Marky.

'If you don't pipe down we *will* have you deported,' said Rory.

'You'll be four days in a container in Jamaica Bay without –'

Marky cut himself off, cocking an ear to a sound that came rushing up the corridor like a phantom. A sound – like somebody singing, doing vocal exercises. The tone was sweet, true, rich, thick – taking up all of the air. And the singer was skilled, gliding among notes with birdlike ease.

The three men, captivated by the music, turned slowly about to face in the direction of the apparent source. Towards it they were pulled, heads forward, mouths agape, feet plodding. They were led to a balcony that looked down upon the grand stair hall.

All occupants of the building had been lured to the hall, or were still gathering, collecting on the floor below and on the other balconies. Their attention was absorbed by the figure on the walkway that vaulted the space. Its arms were awhirl, and it squirted about on its feet by means of a tremulous leg motion, rapt in its own performance, but it was not singing, as it had no mouth. Rather, the sound emanated from its head – which was white, smooth, shiny and featureless, save for an intimation of bone structure – travelling in all directions, evenly, as if pulsating from the peak of a radio transmitter.

But the sound was no longer just a fountain-fall of single notes: now it came as a polyphony, not-human, yet beautiful.

And then a song, only too human:

> *'The head of my love bobs atop the blue waves.*
> *(Come down to us now on the dark ocean floor!)*
> *The closer I'm carried, the further away.*
> *(Feel the salt of the sea in all of your sores!)*
> *I pinch my legs round a white spuming steed.*
> *(Throw him off west of Ushant, untameable mare!)*
> *It expresses me to my homeland of green.*
> *(Wash up on the rocks half a mile below Clare!)*
> *I look for you now in sunshine and rain.*
> *(She was stretched out in white on the dolmen's cold slab!)*
> *I ask an old woman who knows you by name.*
> *(We are the familiars of such wicked hags!)*
> *She tells me, my love, that you are quite dead.*
> *(Tooty toot-toot toot-toot, tooty toot-toot toot-toot!)*
> *And over your grave I unscrew my head.*
> *(Poopy poop-poop poop-poop, poopy poop-poop*
> *poop-poop!)'*

The final note reverberated in the great chamber of limestone and marble and bone, joined only by the sound of scattered outbreaks of weeping. Rory and Marky, on either side of Rickard, were inconsolable.

Bent backwards at the knees, face towards the sky, one hand pressed to breast, the other held out and open in supplication to some god of love, the figure held the pose of an operatic tenor until the last harmonic.

And then it stiffened to an upright stance, causing all to gasp, and many men to faint. 'Gentlemen!' it called out. 'Or should I say, after a fashion, fellow Kunians! For it is I, Denny Logan!'

The assembled swayed as one organ, rippling inwards and outwards like the walls of an upset stomach. Mob sounds began to swell. President Paulus, on the next balcony down from Rickard, spoke for everyone: 'How could it be? Denny Kennedy-Logan was buried in a Long Island cemetery last week!'

The figure swiped the air with a flattened hand and brought immediate silence and order.

'I was not buried in Long Island, or anywhere. What was put in the ground last week was a bag of mince and tallow. A substitute for a dead man. What you see now before you standing is that dead man. I have been brought back to some kind of, what you might understand as, life. Not the life that you all know, ratcheted to rhythms regular and irregular, limited by the outlines of your physical beings, and the rest of it only guessed at. I am boundless and I am free. But I am certain. I am at one with the universal quiddity, I am at one with the truthful immanence. What it is I am.'

The voice of Lancelot boomed up from the floor: 'Are you speaking in tongues? Do you channel the dead?'

'No, Lancelot. What I channel is the truth. The truth is what I have come to tell you about. I have come to put you on that white and lighted path. I have come to show you what might be found beyond the slough of dither and quandary. The truth is in reach of us all.'

A man leaned forward in his Zimmer frame and shouted: 'Are you the New Bab?' A man with a chicken-skin neck cried out: 'Are you The Christ? Or a Christ-like saviour?'

Denny shook with what might have been laughter. 'No, Freddy; no, Solomon. I am not the New Bab, or The Christ, or a Christ-like saviour. But I know of a saviour. He has gifted me the truth.'

'Are you the ghost of Charles Taze Russell,' someone called out, 'finally delivered on that train?'

'No! It's me – Denny! Denny Logan. Look, will you just hear me out for two seconds while I talk to you about the truth?'

A feeling of dread flushed through every cell in Rickard's body. He could not resist:

'How can you know the truth when you do not have a head?'

Without turning to Rickard, Denny replied:

'Because, Rickard, I still have a heart.'

Somebody else shouted: 'If you know the truth, can you tell me what my first wife's maiden name was?'

'No, Benny,' said Denny. 'Because your first wife's maiden name is a fact, it is not the truth. But if I had to guess, I would guess "Otway" or "Attleway".'

'You're right, thereabouts!' the man shouted back.

Another man shouted: 'Can you tell me what the lucky playing card is that I always carry in my inside pocket?'

'Again,' said Denny, 'I think you're somewhat failing to grasp the meaning of "truth".'

Somebody else called up: 'I've just been up to the Whitney. Can you tell me what this whole "modern art" is about?'

'Ah,' said Denny, 'now I'm on firmer ground. It's about materials, it's about context, it's about subjectivity, and it's about the nature of existence.'

The crowd swooned: faces turned to faces, nodding.

'Does a pendulum swing always forward or always backward?' somebody asked.

'Always backwards, Mitchell,' said Denny.

Rickard leaned forwards over the stone balustrade. 'I have a question,' he said, but was drowned out by the shouting of others.

'Shush, men, for one moment,' said Denny. 'Rickard, I think you were fractionally first.'

'Yes,' said Rickard. He felt sure now that, with his question, he would call out the 'truth seer' for what he was: a puppet and proponent of Townsend Thoresen. 'I have a question,' he repeated.

Denny this time turned to face his questioner, and by doing so invited everyone else to look in Rickard's direction.

Rickard, with his hands curling into paws on the stone sill, felt like a man in the dock. 'Yes,' he said. 'Can you tell all assembled here whether they should

364

sell out to Puffball's new CEO, with his offer of a crisp one billion dollars, or whether they should refuse him, and thus clear the way for Townsend Thoresen's innovations to dominate the world?'

Slowly and stiffly Denny turned away from Rickard. The featureless face seemed solemn in its blankness.

'I'm glad you've asked that question, Rickard,' Denny began. 'Because I was going to pronounce on that matter. I understand that the sale has already been agreed on, but the money and deeds have not changed hands. So there is still the possibility that you might be persuaded not to sell. How and ever, in truth – and the truth is all I can give – you would, as a collective, be crazy not to take the money. But, I suppose, you knew that already. I mean – one billion dollars! Take it and enjoy the rest of your lives, gentlemen!'

In astonishment Rickard ejaculated: 'But what would your master say?'

'My "master", if you mean my spirit guide, my dictator of truth, is my equal,' said Denny. 'He can only be truthful too, so he would tell you the same as I have just told you. But in the earth-bound phase of his being he was a man who lived life to its lushest extent, so he would, in any case, say to you all: "Abú! Abú! We're smelling of roses now, me garsoons!"'

'That renowned ascetic Townsend Thoresen?!' said Rickard. 'It doesn't sound like him. Come, come, now. Come out with it! What underhand business is afoot here?'

'Townsend Thoresen?' said Denny. 'Do you think I'd heed a word from that entity? Only the one spirit brings the truth to me – the great John McCormack! It is him and I that are in communion. Now, men. As the man himself, while he was on this earth, might have proposed, what say that we dredge the cellars of all of their wines, before the new owners get their hands on them, and we'll carouse for the rest of the day and into the next?'

* * *

By nightfall, the rooms and corridors of the clubhouse resembled scenes from Hogarth: ruddy-faced men, with their shirt collars loosened and shirt ends loose, and many with their ties tied around their heads, guzzling wine from goblets or straight from the bottle, and sliding down polished walls and slung like saddles across delicate items of furniture. Rickard skulked outside the saloon, sipping a port, absently nodding along to the man who had him buttonholed.

'... no, never been to Ireland. Loch Ness, yes; London, yes; Paris, yes; Scotland, yes; Germany, yes – this all on the one tour thirty years ago – Belgium, yes; the Rhine, yes ... But, yes, been at it secretly for this last year, apparently, this new chief, John Thomas. Laying down this cable. Gives him a trillionth-of-a-second advantage. Gives us a billion-dollar advantage! He talks about a universal brotherhood. You've got to wonder what the sisters will have to say about it ...!'

From inside the saloon came the muffled sounds of revelry: laughter, the din of loud chatter, singing – *singing*; snatches of 'Cogitations of My Fancy' and 'Bring the Boy Home' and 'Come Off It, Eileen'.

The door to the saloon opened a mite, and then wider. A man sidled out, tapping his pipe. Lifting his head, and adjusting his crossed eyes to Rickard and Rickard's hostage-taker, he said, 'Come on inside, for godsakes. There's room for two more.'

Rickard entered to a happy hurly-burly. Denny was holding court at the bar, miming enthusiastic shapes to illustrate the words that his deadened face could not emphasise. His audience loved it – they were beet-root with giddiness, and falling about the place.

'I mean – Cha *Bum* Kun! What kind of name is that anyway? Did anyone ever pause to think about that? *Bum* Kun! *Bum* Kun! Bum! Bum! Bum! Big bouncy wobbly veined Cha *Bum* Kun!'

He held a tumbler of brandy, and would at intervals splash some of it against his face, letting it dribble down and off his chin to even greater hysterics. Two policemen's hats sat on the counter; Rory and Marky were still in tears, but tears of laughter now. Rickard had caught the eye of Marky, who tugged at the sleeve of Paulus, the two of them finding in Rickard's appearance something funnier than even Denny had said.

'Rickard Velililily – the devil himself,' Denny suddenly called out – and at an instant, the high spirits of his drinking companions seemed to level off.

Paulus cleared his throat. 'Rickard, have you started looking for work? Your residency is set to come to a close, you know.'

Denny answered, 'Oh, he'll have no problem, no problem at all finding work. Of a good many talents, is Rickard.'

He pushed through to him, and slid his arm around Rickard's shoulders. Rickard thought he seemed taller, more correct of posture, than when he was alive, when he had had his own head.

'Young man, I'm glad you've turned up. I'll need the youngest, most physically able man in the building to assist me in something. I've been saying to the boys, there's a crate of 1928 Chateau du Superior Vena Cava in the cellars somewhere, I know there is. Would you accompany me, please?'

They left the room – and down the corridor, safely around a corner, amidst cooling shadows and creaking wood, Denny nuzzled his warm plastic face against Rickard's ear; Rickard felt the plastic vibrate.

'O the blather! O the guff! And it's not as if I'm able to intoxicate myself through it. Get me away from here now.'

In the stair hall, he took the keys to the cellar from behind the porter's desk. Under the first flight of the grand staircase, he pushed open the low iron door that led to the steps underground, put one foot over the threshold, and beckoned Rickard to his side again. Down the worn sandstone steps they went, into the vaulted catacombs. He pressed his fingers against the nobble between Rickard's shoulder blades, encouraging him forward, saying 'this way, this way' as they moved among the racks and the dimly glinting bottle ends. Somewhere along the route he had detached a fire axe from a wall.

'Any ideas where we might find this crate we're looking for?' said Rickard, his mouth dry and tasting the charnel air.

'Over there,' said Denny. He was holding the axe by the blade and pointing the handle towards an area of the floor.

'Is it gone?'

'No, no. Over there.'

Rickard moved to the spot that Denny was indicating, finding a flagstone apparently brushed clean of its covering of dust and with the grouting around its edges scraped out.

'Lift it out for me, there's a good lad,' said Denny. 'I chiselled at this all morning.'

With the thin end of the axe blade Rickard worked one side of the flagstone off the ground, then placed a bottle beneath the axe handle and levered it up some more. It was easy to lift out, being made of thin, rough-hewn slate. It was about a metre squared in area, and left a large tamped bed of sandy soil, with a hole in the centre, like the entrance to a fox's den. Denny poked around with the axe, causing soil at the edges of the hole to fall away, making it wider. They stood opposite each other on the flagstones either side, looking down into the hole. Rickard blinked at the darkness, hoping for better resolution, searching for … he didn't know. There was further movement of the soil. Two grey fluffy paws appeared, scrambling for purchase. A platypus – no, a dirty-faced shih-tzu – squirmed out of the ground. Another one, orangey-bearded, followed. The animals sniffed and snorted at the air, and beetled away, flattening their bodies to squeeze under a wine rack.

Rickard looked back at Denny, intending to express disbelief. The old man was holding out both his hands.

'Help me in,' he said.

'What?'

'Help me down. Into the hole.'

'Where does it lead?'

'To Ireland. Eventually.'

'Ireland?'

'It leads to a fault in the schist, a crack, before that crack finally tapers to a close, into which emerges an undersea cable. The cable goes some fifty miles south, wraps three or four times around a spindle outside New York harbour, and then runs north-east until it reaches the south-west of Ireland. It's composed of more or less the same material that human nerves are made of. I'll find my way to that line, and feel my way home, along its length.'

'You'll drown!'

'I won't drown. I don't have a mouth to drink with, let alone drown with.'

Denny's hands felt very frail and cold in Rickard's own, and his body light. He slipped into the ground diagonally, to his elbows, and stopped.

'The axe,' he said. 'Pass it to me. I want to give this cable a few belts along the way, rightly mess it up.'

He took the weapon from Rickard, and slithered further into the hole, to his head.

'Wait!' said Rickard, to the white shining lump.

'Yes?' said Denny.

Rickard opened his mouth, but found he could not say anything. He was not sure what he wanted to say.

Denny remained motionless, waiting.

'Rickard,' he said. 'Stay here in New York. You'll have an important job to do. That voice. Your vibrato. Wonderful control in the upper to middle register. Look after it. There's a truth in your voice such as is rarely found anywhere. You'll change the hearts of men and women and make them human beings again.'

And with that, the head shot beneath the ground, as if the body had let go.